MAZIE

REGINA FELTY

To the Mildred Buxtons and Melba Longs in my life that I never thought I needed when I was young and wise in my own eyes.

What I wouldn't give to sit at your feet and hear your stories of how you survived, how you kept your faith, and how to age gracefully, as you did.

As Mazie would say, "You only get one shot."

I want to make that one shot count.

If you pass me by and notice the load of burdens that I have dropped at my feet, and you stop to help me carry them. First, help me choose which burdens I should not pick up again but that would be better for me to leave behind.

(RLF)

PROLOGUE

YOU CAN RUN from your demons, but they will always find you. In fact, they were never gone at all, but remained lurking in the shadows, nipping at your heels, until you could no longer ignore them.

What brings us all to this understanding—this impasse—is unique for each of us. It may be the loss of a job, a sudden illness, a tough-love confrontation from a lifelong friend, or even your nemesis. It is something that stops you in your tracks and causes you to take inventory of your life and its direction.

It may even be a perfect stranger who steps on the scene at just the right time.

CHAPTER 1

"I ALREADY TOOK care of that last week, remember? Uh, huh. Got it. Yep, I got the keys last night."

Brian leaned against the car door, cell phone pressed to his ear, half-listening while his mother chattered on about how excited she was for him. She offered the same age-old advice that he was sure all mothers memorized and recited to their offspring during important life events.

It wasn't like he hadn't been on his own for several years now and hadn't heard it all before, but this was his first house purchase—and his first time living outside of his hometown of Mobile, Alabama.

He was never so thankful to see his best friend, Finn, pull up in his old red '98 Chevy Silverado. Finn turned the corner and cruised down his street, the blaring of a rowdy country song preceding him from a half-block away.

"Gotta go, Mom. Finn's here. Love ya."

Before letting him go, his mother dropped one last request. He should have known it was coming.

"Don't forget to call your dad to give him your new address," she said.

"Sure, Mom. I'll do that," he told her and ended the call. If she said anything after that, he didn't hear it above Finn's music. He had only agreed to make her feel better anyway. He would never make the call. In fact, he had never even given his dad his previous address.

While he waited for Finn to back the truck into his driveway, Brian noticed movement in his neighbor's yard. It was an old woman wearing a blue sweater—*on a warm day too*—walking with a cane, puttering around in her garden. She appeared to be talking to herself.

Great, he thought. *A senile old couple for neighbors. Probably have yappy dogs or a bunch of stray cats hanging around that they feed.* Sweeping over the yard, he didn't see any animals in sight. That was a good sign.

Well, at least those neighbors won't be bothering me.

"Let's go, dude! This truck ain't gonna unload itself." The tailgate was lowered, and Finn was already tugging out a large black dolly from the truck bed.

Brian shoved his cell phone in his back pocket. "I'm coming, I'm coming."

～

MAZIE STOOD over the rebel weed and silently cursed its existence.

She prided herself in having a tidy garden bursting with glorious flowers and well-trimmed shrubbery. Each carefully tended herb was labeled with her own handwritten wood markers so admirers would know on whom their praise was being lavished.

Every morning, after a breakfast of an extra-toasted whole-wheat bagel and instant hazelnut coffee, Mazie made her way out to her garden to hunt down any unwelcome intruders and pluck them out from the oasis she'd created. She was offended this morning to see that this unsightly jagged-leafed invader had dared to pop its head up on her turf.

"You rotten, little freeloader, trying to sneak your way into my garden and suck all the nutrients for yourself."

Steadying her balance with one bony hand gripped on her cane, Mazie slowly bent over and, with the gracefulness of a crippled penguin, ripped the weed from the ground with a jerk. Leaning heavily on her cane, she unrolled her body, vertebrae by vertebrae, until she was back to a semi-standing position and shoved the limp weed deep into her sweater pocket.

Just as she tugged her cane free from the soft soil, she heard the *thump, thump, thump* of loud music coming from the driveway next door.

Mazie turned toward the obnoxious music and observed a man carrying two large cardboard boxes shuffling up the sidewalk leading to the front of the house next to hers. She could barely make out a mop of black hair over the top of the box tower and noticed the torn denim pants jutting out the bottom, but the man appeared to be quite tall, with long, golden brown, muscular arms clutching the boxes against his frame.

A few steps in his wake strolled a second young man who was much shorter, with hair the color of corn silk cut military-short, sporting a blue tank top and khaki shorts. He struggled with a large dolly, pushing a metal filing cabinet in front of him. He hollered to the tall man over the sound of the music.

"Hey, Brian, throw those boxes on the porch and help me drag this thing up the steps, will ya?"

"Yeah, sure," the tall man—*obviously Brian*—replied.

Mazie was intrigued by the two young men. No one had lived in the house next door for the past two years, the *foreclosure* signs that used to hang on the front door having long since torn off and blown away.

Well now, won't it be nice to have two strong fellas living next door that I can call on for help.

She looked across the yard to where the incessant music pounded and rumbled out of a big red truck parked behind a white car in front of the house. As the clamor drifted over the fence and vibrated her chest, she reconsidered.

Hope they don't plan on playing that god-awful racket every day and disturbing my peace.

Just then, the blond-haired man noticed Mazie staring

their way and lifted a hand to wave, an expression akin to a smirk on his face.

"How's it going?" he shouted over at her.

Mazie was mortified. She'd been caught spying on her neighbors—her barely moving-in new neighbors, at that—like a meddling old busybody poking her nose in everyone's business. She didn't even bother waving back. She would just act like she didn't see the man and head back into the house. But she had to be slick about it. Bending over a rose bush in front of the fence next to her, Mazie plucked off a few leaves, as if that had been the sole purpose for her being out here in the yard, and pushed them down into her pocket beside the rebel weed.

When she straightened, she saw no sign of the two young men, who had clearly made their way into the house, leaving the file cabinet parked at the top of the stairs on the porch. She breathed a sigh of relief. Lips pursed into an unflattering frown, Mazie thought up a way to redeem herself.

Guess I'll make up a batch of sourdough cookies to bring over later, she mused. *It's the neighborly thing to do, after all.*

BRIAN AND FINN sat on the floor in the empty living room, an extra-large pizza box and a two-liter of Coke filling the space between them as they took a break from hauling boxes and furniture all morning. The aroma of pizza grease

and stale air—from the house sitting empty for a few years
—clashed in Brian's nostrils. Finn belched loudly as he
leaned over for another slice of pizza, a long, thin rope of
cheese strung up to his chin. Brian laid his head back
against the wall, a loud sigh escaping his lips.

"They could have at least cleaned this place up a bit
before they handed over the keys," Brian grumbled. "With
all the mouse droppings and old spiderwebs, I'm going to
be scrubbing this place top to bottom for days before I can
even put dishes away in the kitchen cabinets." He
shuddered.

Finn grabbed a cleaning rag on the floor next to him
and used it to wipe his mouth. "Lighten up, bro, you ain't
got nothin' better to do anyway. Maybe Sam could come
and help you out with the cleaning while you get your office
set up."

Sam—short for Samantha—was Finn's twenty-four-
year-old sister. She'd had a crush on Brian since she was in
the fifth grade and was forever finding creative ways to
interject herself into his life, all with Finn's encouragement.

It wasn't just the fact that she was seven years younger
that caused Brian to keep her at bay; it was also because
Sam had a way of exhausting you before you got more than
three words in. As a kindergarten teacher, her energy level
and enthusiasm were a perfect match for her brood of
rambunctious five and six-year-olds, but way too over the
top for Brian's taste.

"Nah, I'm good. I can handle it." Brian watched as

Finn snagged the last piece of pizza and folded it in half, taco-style, before shoving it in his mouth and wiping his hands on his pants.

"Speaking of setting up my workspace," Brian continued. "Can you help me run some wires for the PC? I have a website I need to finish setting up for a client by tomorrow."

"Sure, let's do it," Finn said, already jumping to his feet and heading to the office. Brian stood and kicked the lid to the pizza box closed before trailing behind him.

Brian had started his own graphic design business a few years back as a side job to supplement his income as a layout artist for an advertising agency when the industry started getting tougher and he got sick of competing for design jobs. After he'd established a decent clientele, he'd taken the leap and turned in his resignation, never looking back and with not one ounce of regret.

They worked to detangle wires and set up his office equipment over the next few hours. After Finn headed out and Brian had just booted up his computer, he heard a timid knock on the door, followed by the loud clanging of chimes that he surmised was his new doorbell.

Who in the world?

Brian glanced at his watch. It was just past three o'clock in the afternoon. Panic gripped him when he wondered if Finn had taken it upon himself to go ahead and send Sam over to help anyway. He ran his fingers through his hair and mentally prepared an escape plan to get Sam turned around and back on her way before she made it into the entryway. Just as he reached for the doorknob, the chimes rang again.

Brian made a painful attempt to rein in his irritation before jerking open the door and coming face-to-face with a short elderly woman donned in a white summer dress layered with a light blue sweater and bright white tennis shoes. He recognized her as the neighbor lady who'd been talking to herself in the garden.

Her face was a sea of wrinkles as she smiled up at him and his first impression was that she didn't look as senile as she had from across the fence. Her distinct bright green eyes, which gave her an aura of youthfulness in spite of her advanced age, appeared intelligent and aware. His eyes dropped to a foil-covered plate the woman held stiffly in front of her. He saw her feet inch closer.

"Hello there," he said. "Can I help you?"

The plate was thrust toward him. "Good afternoon. I'm Mazie. We're neighbors!" She tipped her head toward the white picket fence outlining the property between the two houses. "I live next door."

She gave the plate a shake and brought it closer to him. Too close. Brian took a step back.

"I made a batch of sourdough cookies this afternoon and thought you might like some—an official welcome to the neighborhood." Her smile widened, displaying a perfect row of gleaming white teeth.

Dentures, Brian thought. *No one has teeth that good at her age.*

Still, when she smiled, he couldn't help but notice that

the sea of wrinkles softened to a gentle puddle, complimenting her captivating eyes.

He nodded and reached for the plate—a disposable paper one, he noticed—and bent back a corner of the foil to take a peek. The scent of sweet vanilla drifted up to his nose and he could feel through the thin plate that the cookies were still warm. His interest was piqued.

"Hmmm, these smell wonderful! Thank you so much."

The old woman's face flushed with the compliment.

He'd never been "officially welcomed" to a neighborhood before and, since this was his first house purchase after living in rented apartments, he wondered if this was what "domestic" people did for the new folks on the block. He had no idea what he was supposed to do now. *Am I obligated to invite her in and offer her a cup of coffee or something?* Panic tingled in his chest as he fumbled for an appropriate response, but the woman saved him.

"My pleasure!" she beamed. "I won't keep you. I just wanted to introduce myself and drop these off." She pointed at the plate in his hands. "I gave you a paper plate so you wouldn't have to return anything."

Brian shifted the cookies to one hand and offered his other hand to her.

"Mazie...right? I'm Brian. Brian Denson. Glad to meet you and"—he lifted the plate up—"thanks again!"

Her hand was like a soft dough ball and he was careful not to squeeze too hard for fear he would hurt her. With a small shake, she pulled back and tucked her sweater closer against her. Turning to leave, she paused midstep and turned back toward him.

"Are you married, Mr. Denson? Any children?" she asked.

He shook his head. "Neither. And you can just call me Brian. Calling me Mr. Denson is better suited for my father."

She reached for the wood banister and lifted a foot down. Remembering his manners, Brian hurried to her with his free arm to assist her down the stairs, but she waved him off.

"Oh, I'm alright. Just need a bit of help when I come up on potholes and such. I have my trusty cane for that back at the house."

He watched her work her way to the bottom, carefully testing her weight on each step. When she reached the last step, she looked back up at him. "I'll be fine now." She adjusted the hem of her sweater over her hips and gave him one last long look.

"Just you living here alone?"

Brian shrugged. "Just my lonesome self."

He heard her mumble under her breath as she stepped to leave, "That's too bad."

He frowned. *What's that supposed to mean?*

Brian watched her shuffle down the walkway until she was almost to the open gate of the fence.

"Thanks again, Mazie!" he called out.

CHAPTER 2

As SHE TUGGED the limp knee-high nylon up her calf, Mazie thought about her new neighbor.

Poor young man has that whole house all to himself. She had assumed that maybe the other shorter fellow that had been with him when he moved in was a roommate, but she was wrong.

He's gonna get awfully lonely over there.

From outside her bedroom window she could hear baby birds chirping loudly for their mother. She had first noticed the nest of eggs a few weeks ago when she opened the drapes to let the warm sun flood her room. She had made it a point to check on their progress every day after that, feeling that she had a duty to watch over them when their mother left the nest, until she looked one morning to see hatchlings raising their tiny beaks to the sky for food. She couldn't explain it but she felt that same instinct stir in her about her new neighbor. *No one should be alone like that.*

She pulled on the second knee-high.

She brushed her skirt hem down and reached for her black leather loafers. *Did he move here because of a job? Does he have family here?* She thought about the other young man— the blond one with the rude smirk—that had helped Brian move in. *His brother, maybe? No, couldn't be. They look nothing alike.*

Mazie couldn't put her finger on it but she wanted to know more about her new neighbor. The thing was, she hadn't seen him at all lately. She was an early riser herself and was always on the porch with her cup of coffee by six sharp every morning.

She knew the comings and goings of every soul in the neighborhood: the Perkins family across the street with the wild, red-headed twin boys, and Janice, two houses down, who had recently brought her elderly mother to live with her so she could help care for her, and the odd man with the strange little girl who lived on the corner directly across from her new neighbor.

Her mind back on Brian, she wondered again why she never saw him leave his house. He'd been living over there for a few weeks now. She wondered where he had come from and why he was here in Magnolia Springs.

What's wrong with me? Am I getting that bored with life that I'm spying on my neighbors now?

She glanced over at the digital clock on her dresser. It

took her a good twenty minutes to walk to Grace Methodist Church, where she'd faithfully attended every Sunday morning for the last thirty years.

I better get going.

The morning was glorious, with a gentle breeze and the sun warm against her skin. Being out in nature had always been a soothing tonic for her and she basked in the outdoors as often as possible. Careful to watch for pesky cracks in the sidewalk that might send her sprawling ungracefully to the concrete, Mazie took in the freshly planted flower beds outside of a ranch-style house, noting the colorful arrangement of rose bushes sprinkled in each one.

As she walked, she thought again about Brian and what it was like to be young and on your own. Maybe he'd gone through a divorce and moved here for a change of scenery. There was also the possibility that he just *preferred* not being chained down to the responsibility of a family.

Mazie couldn't imagine feeling that way. She had met her husband, Harold, when she was twenty-three. She had been living in Southern California, working to earn extra money as a carhop at an A&W drive-in, balancing on roller skates as she served customers their meals through their car windows.

It just so happened that she failed to stop her skates one Saturday night and ended up plowing right into the side of Harold's turquoise Chevy pickup truck, sending his milk-shake sailing into his lap. They started dating two weeks later but Harold refused to marry her until he could earn enough money to support her. She waited two years.

Mazie never doubted once that he was worth the wait.

But Harold had cashed in on the part of his wedding vows that said *"till death do us part"* and now she was waiting again—this time to join him on the other side of glory. She couldn't help but wonder what God was keeping her around for. Every day felt as if there was a favorite coffee mug missing from life's shelf and that nothing would ever feel right again until she could be reunited with Harold.

No, she just couldn't believe that her neighbor—or anyone, for that matter—actually *liked* being alone.

Arriving at Grace Methodist, Mazie waved up at Karl, the pudgy-cheeked door greeter standing at the top of the steps leading to the church entrance. Seeing that one-third of the church was elderly—including herself—and couldn't make it up the eight (yes, she'd counted them) massive brick steps, she made her way around to the side—*ground level, thank you*—entrance through the Sunday school area. It gave her the opportunity to greet the children on her way in, one of the bright spots in her week.

No, Mazie would have never *chosen* to be alone.

Balancing a disposable paper cup, half-full of lukewarm coffee, in one hand and managing the steering wheel with the other, Brian meandered through the streets shrouded with the dense foliage of massive poplar trees, enfolding him in a warm cocoon of small-town hospitality. He'd been forced out of the house this morning in search of a decent breakfast, since he hadn't had time for a grocery trip yet. He wasn't disappointed.

At the far end of town, he was drawn to a cottage-style coffeehouse and made his way in, tossing his lukewarm coffee into a trash bin parked just outside the doors. The smell of strong coffee and fresh bread washed over him as he pushed open the door and made his way across a wood floor to the counter across the room. A friendly waitress stepped out of the kitchen and greeted him.

"Mornin' hon. You want to sit up to the counter or at a table?"

Brian slid onto a stool at the end of the long laminate counter. "This will do."

He didn't need a menu. He had a craving this morning.

"Do you make omelets here?"

"We sure do. What all do you want on it?"

Brian ordered a sausage and spinach omelet with extra cheese and a large orange juice. He took his time eating it while he listened to the soft hum of voices around him. He was a loner by nature but found himself wanting to be around humanity this morning. After downing the last of his orange juice and paying at the register, he headed for his car. Before he opened the car door, he looked across the road and noticed the river was within walking distance. Pocketing his keys, Brian jogged across the empty road.

Dodging timber and slogging through a deep carpet of dry leaves, he made his way to the river edge.

The Magnolia River drifted lazily under the morning sun as if waking from a long night of slumber. Brian stood on its bank and watched the ripples sway at its center, listening to the gurgles as the water licked against the rocks a few feet from where he stood. The river was as unobtrusive and unhurried as the town itself.

That was part of the attraction for Brian when he considered moving here. That and the memories that he'd had here with his grandmother.

He breathed in the musty smell of wet earth and dry foliage and felt at peace with himself. Closing his eyes, he listened to the birds exchanging chatter in the trees and the gentle bubbling of the river.

Maybe this is just what I needed.

Here in Magnolia Springs, Brian was away from his old life and reminders of painful memories. The flow of the water in front of him was the polar opposite of the stagnant memories that weighed him down this morning. The disconnect he felt with friends and family was soothed by the connection he felt with nature in this moment.

He had no intention of seeking out friends in this new place and, other than Finn and the charming but nosey old woman next door who had dropped by a few times with desserts, Brian had not had a full conversation with anyone here.

He ventured out to the grocery store twice a week, had

CHAPTER 2 | 19

a tire replaced on his car, and had checked out the local hardware store. He was always courteous—he had to keep his options open for future clients—but that was the extent of his exploring. It wasn't that he was a hermit or harbored bitterness against humankind, he just preferred his own company these days. There was plenty of time to explore relationships when he was ready for them. And, right now, he wasn't.

He blinked against the bright sun when he heard a truck pull up on the road behind him and turned to investigate. A middle-aged man wearing a tank top and shorts was heading toward a mailbox mounted on a small wooden pier hanging over the river edge about thirty feet from where he stood. Brian hadn't noticed it was there until now but remembered his grandmother telling him that many residents of Magnolia Springs had their mail delivered via a mail carrier coming down the river. The quaint delivery style had been a part of the town for over a hundred years and was the only river route mail delivery still in use in the United States.

The man noticed Brian as he bent to open the door of a rusty metal mailbox. He waved and greeted him with a chipper "Good morning!" Brian nodded and waved back before jogging back across the street.

～

PASTOR BECKHAM HAD outdone himself this morning, expounding with untethered enthusiasm about the virtues of evangelizing a lost world with the message of hope and salvation.

Mazie was so engaged in the service she hadn't even eaten one of the mints from her sweater pocket. Her heart burned with the residue from the message and she dreaded spending another evening home alone. At least she had Emily's to look forward to on the way home.

Emily's Book Barn stood on a corner just a block and a half away from where Mazie lived and she passed it every Sunday going to and from church, often stopping in after church to see her young friend, Claire, the owner.

The twin metal bells tied to the door handle with jute rope tinkled sweetly as she pushed her way into the bookstore. Claire was talking on the landline at the front register but waved and held up a finger to let Mazie know she would be right with her.

No worries, she thought. *I'll just go peruse the muffin selection.*

Making her way around a large owl statue displayed next to the *New Releases* bookstand, she shuffled over to an antique sideboard where the coffee and pastries were housed. She paused to tap a book back into place that was jutting out from a bottom shelf with the end of her cane before moving on.

She could smell the rich coffee and immediately felt a familiar contentment settle over her as she headed toward the cozy armchair next to the sideboard. She'd wait here for Claire to finish up her business, since she always poured the coffee for them anyway.

Emily's Book Barn was a staple in Magnolia Springs for new and used books and folks drove from several nearby towns to browse the sizable book collection.

It was Claire's grandmother, Emily, who had purchased the old, dilapidated insurance office a decade ago and given its walls a fresh coat of paint and filled its rooms with books. Since she had scrimped and saved up the money to buy it on her own, she thought it only right to name the place after herself. Emily's Book Barn had been a beloved fixture for faithful patrons who had often come to visit with Emily as much as they came to purchase and exchange books.

Two years ago, she'd suffered a minor stroke and had turned the business over to Claire, who had spent much of her time coming by after work to help out with stocking shelves, dusting, and other housekeeping tasks. Emily was often heard saying how she couldn't manage the bookstore without her help and was always telling people that Claire was her favorite granddaughter, to which Claire always chuckled and remarked, "I'm your *only* granddaughter, Nana."

Claire began taking over more and more of the bookstore responsibilities, while Emily puttered about dusting shelves and chatting with the regulars, until, last year, she decided to just stay home and bake pastries for a few local restaurants. Her chocolate chip cookies often appeared on the coffee bar muffin tray, but Mazie was too polite to mention that she thought her own cookies tasted much better.

Mazie sunk deeper into the buttery-soft chair cushion, stiff muscle tissue and achy joints soothed in the strong arms of the oversized chair, the hook of her cane a perfect fit over the chair arm. Along with the bold coffee aroma, she inhaled the subtle scent of the earthy, musky smell of old books that permeated the air. Tiny dust particles danced in the shaft of sunlight that peeked through the lace curtains behind the looming sideboard, making her suddenly feel drowsy.

She didn't even hear Claire approach until several *thuds* broke the serenity of the moment and caused Mazie to jerk sideways in the chair.

"Oopsie! Sorry, Mazie. I'm so clumsy today."

Claire scooped up several books scattered on the floor and balanced them on the top of a small pile already stacked in her arms. She walked over and unloaded the dusty tower on the far edge of the sideboard and reached for the roll of paper towels next to her. Tearing off two, she wiped her hands and gave her neck a swab before tossing them in a wicker basket at her feet.

"How was church this morning?" she asked, looking over her shoulder at Mazie.

Mazie lifted herself higher in the chair and pulled the hem of her cotton dress down where it had crept up above her knees. It wouldn't do for Claire to catch her nodding off, but, thankfully, she had already turned back and was busy wiping out two mugs with a clean towel.

"Good! Pastor Beckham delivered a fine sermon this morning." She allowed for a long dramatic pause for effect.

"It really is too bad that you have to work on Sunday mornings or you could come with me," she slipped in. She'd been hinting to Claire for months now that she should close up shop on Sundays like most other local businesses did. That way, she would be free to attend church. Claire had disagreed, arguing that Sundays were the best day for bookstores because that's when most people had time to relax and enjoy some downtime.

"A bookstore is one of the first places people want to go to relax, Mazie," she had argued.

Claire looked back at Mazie and gave her a noncommittal smile.

"Creamer?"

"As always," Mazie sighed. "A teaspoon of sugar too."

After setting Mazie's cup down on the drum-shaped table next to her, Claire sat across from her on a simple hardwood dining chair and crossed her ankles in front of her.

She had hoped Claire would lead the conversation back to church, and Mazie wrestled with how to slip it back into the conversation, but Claire had already moved on.

"Did you get that section of fence repaired?" Claire asked.

A recent storm had come through and knocked down a

small section of fence between Mazie's house and the neighbor's—Brian's house, actually—and had broken two of her Japanese Wisteria vines.

"Oh, yes," she said. "A worker came out last week and repaired the broken section. He even found white paint that matched the rest of the fence perfectly. He even charged me less than he had quoted me over the phone. Probably felt sorry for a little old woman like me."

Claire giggled. "Right, Mazie. You probably hobbled around, telling him you were barely surviving, eating cat food just to get by, so he'd have pity on you."

Mazie winked. "You got me all figured out, young lady."

While they talked, minuscule wheels began to turn in her head, churning out a wee little spark in her mind. It came so softly, she almost wondered if the Lord himself had planted the seed in her imagination. It *had* seemed like such a spiritually enlightening sort of morning so far. Not one to quench the moving of the spirit, with the best of intentions she tiptoed her way into uncharted waters.

"I have a new neighbor."

Mazie studied the young woman across from her over the top of her mug as steam crept over her cheeks and tickled her nostrils. Claire had slid a rubber band off her wrist and had her fingers tied up in her hair as she worked it into a ponytail. Her chin bobbed as she acknowledged the casual announcement.

"Oh, really? The empty house on the corner—the one

that shares the fence that you just had fixed?" she asked.

Mazie lowered the cup and slid it onto the side table, searching for direction from the Lord—from *anywhere* honestly—she wasn't picky.

"Yes, the corner house. It's been vacant for the past few years since it went into foreclosure on the last owners. A real eyesore too with that overgrown tree dropping leaves all over my yard and the grass dead and brown. A graveyard would be nicer to look at than that lawn."

She shuddered. She was so meticulous about keeping her yard trim and neat—paid a nice fee for a landscaping company to keep it that way too—that the languishing view butted up against hers was like a festering thorn in her side. Brian had recently started cleaning the yard up a bit but it still had a long way to go in her eyes.

"So...a young man moved in a few weeks ago." She cleared her throat. "Such a polite and *handsome* fellow. I've dropped off baked goods a few times, you know, to check up on him, and make him feel welcome."

She wanted to share more about Brian. Roll out a list of his appealing attributes and charming personality but, truth was, Mazie really didn't know a hoot about him. She was almost disappointed in herself.

The first time, she'd brought him sourdough cookies, another time it was macadamia nut bars...oatmeal raisin cookies the day before yesterday. He'd *oohed* and *aahhed* respectfully over each lovingly baked offering, asked politely about her day and other appropriate small-talk gibberish and she'd nodded and blubbered out the standard, *You're welcome…Just thought I'd share….Nice to see the property getting back in shape…You have a good day.*

Not once did she ask about where he'd come from, what had brought him to Magnolia Springs, did he attend church (although she calculated that he didn't since she never saw him come or go on Sundays either) or what he did for a living. Well, maybe the last question would be a little too bold. She smiled at Claire.

"Anyhow, his name is Brian. Kind of quiet though. Keeps to himself." She didn't know why she said it, but thought it might help the cause by adding the small white lie, "I believe he does some kind of undercover work or something like that, although he hasn't come right out and said it…" She trailed off.

Making it appear as an afterthought, she let her eyes roam over Claire's face, giving her a careful study, and added, "As a matter of fact, I think he's close to your age."

Claire wasn't buying it. One eyebrow arching upward, she grinned. Her head gave the faintest shake and her hands were neatly folded into her lap.

"Huh, that's nice." She popped out of her chair and reached for Mazie's coffee mug. "Need a refill?"

Mazie sighed softly. She had tested the course and had slammed face-first into a wall. But that didn't deter her. Once she set out on a worthy mission, she wouldn't rest until she'd seen it through to the finish line, or, at least, until the path broke off in a dead end.

CHAPTER 3

BRIAN'S NOSTRILS burned as he studied the words on the page.

Do I smell smoke?

His brain was on overdrive as he stared at the computer screen in front of him. *Nah, I'm starting to imagine things. I seriously need to start getting more sleep.*

He blinked several times, trying to clear the floating clouds in his vision. The brochure he'd been working on for a client for the past several hours was starting to blur into a haze of colors and text that was no longer making sense. He'd already spent much of the night updating another client's website and had gotten only a few hours of sleep and a late lunch before launching into this project.

Pushing away from the desk, he allowed his head to drop back against the chair, his eyelids slowly blanketing his tired eyes. "Time for a cup of coffee," he mumbled into the vacant room. The tantalizing aroma of a fresh cup of strong coffee teased at his senses, as if a pot were already brewing, luring him to the kitchen. His eyes shot open.

I do smell smoke...

He was on his feet and sprinting down the hall before the desk chair had stopped rolling behind him. Skidding to a stop in the kitchen, he glanced to the stove. *No flames.* Skimmed the perimeter of the kitchen. *Everything's fine.* By instinct, he was drawn to the open kitchen window.

Moving toward it, the burning stench grew stronger and a soft haze hung in the air. Inching closer, he peered through the window screen and noticed a plume of dark ashen smoke drifting over the back fence. It looked like it was coming from the neighbor's backyard.

Mazie's yard.

"Oh, boy." Brian shot out the back door, slipping on a pair of flip-flops next to the doormat, and ran toward the high wood fence separating the two properties. It wasn't easy trying to run in the flimsy rubber sandals but he managed to race through the grass and hike himself up over the tall planks like an Olympic marathoner, landing rear-first in a large bougainvillea bush that he was sure would leave deep scratches on his arms and legs.

After untangling himself from the thorny mess, Brian spotted Mazie standing dazed in front of a large black charcoal grill that was spewing out billows of smoke. Sporadic flames shot from the grill while she stood frozen and continued to stare into the fog.

"Mazie! Get away from there!"

Brian covered the distance between them, snatching the spatula from Mazie's grip and giving her a not-so-gentle shove backward.

"Stand over there," he commanded. "Where's your hose?"

Brian's rough handling seemed to pull Mazie out of her daze and she fluttered about, pointing to the hose, waving her hands frantically to clear the smoke surrounding them, coughing into the long sleeve of her dress.

"Oh, my. Oh, my," she fussed. "I'm not sure what I did wrong. I...I put the meat on and, then, just went into the house for a minute..."

Brian doused the flames with the hose. It was a charcoal grill and not a propane one, for which he was thankful. The flames hissed and sputtered as they succumbed to the deluge flooding down on them. The metal grill was a mess —a huge black gaping mouth, streams of water drooling over its sides and onto the flooded grass beneath it.

When everything seemed to be under control, Brian released the hose lever and the spewing water ceased. Only then did he place the hose on the ground and release his breath. Fists planted hard against his hips, he watched the last ropes of smoke drift lazily into the air. Sweat dripped down into his eyes as he felt the adrenaline seep from his body.

"Whew, that was close. You okay?" he said, turning toward Mazie, who stood quietly behind him. She was staring at the sputtering grill as if she were trapped in a state of shock and couldn't break her gaze from the horror of the scene. She was also crying.

Brian's hands dropped to his sides as he stepped toward her.

"Mazie? Are you alright?" He followed her gaze to the black mess, then looked back at her. "Everything's out now —you're safe." *Did it really shake her up that bad?*

Blinking, Mazie turned her eyes to him. "Harold...well, he...he always did the grilling. I...I didn't think it was that hard."

She looked down at the ground, her hands twisted into the front of her dress with white-knuckled fists, which Brian noticed were also trembling. Not having much experience with women in distress, he wasn't sure what to say or do next. Mazie saved him the trouble.

"Harold, my husband, he—" She took a deep breath and released her grip on the dress, smoothing down the bunched material as she spoke.

"My husband died two years ago."

She didn't seem to feel the need to explain any further or even need him to respond. But Brian felt even more lost at this point.

A widow.

Brian hadn't realized she lived in this big house all alone. And, now, she'd come close to burning the place down. He considered that there must be a lot of uncharted waters for her that she still needed to work through.

He shoved his hands into his pockets. He could smell the stench of sweat and smoke clinging to his skin and clothes and felt itchy all over. But he couldn't very well just leave her standing in her yard with a scorched grill and having just laid her heart out at his feet. He said the first thing that came to his mind.

"Wow, I'm…really sorry to hear that, Mazie."

He gazed around the property instead of at Mazie, partly to avoid her seeing the pity in his eyes and partly to get a look around and judge how he could leave the yard in some kind of decent order for her—maybe clean things up a bit. He knew he should leave the grill to cool off until tomorrow, at least, then decide what to do with it. Honestly, there wasn't a whole lot he could do right now. He turned his eyes to Mazie, who still stood in front of him with a shell-shocked expression on her face. *Sheesh, here I go…*

"I had planned to order pizza for dinner. Since you don't"—he avoided glancing back at the offending reminder behind him—"have dinner now, you wanna come sit on the porch and visit while I order us something?"

He didn't know what had possessed him to submit such a proposal to the old woman. I mean, sure, he felt awful that she had just been through a traumatic experience and lord knows what she would have done had he not come flying over her fence like a superhero, but inviting her over for pizza seemed a bit drastic. *Oh, well, I'm committed now.* He felt like kicking himself.

He knew he'd said the right thing when she smiled at

him and brushed the tears from her cheeks with sooty fingers, leaving a comical black streak under one eye.

"Sure you don't mind an old lady having dinner on the porch with you? The neighbors might talk." She sniffled, then grinned.

He grinned back.

"I don't know anybody in this neighborhood besides you. I'll manage."

"Alright," she said, then looked down at her dress, which was also streaked with dark smudges. "I'll go in and change. I smell like a coal miner."

Brian was glad to see she had pulled herself together. He didn't think he could handle any more drama right now.

"Oh, and I just made a batch of cinnamon rolls! We can nibble on those while we wait for the pizza. I'll pitch in a few dollars too."

Brian headed toward the front of the house—he wasn't going back over that prickly bush and fence again. "No, Mazie, I got this. Just go change."

MAZIE PEERED over at the young man sitting across the porch table from her. She noted the dark waves of glossy, black hair and the fine chisel of his narrow chin. She guessed him to be around twenty-eight—maybe thirty.

She was still curious about what he did for a living but

put the wayward thought on the shelf for now. He was obviously paying for his house and the vehicle sitting in his driveway, so he had income coming from *somewhere*. Mazie cleared her throat—rather loudly at that—and dabbed at the edge of her mouth with her napkin.

"Thank you, Brian, for saving my life and home tonight. I don't know what I would have done had you not stepped in. Or should I say *jumped* in?" She giggled.

It hadn't dawned on her until she was standing in her bedroom changing into clean clothes, reliving the scene in her mind, that he'd come sailing over her fence and bounced off her bushes to help her.

I guess it was faster than coming up the front driveway and through the gate.

A hunk of pizza crust dangled from his fingers as Brian stared at Mazie. He blinked a few times and she could tell she had left him speechless.

He's humble, she noted with satisfaction.

"Uh, well, Mazie, to be honest, I don't think my running over and putting out a grill fire for you was all that heroic." He set the crust down on his paper plate and sat back in his chair. "I'm pretty sure your life and home weren't in any imminent danger either."

The look on his face was the perfect picture of clueless, which made things a whole lot easier for Mazie.

"I owe you, Brian. In fact, I have a splendid idea. Do you like lasagna?" she asked, not waiting for an answer. "Well…I make a wonderful lasagna and I insist on having you over for dinner—cooked *inside*, of course—say, this next Friday night?" Harold used to tell her that he could never resist her when she batted her bright green eyes at him. She batted them now.

Brian looked confused, dazed even. It took him a few throat-clearings before he could reply.

"That's...uh...that's kind of you. Really, it is. You don't *owe* me anything, Mazie... anyone would have..."

She was already waving his excuse away with her hand and gathering up her paper plate and napkin.

"Perfect! Next Friday night it is. Does six thirty work for you?" Her sharp mind kicked in just in time to throw in the question she was dying to ask. "Unless you have to work...?"

Brian scooted his chair back and stood, reaching for her plate. "I can take that..." She handed him her plate, throwing the napkin on top.

"No, I mean *yes*." Face flushed, he blew out a heavy breath. "Sure, yeah, six thirty will be fine. I usually don't start working on client projects until after nine. I prefer to work later at night."

Mazie smiled innocently. "Oh, you work at home then?"

He looked down at the plates in his hand and, for a second, she thought he wasn't going to answer.

"Yes, I do. I'm a graphic designer. Uh, you know, computer work."

He's covering something up, she thought. *Look how he fumbled with his answer, like he made it up on the spot.*

Mazie plastered on a pleasant expression, burying any hint of skepticism that might be obvious on her face.

"Well, thank you, Brian, for dinner. I haven't had pizza delivered in years. You've been so kind." She stood and straightened the cushion on the chair. "I'm really looking forward to next Friday."

"Yes, ma'am. You're welcome." Brian set the plates back down and moved to help her. Tucking her arm into his, she let him lead her down the steps. She paused when they reached the bottom.

"We'll see you next Friday then," she said, releasing his arm and turning to him. "And if you have a lady friend or a girlfriend, you are welcome to invite her along as well."

Brian threw both hands up, palms out, and shook his head.

"That's kind of you but I'm not seeing anyone right now."

Two motorcycles passed, their thundering pipes briefly drowning out all conversation. When they had passed, so had the chance to pry for more information. Brian was already turning toward the house.

"Thanks for the cinnamon rolls," he called back. "They were top-notch."

As she ambled back to her house, Mazie's mind was already buzzing with determination. She'd taken a chance throwing that line out there about Brian inviting a girlfriend on Friday. How else was she going to get it out of him? Thank goodness he said that he was unattached.

Now to find a way to get Claire to dinner next Friday…

THE PHONE WAS RINGING when Brian made his way back into the house. Jamming his foot down on the trash can pedal to lift the lid, he dumped the pizza plates and trash in and let the lid slam.

He grabbed the phone on the fourth ring.

"Hello?"

"Hey, sweetie! How are you?"

It was his mother. He glanced at the clock: *7:52.*

"Hey, Mom. I thought you didn't get off work until nine?"

Brian's mom had been a waitress at Spencer's Bar & Grill for the past nineteen years. It had actually been Finn's mom who had gotten her the job the year after his dad left and she had needed to go back to work to support herself and Brian. Unfortunately, it was also a place frequented by a lot of distasteful men looking for lonely women. His mom had gone through a string of loser boyfriends over the years.

It made Brian's stomach burn with anger against his dad every time he thought about it. Of course, he knew the divorce wasn't just his dad's fault, but leaving them without hardly any money to live on and forcing his mom to work in a shady establishment was definitely something he could have helped avoid.

Brian heard her yawn on the other end of the line.

"Yeah, things were slow tonight so Steve let me leave early," she said. "Finn dropped by yesterday for that side table of Grandma's that you wanted. He said he'd bring it when he came out to see you sometime in the next few weeks. He also told me your place is pretty nice. I hope to get out to see it when I get some time off... If you don't mind, of course."

"Oh, yeah...thanks. I appreciate it. The place is a little bare and I need furniture to fill it up. It's bigger than the apartment was so I have a lot of empty space." Brian paused. He didn't really want to say it, but knew she expected to hear it. "And, Mom, you know you're always welcome to come."

They talked for a few more minutes, ending with his mom's promise to check into her schedule for a future visit.

After hanging up, Brian stood in the kitchen, realizing how still and quiet the room felt all of a sudden. At least living in apartments had provided some level of noise, whether it was one of the neighbors below him or next to him. He could almost understand why his mom kept latching on to new guys whenever a relationship didn't work out. Maybe the silence in her own house had gotten to be too much for her as well.

He felt bad for his mom—even a little guilty. He loved her, appreciated all she'd sacrificed to take care of him, but talking to her always left his stomach feeling like it was filled with lead. He knew he couldn't avoid her coming to see him *sometime* but wasn't ready for that to happen for a while. He had come to Magnolia Springs to put space between his old life and the one he was trying to forge for himself. Independence, distance, obscurity…that's what he craved right now in his life.

He thought about Mazie inviting him over for dinner on Friday and how she mentioned that he could bring a "lady friend." He hadn't had a *lady friend* in a long time and, to be honest, he didn't want one. Not after seeing how ugly the breakup between his mom and dad had been and how many times he had needed to comfort his mom whenever another guy dumped her or turned out to be a jerk.

No, he'd much rather live with the silence than an unwelcome heartache.

CHAPTER 4

SHE STARTED on her mission the very next morning.

Mazie mulled over calling Brian to help her clean up the mess in her backyard but decided against it. Better to not overtax her young neighbor's generosity. She'd just have someone haul the scorched grill to the dump and pay the landscape guy to put a raised bed of flowers in the vacant spot. She had other pressing things to tend to today.

After she'd dusted the final bagel crumbs from her housedress and checked for any more unwelcome weeds in her garden, Mazie changed into a pretty floral printed dress, slipped on her loafers, grabbed her handbag and cane, and made her way to Emily's Book Barn.

A midweek visit to the bookstore was unusual for her and she was lucky to find Claire working behind the counter when she walked in. Shock registered on Claire's face as she set aside the book she had been mending with binding tape.

"Mazie!" Claire called out and made her way around the counter. A customer standing nearby—an elderly gentleman with a newspaper rolled under his arm who was browsing the westerns—glanced over and frowned at the sudden outburst. Mazie paid him no mind.

"Good morning, Claire! I thought I'd drop by and say hello."

She leaned in for the hug offered by the younger woman, who still looked a bit surprised to see her on a weekday.

"Got any coffee on by any chance?"

She'd already had her morning coffee, just like every morning she woke to God's new day, but this was a special visit and, well, conversation just seemed to flow smoother over a cup of coffee.

Claire glanced over toward the sideboard where the coffee was kept.

"Actually, you're in luck. I just put a pot on to brew. I don't usually start brewing coffee too early in the day with no customers right off—coffee gets bitter if it sits too long. It might be a few minutes, though, before it's ready."

Mazie made her way to her favorite chair, hoping some old coot hadn't already taken residence in it. She gave a small sigh of pleasure. It was empty, just waiting for her.

You must be orchestrating this whole thing, Lord. Seating

herself comfortably, she turned her brightest smile up to Claire.

"Do you have some free time to join me? I would love a few minutes of conversation. It's been such a dull morning."

Claire glanced behind her, back to Mazie, then back toward the front of the store.

"Hang on, let me check on the gentleman up front and lock the register."

When Claire was finally seated across from her, Mazie scooted to the edge of her seat, pinning Claire with her stare.

"I have a confession to make."

Mazie tried her best to appear serious about the request she was about to make but was pretty sure she looked more like a five-year-old caught with a fistful of stolen candy.

"I actually came here to ask…well, to see if you'd like to come over for dinner."

Claire leaned toward Mazie, an awed expression on her lovely face.

"Really? Wow, I didn't expect that!" Claire slapped a hand to her forehead. "By the surprise visit and the look on your face, I thought you'd come to confess to a bank robbery or something."

Mazie laughed. "Sorry about that, dear. I didn't mean to seem so serious."

Claire shook her head, smiling. "I'm just teasing. But that is so sweet of you, Mazie! I would love to plan…"

"Friday night," Mazie interrupted.

"Oh, um, let's see. Friday night." Claire looked around as if searching for a calendar on the wall to refer to. Of course, there were none. She turned back to Mazie.

"I…would need to check. I mean, I don't *think* I have anything going on Friday night but…"

Mazie's remorseful five-year-old expression shifted to a convincing pout. She had to persuade the young woman that she would be heartbroken if she said no.

"Oh, I would so love it if you could, Claire. I'm making my homemade three-cheese lasagna. Not to brag, but everyone always begs me to make it for all the church potlucks," she added.

Before Claire could launch into another potential excuse, Mazie reached into her handbag and produced a small pad of paper and a pen. She jotted her phone number down and tore off the page, handing it confidently to Claire.

"Here's my number. Let's just plan on you coming, say around six fifteen?"

Her smile was infectious, judging by the grin forming on Claire's face. Figuring this was the best time to make her exit, Mazie stood, tucked her cane and handbag against her, and made her way to leave. As Claire escorted her to the door, peeking in on the gentleman who was engrossed in a book while he stood in the aisle, Mazie turned to her once more.

"Please let me know by tomorrow if you can't make it. I

want to shop for everything I need ahead of time. I just can't stand trying to pull things off at the last minute."

Claire shook her head and giggled. "Fine. I'll be there, Mazie. What can I contribute?"

Mazie could have sprouted wings and flown right out of the bookstore entrance from the joy coursing through her body. She would be singing the praises of the Lord all the way home.

"Nothing! I've got it all covered. We'll see you Friday at six fifteen!"

She slipped through the door Claire held open for her and scooted—practically skipped—down the sidewalk, cane and all. She was halfway to the corner when Claire called out to her.

"Hey! You never even got your coffee!"

Mazie turned and shrugged, giving a little wave of her fingers.

"It's alright, dear. I'll take that coffee on Sunday..."

MAZIE NEEDED to get a hold of herself.

She'd been sitting on the end of the bed for over a half hour carrying on like a baby. She woke up feeling a little out of sorts already this morning, having not slept well last night.

Then, when she remembered that she hadn't looked out the bedroom window for almost two weeks, she was shocked to see that the nest with the baby birds was abandoned, the nest in disrepair, with just wisps of feathers clinging to its shell. It had made her sad that the fledglings had all left and no longer depended on their parents for sustenance and protection.

She'd gone from the window to trying to retrieve a pill she'd dropped off her nightstand that had rolled under the bed. She had gotten down on her knees—quite a feat for her these days—to look for it and had discovered the slipper that Harold had lost at least three years ago. She'd have to ask the housekeeper why she hadn't been vacuuming under the bed. But the slipper had done it for her. On top of being tired and a little emotional over the empty nest, she had been missing Harold a lot this week.

Hence, the reason why she was sitting on the end of her bed weeping, caressing a dusty slipper.

Harold had overreacted about it too.

"Why are you always moving my things, Mazie!? I put my stuff right where I know where to find them and you are always taking them!" She could only stare at him while he raged, knowing full well she hadn't touched his slippers, or any of the other things he had been accusing her of moving all week.

She tried to answer calmly. "I'm sorry, Harold. I was cleaning and somehow misplaced one of them," she lied. "I'll look for it. If not, I'll buy you a new pair."

When he tore the house up later that evening looking for the car keys, he turned on her.

"You hid the car keys. Why? Give me the car keys, Mazie, or I'll call the police."

Yes, she *had* hidden the car keys. He had no business driving right now. She calmly finished washing the last dish in the sink and turned the water off. She hoped he would calm down and get himself under control. He was being completely unreasonable. What broke her heart the most was that he didn't even realize it.

Harold had never raised his voice to her. Had rarely even gotten angry and, if he did, he got over it quick. He was so gentle with her that, at times, she wished he had a little more fire in him just to keep things interesting. But it was his goal in life to make her happy. He always insisted that she be the one to pick where they went to eat and if she even so much as mentioned a new kitchen gadget she wanted, it would appear in her kitchen within a week.

Harold's world revolved around Mazie—and she had loved every minute of it.

But she didn't recognize the man he had become. They had warned her of the behavior changes, the erratic temper, depression, and mood swings. The deceptive pendulum between a loving husband and a violent stranger.

She reached over for the towel and dried her hands off while he tore apart the kitchen drawers and slammed cabinet doors closed.

"Where are the car keys? I want them now!" he raged as he stormed around the room.

"I'm sorry, Harold. Let me finish what I'm doing and

I'll get them," she lied again. She was stalling, hoping he'd move on.

That's when he struck her.

The large hand that swallowed hers when they went on walks and that lovingly wiped her brow when she raged with a fever one summer came down hard across her face. Overcome with grief more than pain, she reached into her apron pockets and handed him the keys, thinking to call the police to go after him if he drove away—letting them know that he wasn't safe on the road.

But he'd sat in the dark driveway, never even turning the car on, while she watched anxiously out the window to see what he would do. After a while, he came back in, set the keys on the counter, and went to bed, fully clothed.

She made the phone call the next morning. Not only was her heart breaking watching Harold deteriorate a little each day, but now she was also afraid.

THE TREE TOWERED above him like the never-ending vine from "Jack and the Beanstalk" as Brian stood beneath it, huffing from the exertion of sawing off its lower branches in an attempt to tidy the untamed behemoth into a more presentable display. The only grooming he had managed to accomplish was to leave unsightly nubs sticking out every which way from its massive trunk.

"I am no match for you big fella—or lady, whatever…"

he called up through the thick tangle of branches that seemed to mock his feeble efforts. Sucking in a heavy breath, Brian tossed his handsaw by the scattered mess of hacked tree parts around him and turned to go into the house.

"Yep, time to call the professionals in. Probably gonna cost me a fortune." He huffed under his breath.

And, here I am, talking out loud to a tree. Maybe I'm the one needing a professional.

Sitting on a worn wicker chair on the back porch, he unlaced his work boots and set them by the back door to air out. Judging by the soggy socks, he knew his boots would be drenched in sweat as well.

All I want is a long shower and a pitcher of ice-cold lemonade.

He knew he didn't have the lemonade, but the shower was definitely within reach. Glancing down at his watch, he saw that he'd been working several hours already.

It's already 5:28. Where had the time gone?

Like a bucket of ice water, it hit Brian cold in the face: *Mazie!* He had completely forgotten that he was supposed to have dinner at her house at six thirty. He had an hour to get cleaned up and…

Oh, no! I didn't even think to ask what I could bring to contribute.

He felt like a world-class heel for procrastinating and— yeah, who was he kidding?—he just plain forgot. It wasn't like entertaining an old lady for the rest of the evening was high on his priority list. In fact, if he had not let it slip his mind until it was too late, he would have gone over and made some excuse to get out of it. *Oh, well, I'm roped in now.*

Popping off the chair, Brian jerked the back door open. Racing into the kitchen, he started yanking open cabinets, searching frantically for a box of crackers—*Crackers? Really?* —or a boxed brownie mix. *Anything* that he could throw together so he didn't show up to dinner at Mazie's empty-handed. He was going to have to put on his game face as it was. He didn't want to look like a total loser on top of it.

Coming to the last set of cabinets above the stove, he spied the small white box sitting on the edge of the counter. The one with his mother's homemade peanut brittle that she'd mailed in her care package this week. The one that also had "Miss you, son!" written with a black marker across the top of it in her lovely cursive writing.

Yep, perfect!

He turned sharply to a cupboard behind him and scanned his plate collection, which consisted of only four mismatched ceramic plates he'd picked up for less than twenty bucks at the Dollar Store. He was a bachelor, for crying out loud, not a Better Homes and Garden featured dinner host.

Sliding a brick-red plate off the top of the stack, he set it on the counter and reached for the peanut brittle box. Peeling back the lid, he lifted the plastic wrap away from the contents, tipped the box over the plate, and gave it a gentle shake, careful not to shatter the peanut brittle into a thousand shards.

After wrapping the plate with a sheet of foil and shaking his head at how subpar his contribution to dinner appeared, Brian jogged off to shower and dress. He had forty minutes left.

SHE WAS PRACTICALLY GIGGLING and that was something a woman of her age didn't normally engage in, but she hadn't felt this tickled in years. In fact, she hadn't felt this *alive*—this invigorated with *purpose*— since she'd headed up the Children's Ministry annual fundraiser at church.

Her company would be here in twenty minutes and everything was in perfect order. Her three-cheese lasagna had come out beautifully—with the cheese bubbly and toasty brown—and was cooling on the stovetop. The homemade crusty bread was due to come out in fifteen minutes. The house smelled like an Italian restaurant, complimented by the crooning of Dean Martin's Italian love songs drifting from the CD player on top of the microwave.

She walked over to the refrigerator and peeked in on the homemade tiramisu cheesecake encased in a glass cake stand on the top shelf. Chocolate ganache drizzled teasingly down the sides and the delicate peaks of mascarpone sprinkled with cocoa were just the right touch to the masterpiece.

It's almost too pretty to eat, she thought.

Mazie was pleased with dinner's progress so far. One

didn't serve dinner the minute company walked in the door. Better to give them time to sit and visit, or, in her experience with this younger generation, expect that they might even be a few minutes late.

And company tonight was plural. She grinned up at her reflection in the china cabinet glass across from the kitchen island, where she stood dicing cucumbers for the salad. Even after a tiring week of planning for dinner, catching a ride to the grocery store from her neighbor, Janice, and keeping tonight's company in the dark about each other, the whole experience was inspiring for an old gal like her.

She was really hoping her plan went smoothly. She felt a twinge of guilt at misleading Claire about Brian, trying to make him sound more interesting to draw the girl's attention. She felt even more guilty with the fact that she had lured both of them to dinner tonight without disclosing that either one was coming.

Forgive me, Lord. I'll handle things better next time.

Meanwhile, she needed to touch up her hair before her company arrived.

CHAPTER 5

BRIAN SAT on the loveseat across from the petite blonde, who studied the pictures on the walls, leafed briefly through the coffee table book with colorful photos of unique birdhouses, stared at the area rug under her feet—anything to avoid looking at him. She looked as awkward as he felt.

He could hear Mazie humming in the kitchen. She'd already refused both of their offers for help, insisting that she "only had a few things to finish up" and shooed them into the living room until she called them for dinner. She'd barely even glanced at the plate of peanut brittle Brian had shyly handed her before turning to introduce him to the woman who sat across from him now—Claire was her name. It was obvious by the stunned look on her face that he was just as unexpected as she was to him.

Mazie, however, was as chipper as ever—*even giddy*—and Brian wondered briefly if there were cameras hidden somewhere and they were on some kind of a reality show about how people react when placed in awkward situations. Not only did he feel awkward, he was also seething inside.

He would be having a chat with Mazie about this later.

So, here they sat, avoiding eye contact and conversation like two enemies thrown together in a foxhole in the middle of a warzone. *This is dumb*, he thought, *she looks as shell-shocked as I am*. Brian cleared his throat.

"So…are you related to Mazie? Her granddaughter…?"

At least Claire was looking his way now, even if she stared at him like he had a third eye. It was still better than the silent waltz they'd been attempting for the past ten minutes.

Brows puckered, she shook her head. "No, not at all." Settling back against the couch, she seemed to relax now that Brian had broken the ice. "Mazie is a customer who comes to the bookstore where I work and well, she's a good friend too."

Her words drifted off and her gaze dropped back to the rug. Brian figured the brief exchange was over until he spied her peeking up at him, a curious expression on her face. Her bottom lip tucked in and she chewed its corner as if she was burdened with a heavy secret and was puzzling on whether to let him in on it.

"Are you…" A pale hand lifted to her mouth and she nibbled delicately on her thumbnail. "I mean, Mazie mentioned that her neighbor did some kind of undercover…or, I don't know, secret service, work or something. Was she talking about you?"

Brian did some fast calculating. Unless she was referring to someone down the block, the neighbors he'd seen that lived in close proximity to him and Mazie didn't seem to fit the job description—the rotund guy across the street who was always yelling at his kids in the front yard, the woman a few doors down who Brian had only seen in a 1950s parade of house dresses.

Then again, he thought, *it's not like you can stereotype under-cover law enforcement. In fact, maybe the housedress lady was secretly working on busting someone babysitting more than three kids in their house without a daycare license.*

He had to bite hard on his inner cheek to keep from saying something rude pertaining to Mazie's advanced age causing her to be delusional or something.

Where had Mazie come up with this exaggeration?

The best he could do was fake a light cough to cover up an irritated snort.

"No, ma'am, I'm positive she wasn't talking about me and, to be honest, I have no idea *who* Mazie was referring to as far as our neighbors."

Speaking of Mazie, the guilty culprit popped out from the kitchen doorway with remarkable spunk.

"All ready! Let's eat!"

Yeah, he was most certainly going to be asking Mazie a few things later on.

~

"GREAT DINNER, MAZIE."

Brian reached for his second piece of bread and looked to Claire to see if she wanted one as well. She held up a hand.

"No, thanks. I couldn't eat another bite." She smiled over at Mazie, who studied a lasagna noodle she was pushing around on her plate, seeming to be a hundred miles away instead of at the table with them.

"I'm with Brian. The meal was amazing, Mazie."

Mazie speared the noodle and popped it in her mouth. She beamed up at them both. "My pleasure, dears. I'm so glad you enjoyed it." She pulled the napkin from her lap and dabbed at her lips.

"I hope you saved room for dessert. It's a tiramisu cheesecake. This was my first time trying the recipe but I know it will be delicious—I licked the spoon." She grinned.

With that, she stood and began gathering their plates. Brian started to rise to help but Claire stood up before he could.

"You go ahead and have a seat, Mazie," Claire said. "I've got this."

Brian sat back down.

"Oh, no," Mazie said. "You let me take care of this while you two enjoy each other's company. I'm just going to load these into the dishwasher."

Claire started to protest but Mazie insisted. "Go on." She pointed Claire back to her seat.

Claire lowered herself to her chair. Brian was surprised when she reached for the last piece of bread.

I thought she couldn't eat another bite?

Neither one of them could think of a thing to say—at least Brian couldn't anyway. Maybe Claire had a lot of things to say, but not to him. From the corner of his eye, he watched her finger the cloth napkin in front of her and pretend to study a picture of an old barn on the wall across the room.

Brian wiped a finger down the condensation on his water glass, then brushed away an invisible hair on his forehead as the uncomfortable silence hung between them like a laundry line of wet clothes. The only sounds in the room were the clinking of dishes as Mazie loaded the dishwasher and the music drifting over from a CD player on the microwave. He could hear fragments of Dean Martin crooning about being lonesome and begging his lover to return.

Brian was about to start chewing on the ice in his glass just to have something to do when Claire shifted in her chair to face him.

"So, what brought you to Magnolia Springs?"

The question caught him off-guard. He was surprised that she would initiate a conversation, since a moment ago she had looked like she wanted to crawl under the table.

He almost wished they had continued on in silence.

There was no way he was going to expose the real reasons he'd made the move to Magnolia Springs: escaping the drama of his mother's turbulent relationships with men and the memories of growing up in a run-down part of Mobile, Alabama with a single mother. It still left a bitter taste in his mouth. Not that Mobile itself was bad—he loved a lot of things about it. Finn still lived there and so did a lot of other good friends he'd made while growing up. But it was what he *lacked* growing up that made the memories painful for him.

It would make him sound like he was running away from something…which was exactly what he was doing.

His parents had gone through a messy divorce when Brian was eleven that separated him and his brother, Derek, who was thirteen at the time. Derek went with their dad and he had stayed with their mom. Like an old, threadbare cloth that no longer held any value, the family was torn right down the middle.

Brian hardly ever saw his brother or his dad after the final papers were signed, especially after dad and Derek moved to Florida, widening the gap between them—a gap that had remained an empty canyon in his life ever since.

It was part of the reason Brian shied away from relationships. It wasn't that he didn't want to settle down with a nice girl and start a family—he just didn't want to mess it up like his parents had. Having dated a few girls here and there who always seemed to either be just interested in having a good time or dragging him to the altar had also quelled his enthusiasm for investing in a relationship.

Dating and relationships were just too complicated to bother with. Besides, when he decided to go into business for himself a few years ago, he knew he would want to be well-established first before even considering settling down. Since his business was remote, he could also work from anywhere—in his case, his own home office. That made moving away from Mobile a whole lot easier for him.

Magnolia Springs was the perfect place for him to start fresh. His grandmother had lived here for many years before moving to an assisted living facility and he had always loved visiting her when he was growing up. Moving to Magnolia Springs was a good change of scenery for him.

But he wouldn't tell Claire all that backstory.

"My grandmother used to live here and I always enjoyed visiting her during the summer. It just seemed like a nice place to relocate to."

"Oh, that's nice." She nodded thoughtfully. "Yeah, Magnolia Springs is a great place to live. It's easy to fall in love with it."

Brian searched for a question he could ask her to keep the conversation flowing but came up blank. He was relieved when Claire hopped to her feet and reached for the empty bread plate to carry to Mazie.

"Mazie," she said, making her way across the room, "should I get the dessert ready?"

CHAPTER 6

It was Thursday and she was running late, something akin to a sin in Mazie's "rule book for life."

She'd had to rush through her bagel, even abandoning a chunk of it to the birds when she went out to water her roses, and she dumped the last few sips of her cold coffee into the sink. What had gotten into her this morning to put her so behind schedule?

Tugging on her blue sweater—which, she noticed with agitation, had a snag on one sleeve—Mazie knew the answer. She'd had another rough night, tossing and turning until, sometime after three in the morning, she had given in to the grief and had herself a good cry.

Today was her and Harold's wedding anniversary. Well, it *would* have been if he hadn't up and died on her, leaving her to face the echoes of her own voice bouncing off the walls of this big house. They had been married forty-four and three-quarter years.

Couldn't have hung around a little longer to make it a flawless forty-five, she pouted.

She was glad for that many years, though.

At least he didn't have a heart attack right after a spat between us. Then we would've never had a chance to say "I'm sorry" and would have had to wait to make things right on the other side of the pearly gates.

No, it didn't happen like that at all.

It was a slow death for Harold that ate at his soul before it was even evident in his body, and a part of her died with him every day that she lost him to the darkness of his mind, his forgotten memories. The stab of pain and hopelessness that pierced her soul the day they got the diagnosis replayed over and over in her mind this morning as she drifted through the house getting ready for her day.

"The tests are indicating Alzheimer's, Mr. Ellinger."

Dr. Harper pronounced the death sentence with as much gentleness as if he were breaking the heart of a child, his chair pulled close to Harold's, eyes brimming with compassion, his voice low and soothing.

Harold held tight to Mazie's hands, his thumb gently rubbing her skin, as if that small act alone might shield her from the grievous burden being placed on them.

"It's okay, Mazie. Everything is going to be alright," Harold whispered—always the strong one, the steadfast optimist.

She didn't know why, but instead of giving her attention to Harold in that moment—when he needed her the most —her eyes were drawn to the open window across the room where the sky had been darkening each hour with clouds ever since early morning when the two of them had sat on the porch together. Perhaps the world was preparing to weep with her—if she could even find the relief of tears. In that moment, her emotions were frozen in time.

No, Harold, everything is not going to be alright.

The signs had been there, but they hadn't understood what was happening. When they went to their favorite restaurant a few months before, Harold had gone to the restroom and couldn't find his way back to the table. Their waiter found him standing in front of the live lobster tank, looking dazed and confused. After being led back to their table, she had laughed and teased him, saying something about him getting old and forgetful.

Then Harold had stopped singing. He was forever singing around the house, while helping her with dishes and loudly in the shower, humming while he read the news-paper sitting on the porch next to her—which always irri-tated her when she tried to read her book—and making up silly lyrics to instrumental classical songs on the radio. As if spending a whole day at work around music wasn't enough for him.

She noticed the silence first. Then she noticed how he brooded and how he got so angry with her over the most trivial things. Things that never bothered him before. When they started getting late notices and phone calls about missed payments on bills, she confronted him.

"Harold, what is going on with you?" She scolded when he left the stove on one afternoon and then left the milk to warm on the counter later that night.

He didn't remember the stove or the milk.

She made the appointment for him. After an exhausting circus of visits to their primary care doctor and two neurologists, mental cognitive testing, and brain scans, they had arrived at this: *The tests are indicating Alzheimer's, Mr. Ellinger.*

Shocked and numb, they left Dr. Harper's office holding hands, resolving to live each day to its fullest. They walked for hours in the park after leaving the clinic until the clouds that had threatened from overhead all morning finally broke forth with a torrent of rain and they had been forced to go home.

Her darling husband, best friend, and love of her life started his death march from that day forward, whether he tried to deny it or not. And—as it often happens with soulmates who share a lifetime together—so had she.

Mazie finished tucking her feet into her loafers and reached for the cane hanging on the bedpost. She debated whether she wanted to bother with it this morning, but the walk to Magnolia Children's Hospital was long and treacherous in places. *I better not chance it.* She pulled the cane to her and stood.

Her head felt heavy from lack of sleep and her chest felt

bruised with aching. She should just call Rebecca and tell her that she wasn't feeling well today. And it would be true.

What do they call it nowadays? Taking a mental health day.

No, she wasn't gonna start that nonsense. She hadn't sat around feeling sorry for herself hardly at all these past two years since Harold passed and she didn't plan to start now. Okay, that was a lie. She did have her moments—quite a few, actually—but she was quick to give herself a pep talk and move on. This morning's "pep talk" on the porch over breakfast hadn't gone so well and now she was running late because of it.

It took her another ten minutes before she was actually out the door after washing her coffee cup (she couldn't stand to leave dirty dishes), digging through the pantry for the bag of gummy bears she *thought* she'd put in a place where she'd remember it, and another trip to the bathroom since she couldn't seem to hold her unpredictable bladder for more than thirty minutes anymore. After tucking her keys behind the angel statue and adjusting the grocery bag on her arm that held her coin purse and the bag of gummy bears, Mazie guided her cane down the steps and hurried on her way.

Janice was out walking her dog up ahead on the sidewalk. If she wasn't already behind schedule, Mazie would call out for Janice to wait up so that she could catch up on how her ailing mother was coming along, but that wasn't an option this morning.

Maybe I'll drop by on my way home.

Thinking about showing up on Janice's doorstep with nothing in her hands gave her pause. *No, that won't do. I need to plan a time when I can bake a little something to bring over first.* She watched as Janice tugged her dog off a patch of grass and made her way around the corner.

The morning was crisp and lovely. Not too chilly at all. Mazie enjoyed the sounds of birdsong and the hum of distant traffic as she swayed down the sidewalk. Someone was playing the piano and the sweet chords of an old hymn she recognized drifted from the open window across the street. She smiled and a deep sigh escaped her.

I sure do hate walking alone, Harold. And on our wedding anniversary too.

The memories just wouldn't let go this morning, but had buried their talons into her spirit and held her captive.

For the past ten years, Mazie had faithfully volunteered a few mornings each week on the children's cardiac floor at Magnolia Children's Hospital. Being around all the children—even when they were sick and hurting—made her feel young, and easing their suffering and shouldering some of the burden from the staff's shoulders made her feel useful.

She knew she wasn't a big help, of course, with her limitations, but she could sit and visit with fussy toddlers who fought being imprisoned in a caged hospital bed so the nurses could finish their rounds or sit in the playroom with a bucket and bleach water to sterilize the toys once a week.

Harold had always joined her on her walks to the

hospital on those mornings, mostly complaining that they had a dependable car sitting right in the garage that he could transport her in. But she always brushed him off, preferring the fresh air.

You'd think he would have given up on asking after all those years of me refusing. Only if the weather was bad would she let him drive her.

At the front steps of the hospital, Harold always gave her cheek a light peck before watching her disappear through the sliding doors and had another peck ready when he picked her up a few hours later. They'd talk all the way home, mostly her updating him on little Anna's progress or how she'd cajoled three-year-old Colton into eating his mashed potatoes by letting him suck them up through a large smoothie straw.

It was a few weeks before she returned to volunteering after Harold's death, and several months to accept the tortured silence of walking there alone. Over time, though, she'd learned to retune her ears to the sounds of the world around her that had been drowned out by the ebb and flow of talking with her sweetheart.

Speaking of sweethearts and conversation...

She felt the nostalgia and grief lift as she tugged her thoughts toward something more pleasant, like dinner last Friday.

Mazie grinned and fluttered like a peacock as she thought about how well dinner had gone. Her three-cheese lasagna had turned out perfect, Brian and Claire gushing out all the proper "Oooohhhs" and "Delicious!" compliments she'd grown used to over the years whenever she served it. But it was the delightful connection that seemed to take place between the two that tickled Mazie the most as she stood waiting for the "Walk" signal to blink from the pole across the street.

They seemed to hit it off so well.

Sure, she'd interjected a comment here and there so it wasn't so obvious that she'd orchestrated the whole meeting, but not so much that the attention was drawn to her instead of, well…each other. Claire had even thanked her a second time when she'd dropped by the bookstore on her way home from church on Sunday.

She noticed that Claire didn't mention Brian at all while they sipped on their coffee, but Mazie just contributed it to shyness.

She nearly chuckled aloud over her cleverness, but the blinking green permission to "Walk" had been granted and Mazie noticed a few people in their cars at the stoplight were giving her odd looks, so she fixed her expression to appear more *elderly* and *stoic*—whatever that looked like—tugged the gummy bear bag closer to her, and stepped off the curb into the crosswalk, her trusty cane leading the way.

CHAPTER 7

"No way, man! I didn't know you had a photo of Kelly Feinbuster!"

Finn did a flip over the back of the couch where he'd been browsing through a box of old photos Brian had left sitting on the coffee table. He slid into the kitchen, where Brian was dicing up hot dogs to add to a pot of macaroni and cheese.

He knew it was a lame dinner but, hey, this is what was left in the house. Besides, how much could one expect from a bachelor? Finn didn't care. He got almost as excited over macaroni and cheese as he would be if Brian had served filet mignon on china plates. Finn just liked to eat. Period. Brian dropped the knife down on the cutting board and walked to the sink to wash his hands.

"Hey, grab the ketchup out of the frig, would ya?" he hollered over his shoulder. He didn't care what other people thought either. Yeah, he poured ketchup on his macaroni and cheese too. *So what?*

One hand still clasping the wallet-sized snapshot of Kelly, Finn pulled the refrigerator door open and reached for the ketchup on the door with the other. It wasn't hard to find. Besides a bottle of hot sauce, it was the only other item on the door.

Finn snatched up the bottle and pushed the door closed with his shoulder.

"Dude, seriously, *why* do you have a pic of Kelly Feinbuster anyway? She was way out of your league."

"Kelly and I did not have a *thing* going. We were just casual friends who happened to also be in band together."

He fished two plastic bowls out of the cupboard and set them next to the stove.

Brian had to chuckle. True, Kelly was the most gorgeous girl in their senior class and also the sweetest girl in high school, but Finn was right—she was way out of Brian's league as far as romance went.

Brian dumped the hot dogs into the pot of macaroni and cheese and gave everything a quick stir. He reached for the bowls. Finn hunted for spoons, a scowl on his face.

"As much as I'd love to claim a clandestine love affair with the hottest girl in Brenner High School, my friend, it isn't true," Brian sighed. "Kelly played the trumpet and I was a saxophone player. We teamed up as a duet to play a love song for the talent show our senior year. You would know if you hadn't skipped school half the time."

Finn jammed his spoon in his bowl and grabbed the photo off the counter, staring down at the gorgeous brunette with soft blue eyes and a dazzling smile. He looked back at Brian, then down at her image again.

Brian bumped Finn with his elbow as he passed him on the way to the living room to eat his dinner.

"Get your head out of the clouds...and don't get cheese on that photo either."

BRIAN STRETCHED the last of the packing tape across the final box and lifted it to his growing stack of boxes to be stored in the attic later.

He and Finn had spent most of the evening reminiscing over long-ago memories of their youth as they sorted the photos from the box. The same box Finn had fished Kelly Feinbuster's photo out of. Finn had even kept the photo separated on the end table next to him, glancing every so often at it. Brian had finally leaned over and snatched it to toss it back into the box. He started to suspect Finn was going to pocket it and take it home with him.

He'd probably hang it on his frig so people would think it was his girlfriend, he thought. *Then again, the only visitors Finn had at his place were his mom and sister...and they both knew better.*

Scooping up the empty bowls from the coffee table—Finn never cleaned up after himself—Brian allowed his thoughts to transport him back to his high school days as he moved toward the kitchen: *awkward, going home to an empty house because his mom was always at work, gym room locker that always jammed, hitching rides to school, band geek...Kelly Feinbuster.*

He'd only dated one girl in high school and that was for barely two weeks his junior year until he got bored with the drama of dealing with her friends and her expectations for him to shower her with little trinkets. He didn't have a job back then and didn't have the money nor the interest to cater to a girl's demands. After that, he'd spent plenty of energy flirting, but never bothered to pursue a girl seriously for the rest of his high school career.

He set the dirty bowls down into the sink, dumped dish soap over them, and turned the hot water on.

Mesmerized by the glossy rainbow hue of the soap bubbles as the bowls filled, Brian felt nostalgic and, perhaps, a tad bit regretful. Here he was, thirty-one, having only dated a handful of girls since high school and college, aimlessly drifting along in his bachelor life.

Finn—two years his junior—was developing an annoying phobia of being single the rest of his life and was constantly asking girls out in pursuit of his "soul mate." If a girl gave him any special attention or talked to him for more than five minutes, Finn was on it.

Like that poor cashier at the gas station who had mistaken Finn for an old neighbor and lavished her full attention on him until he asked her what her name was. Understanding crept into her eyes and she spent the next two minutes apologizing for her mistake before busying herself with reorganizing the cigarette display behind her.

Finn wasn't a super responsible guy—he spent every penny he earned on worthless junk and fast food, played endless video games when he wasn't working at the computer, never remembered anyone's birthday—but he'd been Brian's best friend since the eighth grade when Finn had rescued Brian from a bully by knocking him into a water fountain.

Finn wanted to get married, have a boatload of kids, and sail into his twilight years sitting in matching recliners with his bride. Brian knew it would happen for his friend someday, but it would take a special woman to love Finn.

Brian, on the other hand, was content just being single. There was no rush to find romance and float off into the sunset on the love boat.

He didn't need that kind of distraction in his life right now anyway with working late into the night on design projects for clients and sleeping most of the early part of the day. Midday to evening was filled with household projects, errands, or checking on his grandmother, who lived less than forty minutes away on the outskirts of the Orange Beach coast in an assisted living facility that cost an arm and a leg but was well-maintained and kept her busy with activities and socialization.

She has more of a social life than I do, Brian realized.

He also enjoyed reading in his free time. Just lounging on the couch with a creepy thriller book—the kind that made you look over your shoulder for the boogeyman—and losing himself for a few hours. No, the way he saw it, he didn't have *time* for love.

Brian pushed a noodle down the drain and shut the sink water off.

Man, I'm hungry.

The mid-size bowl of macaroni and cheese from three hours ago had long ago digested and his stomach grumbled. Come to think of it, he hadn't had a decent meal since…well, last Friday. Mazie's lasagna. What he wouldn't do to have a huge helping of that right now, complimented by a fist-sized chunk of that homemade bread she'd slid onto the table, heat radiating off of its golden crust. He would have to find more opportunities to rescue Mazie so she'd feel obligated to have him over for dinner more often.

Then again, maybe not.

He never *did* get to have a chat with her about her obvious attempt at matchmaking and the ridiculous fabricated story about the "neighbor" who was some kind of an undercover law enforcement agent.

He considered the *other* dinner guest that had also been invited: Claire.

Wonder what she did to deserve a special dinner invitation—give Mazie an employee discount on a cookbook at the bookstore?

He grunted at his own joke, remembering how Claire had inquired if he was "the neighbor in the secret service" or whatever she'd asked. Mazie had come waltzing in right after he'd denied being *that* neighbor, so he'd never really had the opportunity to clarify what his real job was. Maybe Claire had already asked Mazie, who was obviously more than happy to share her wealth of knowledge about him, whether it was accurate or not.

Why did he even care anyway?

Brian grabbed his iced tea from the counter and made his way to the office to start his work for the night.

Secret service, indeed, he huffed.

BRIAN FELT like a wad of cotton had been shoved to the back of his throat as he sucked in gulps of air. His heart thudded recklessly against his T-shirt as gray, hazy spots clouded his vision and his head filled with fog. His pulse raced wildly and his palms were slick with sweat. He couldn't go on…he had to end this right here and now. He stopped and bent his head to his knees.

Come on, man, it's only been two miles.

Only two miles into his first jog in months—*or was it longer?*—and Brian felt like he was about to have a heart attack.

I didn't realize how out of shape I was.

He had always had a desk job, sitting for long hours with minimal physical activity and everything he needed within arm's reach. But he never felt as much like a slug as he had lately. Of course, back in Mobile he'd been surrounded by his buddies and was always on the move and doing things outside of sleeping or working. He'd kept busy enough that extra exercise wasn't a necessity. Then again, he wasn't as young as he used to be either.

He thought about his inadequate dinner last night of macaroni and cheese with hot dogs. If he kept eating like that, he'd have high cholesterol to add to his problems.

On top of eating poorly, moving his body these days consisted of maneuvering his tall frame under a narrow sink in order to fix a broken pipe or hacking away at overgrown trees and shrubs around his property. It wasn't that he had gained a lot of weight, it was the fact that he had no energy or inspiration to do anything with his free time and basically had no social life.

He couldn't do much about his social life right now, but he *could* do something about his health. It was why he had decided last night that he was going to go for a run this afternoon. And, here he was, gasping for air like a vacuum cleaner on steroids.

Sucking in one long last gulp of air, Brian raised up and rolled his shoulders back. He was just lifting his arms above his head to let more air into his lungs when he spied a young girl from the corner house across the street staring at him through her fence, a bored expression on her face.

Short and roundish with bright pink cheeks and a pointy knit cap jammed down over her fluff of black frizz, the little girl could have easily passed as a garden gnome— minus the long, white beard, perky mustache, and big ears —as she sat perched atop a flat rock close to her fence.

Brian dropped his hands to his sides, then reached down to touch his toes, like stretching on the sidewalk in front of his house was a common ritual for him. He stood and raised his eyes to hers once more.

She blinked. Slow and disinterested, like a cat observing an insignificant stray dog.

Brian went with his initial reaction. He waved.

"Hello there!"

It took her so long to respond that he thought maybe she hadn't heard him, but she couldn't have missed the obvious wave he gave her since she was staring right at him. Just as he was about to turn away, one small hand lifted briefly from her pant leg and a half-hearted wave was sent his way. No smile or change of expression whatsoever. Her face was so set it could have been stone.

Like a gnome—just like I thought.

He stood there with a stupid smile plastered on his face, bewildered as ever, before clasping his hands together in front of him and faking another stretch. Giving the gnome girl another wave, he turned on his heel and made his way up the sidewalk to his house. Only after he'd pushed the door closed did he turn and peek back through the peephole.

The girl was still sitting there like a statue, but instead of staring his way, her face had turned downward, looking at her lap. He couldn't calculate why, but Brian felt a wash of pity flood over him for the young girl who he hadn't even known lived across the street from him until today.

Wow, that was weird. Maybe I'm better off staying in the house.

One step away from the door, Brian felt a stabbing pain shoot up his calf, radiating deep into his thigh muscle, before his body tipped hard against the entryway wall.

Cramp!

CHAPTER 8

IT WAS TRASH DAY. Brian had forgotten to take it out last week and had almost forgotten it again.

He was still getting used to putting his trash can out on certain days of the week. Living in an apartment, he'd always just walked his trash over to a shared bin in the complex parking lot before work in the mornings. Owning his own home was proving to be more of a challenge than he thought: buying a lawnmower for the first time, painting his own walls (he wasn't allowed to in an apartment), fixing his own broken pipes, and so many more unexpected surprises that came with home ownership.

He tugged the heavy plastic bin to the curb and wrestled it around to the right position for the truck's hydraulic arms to easily haul for dumping. When it was situated, he wiped the sweat from his brow and glanced across the street.

There she was again, the *gnome girl*. This time she stood at her fence, staring at him. The same knit cap was shoved down on her head but her wild hair had at least been tamed into a low ponytail in the back. She held a baby doll with no clothes on in one arm, pressing it between her and the fence. It was as if she had forgotten she was holding it.

It was intimidating having the strange girl stare at him like that, not saying a word. He hoped she wasn't going to make a habit out of staring at him every time he left his house. He'd only noticed her for the first time yesterday, but who knows how many other times she'd been looking over his way.

Has she been spying on me since I moved in here?

He cleared his throat. "Why are you staring at me?!"

He had only meant to holler loud enough so she could hear him but it came out more like a burst of thunder.

Brian felt bad when he saw her quickly drop her eyes, but she didn't run away like he expected she would. He waited in case she was working on the courage to answer him, but she just stood there with her gaze locked on the ground. The whole scene was unnerving: the girl locked in some kind of a trance with a nude doll's face distorted from being smashed against the links of the fence. It was like a scene from a horror film.

Yep, I'm totally creeped out. Maybe her parents warned her not to talk to strangers, which was probably wise in these current times.

He brushed his hands off on his jeans and hurried inside.

~

THE CHILDREN'S cardiac ward was a flurry of activity this morning. Mazie stood at the nurses' station as she finished working the pin of her name tag into her sweater and closed the clasp.

She could usually find Rebecca, the volunteer coordinator, fluttering around the nurses' station, getting updates of how the day looked and which patients were being admitted or discharged, ordering supplies for the Family Accommodation Area, planning where volunteers were most needed throughout the day, or even if a parent was having a hard time and just needed a hug.

Somewhere in her forties, to Mazie's experienced eye, with a cheerful mop of red curls piled in a high ponytail on top of her head, a soft spray of freckles across her cheeks, and expressive hazel eyes that turned grayish with compassion or twinkling green with delight—depending on what the moment called for, Rebecca Mollison was a paragon in meeting the needs of patients, family, and staff at Magnolia Children's Hospital.

Mazie poked her head around the large filing cabinet next to the copy machine but didn't see Rebecca anywhere. Actually, she didn't see anyone other than a staff member in green scrubs pushing a cart of dirty trays toward the utility elevator. No bother, Mazie would just go make her rounds to check on her kids—and every child on the ward on any given day was her "kid"—then come by and see if Rebecca had anything special she needed her to do.

Leaving her cane leaning against the back of the filing cabinet, Mazie made her way down the long corridor, the rubber soles of her loafers emitting subtle squeaking noises against the high-polished linoleum floors. As she passed the first room on her right—the one just next to the nurse's station, the one that had once been a patient area but was now converted to a conference room—her steps slowed.

She was remembering another room close to a nurse's station many years ago. The memory still left a hollow pit in her stomach when she thought about it. It was in another hospital cardiac ward a few miles from here—close to forty years ago—before this hospital was built. A room where she and Harold spent the last days of their sweet little Jacob's life before he was torn from them.

Two years...that was all they'd had their precious son for after waiting four grievous years to finally be able to have a child.

The doctor thought he heard a heart murmur shortly after Jacob was born but could detect nothing at his six-month appointment and assumed it had corrected itself.

But, at two years old, Jacob wasn't thriving and had bouts with breathing trouble. A series of tests revealed an undetected ventricular heart defect that developed into congestive heart failure. In a matter of weeks, he was hospitalized for a lung infection and the battle for his life began.

They wrestled with the infection and beat back every demon in hell for days to keep Jacob with them.

When Harold slept—most often with his head resting on the edge of Jacob's hospital bed and one hand holding his son's hand—Mazie would creep off to the small chapel on the floor below and cry out to God for mercy. But, on the sixth day, they lost him. Grief descended like a storm cloud over their lives.

After months of locking herself in a mental cocoon and clawing her way out of grief, it was Harold who had suggested volunteering at the hospital, thinking that it might be therapeutic for her to reach out to sick children. She was horrified.

"I don't know how you can even suggest it, Harold," she spit out. "That's the last place on earth I want to go back to."

She couldn't remember why she changed her mind, but she did. Mazie spent almost thirty years volunteering at that hospital with pediatric cardiac patients. She found that, somehow, it made her feel closer to Jacob.

When Magnolia Children's Hospital was built closer to where they lived ten years ago, she came to volunteer here instead. Harold had been right. Being there for the children, bringing them comfort and a smile where she could, had been a healing balm to her shattered heart.

A family was walking her way, so Mazie quickly brushed away the tear that had escaped down her cheek. She shook away the memories and concentrated on her task.

Her first stop this morning was room 144B: Lena Thomas.

Lena had first showed up in the cardiac intensive care unit over four years ago, immediately after making her way into the world three weeks earlier than expected. Neonatologists, critical care nurses, and a parade of cardiac physicians were the first faces baby Lena saw before even meeting her parents and two older brothers.

Born with Hypoplastic Left Heart Syndrome, or HLHS, where the left side of the heart, which pumps fresh oxygen from the heart to the tissues in the body, is underdeveloped, Lena had fought to live from her first breath. In the four years since her birth, Lena had already undergone two surgeries to reconstruct her damaged heart.

Tomorrow, she would face her third—and hopefully final one—in which the cardiac surgeons would complete the rerouting of the blood movement through the lungs and heart. The right side of her heart would take over all the blood-pumping duties. Although Lena would probably face a lifetime of struggles and likely further surgeries in her future, Mazie prayed that the little girl would have respite from the doom and gloom for a long time to come.

Mazie paused in the doorway of 144B and gingerly poked her head around the corner to view the tiny, pale figure laying on the bed, bundled in a shroud of purple fleece.

Lena's favorite blanket.

Chocolate saucer-sized eyes were already looking her way, as if Lena had been expecting Mazie the whole time.

"Boo!" Lena whispered, her fairy voice floating around the bare walls of the room. Bubblegum-pink lips formed a grin. With her long brown hair tucked up into a green bouffant cap, she looked like an underdressed clown.

Mazie chuckled as she slid the rest of her body into the room and made her way to the head of the bed. Setting her bag down on a chair behind her, she turned back to Lena and poked a crooked index finger on the tip of her button nose.

"Boo, back to you, little one," she clucked.

Lena giggled. The fleece blanket was tucked up under her chin as her delicate fingers gripped its satin edge against her cheeks.

Lena's gaze broke away and she peered past Mazie to where the plastic grocery bag lay on the chair. Her brows rose with curiosity.

"What's in that bag?" she asked, her blanket sinking to her shoulder.

Knowing that Lena had surgery tomorrow morning, Mazie knew the child couldn't have the treat she'd brought in the bag until after her procedure.

"Gummy bears."

She saw Lena's eyes brighten with anticipation—the way to a child's heart was almost unanimously through an offering of candy.

"But," she interrupted, already knowing the request,

"you have to wait a little longer before I can share them with you." She watched as the corner of Lena's lip sucked in as her face puckered.

As Mazie leaned in closer, giving a soft brown curl that had escaped the cap a gentle tug, she whispered, "Here's what I'm gonna do. I'm going to put some aside in a little bag to be saved just for you when the doctor says it's okay for you to eat it. Sound like a deal?"

She gave Lena a reassuring smile and was reciprocated with a small nod.

"Okay. You promise?"

Mazie put a finger to her lips. "Shh...only if you promise not to tell the other kids. I don't bring candy for just anyone, you know."

She wasn't being a hundred percent honest about that. She had more candy where that came from to share.

Lena's giggle filled the room and Mazie knew all was right in the universe again.

Rebecca was at the nurse's station when Mazie made her way back an hour later. The remnant of a sticky cinnamon roll sat on a napkin at her elbow and her feet were kicked up on a rolling chair in front of her. A few fiery curls had escaped her ponytail and drooped lazily against her left check. Her eyes were closed even though she sat perfectly erect in her chair.

Must have been a rough morning.

"Good morning, Rebecca." She pushed around the edge of the station desk and walked over to the water cooler close to Rebecca's chair. Mazie plucked a paper cup from the attached dispenser as she watched her. Rebecca's eyes opened as her legs pulled from the rolling chair and settled on the floor.

"Mornin', Mazie. Sorry I missed you when you came in. I was tied up with an admission."

Picking up the last of the roll, she nibbled off a small corner, then held it up to Mazie. "There's donuts in the lounge."

Mazie nodded. "Thanks."

"Yeah," Rebecca continued. "It was a long night for the little fella. Just came on the floor early this morning. Parents are frantic and anxious, of course. I don't blame them. They just moved here from Northern Ireland a few months back, so everything is new to them," she said, her expression sad. "I called Mona in after I got everyone settled in the patient's room. She's with them now."

Rebecca rolled her napkin into a tight ball and tossed it neatly into a nearby trash can, then tucked the loose curls behind her ears while trying to hold back a yawn.

Mona was one of Magnolia's parent liaisons who offered families emotional support when their children were brought in for care. Having been in the same situation in the past with their own children in the hospital, they offered a sensitive and unique perspective of coping strategies and understanding that most others couldn't.

Mazie stood quietly absorbing the information, waiting before asking questions. Knowing that Rebecca would probably answer them before she did anyway. Her guess was accurate.

"Little guy's name is Ashton...Carter." She scanned a page next to her. "Yes, Ashton Carter. Anyhow, he came into the ER last night with a fever and trouble breathing. Since he has a minor heart defect"—she glanced over at the paper again—"a valve defect as a result of rheumatic fever when he was three, they looked at that first. They're scheduling him for an echocardiogram to see if the infection is originating with his heart. Could be bacterial endocarditis." A deep sigh escaped her.

"Well, anyway, let's hope not." Standing and reaching for a chart from the wall, Rebecca yawned again.

"How old is he?" Mazie asked. Rebecca had left that part out.

Seeming not to hear her, Rebecca filtered through some papers in a file, pulling one out and handing it to Mazie.

"Not much else going on but check in on these patients and see if they need anything—games, a book to read... Oh, and the game system is back from repairs. I'm heading over to talk to Emma about rushing some insurance paperwork for me. Thanks, Mazie."

Rebecca patted her arm as Mazie reached for the paper.

"I got this. You do what you need to do," Mazie assured her.

Rebecca smiled wearily as she walked away. Turning back to Mazie, she addressed her question.

"He's six years old."

CHAPTER 9

"Mazie! Can you hold up a sec?"

Mazie had just reached the doors leading into the main church sanctuary when she heard her name. She turned slowly—it wouldn't do to throw herself off balance by whipping around too fast—and watched as a tall brunette tapped across the linoleum toward her, a large ring of clanking keys with a strange puffy ball dangling from it swinging on her wrist.

She stopped when she reached Mazie and rested a hand on her shoulder. Her hand felt like it weighed fifty pounds. She was tall and Mazie had to lift her chin to look into the woman's face. She also couldn't remember her name.

"Sorry," the woman started, "I didn't catch you before you walked away. I was cleaning up a bucket of crayons that got knocked over. Anyhow, we're in an awkward situation this morning. Sheryl called and can't make it today, something about being stuck at work for an extra shift."

A wide smile spilled generously across her face and the fifty-pound hand on her shoulder gave a little squeeze. Mazie wasn't sure she trusted people who smiled impulsively during a pause in conversation.

"Well, I was wondering," she continued, "if you'd be interested in filling in for the preschool Sunday school class this morning?" The smile didn't budge an inch.

The shock in Mazie's voice came out sounding like an out-of-tune violin. "You want *me* to teach *preschoolers?*"

She stared up at the young woman, making sure she had her full attention, providing her a chance to see the error of her ways: *tiny humans...old woman.* Clearly, she was missing it. The woman gave her another quick shoulder squeeze before her hand slid off Mazie's shoulder and pressed against her own chest.

"Oh, you would do *wonderful* with the kids, Mazie! They all just looove you!"

Why can't I remember this lady's name?

"Besides, you won't be alone. We have a high school girl —you've met Gabby, right?—who helps out, but she's under eighteen and can't be left alone with the kids."

Her hand reached out again but, mercifully, landed on Mazie's arm this time. "We need to have an adult in there with the kids too. Can you help? It would just be for an hour."

Mazie twisted the rubber tip of her cane into the hard floor as she peered up at the woman.

Goodness, she was tall... Heather! That was her name.

At least fifteen years had passed since anyone had dared ask her to babysit any youngsters, if she didn't count her neighbor, Janice, who had asked her last year to watch her dog for a few hours while she took her mother for a medical procedure. She remembered thinking the dog looked like an overstuffed couch pillow. It was a bichon frise with a ridiculous show cut that reminded her of a gigantic cotton swab with raisins pushed into it for eyes.

The dog had parked itself on her favorite armchair the whole afternoon and growled at her every time she walked by. Afraid it would bite her, she left the cotton swab alone until his owner finally retrieved him.

She had to admit, it felt good to be needed.

Lifting her cane to indicate that Heather should lead the way, Mazie dropped the fake smile. "Sure hope you know what you're asking...but I'll do my best."

CLAIRE'S COFFEE was dangerously close to spilling over the edge of her mug—she was laughing so hard. Shoulders hunched, she held the cup safely away from her as she attempted to control herself.

Mazie couldn't understand what the young woman found so amusing.

"I cannot believe," Claire snorted, "that you actually made those poor kids walk around with paper towels stuck in their collars! What a sight that must have been!"

Pulling her coffee back for a sip, Claire looked at her over the rim of her cup and Mazie could see that her cheeks were flushed. Looking like she was about to break out into another bout of laughing, she asked, "What did the parents think when they came to get their kids and they had those...*bibs* on?" Another snort.

Picturing the scene, Mazie couldn't help but snicker herself. She'd thought it perfectly practical at the time to bib up the children with the paper towels, but now that Claire put it that way, well...maybe the kids *did* look a bit silly.

"Oh, come now, Claire," she grumbled. "It's not *that* funny. What's with these parents anyway? Sending a four-year-old to Sunday school in a three-piece suit or an impractical boutique dress that probably cost more than a month's supply of my arthritis medication. For what? Just to do crafts for an hour?"

She huffed. "Mind you, they *were* cute as God's little lambs but, today, of all days, they were going to be using finger paint—*finger paint!*—to make thumbprint trees for the Garden of Eden bulletin board display! Their parents should have thanked me for trying to keep their clothes protected, Claire."

"You know, it was probably washable paint, Mazie."

After a brief second of silence, "And…?" Claire ventured, one eyebrow cocked. "You didn't answer about what the parents thought when they showed up and the kids had bibs shoved down their collars." She bit down on her bottom lip but the smirk was still evident.

Mazie hesitated to answer, knowing it would be exactly as Claire imagined it would be. She couldn't hold back the frustrated sigh.

"They had them off and tossed about the room before the parents showed up." A stern finger pointed at Claire, "And don't you start laughing again."

Right on cue, Claire giggled. Mazie rolled her eyes.

Well, goodness, if she thinks this is a hoot, I won't dare tell her about confiscating the toilet paper to dole out after discovering that naughty boy had pulled out half the roll and stuffed it up into the electric hand dryer.

"Oh, Mazie, you make me laugh. What would I do without our Sunday coffee chats?" Claire's grin over the rim of her coffee cup was contagious.

Mazie grinned back. "Same here, dearie. I'm glad I'm so entertaining," she added, sarcasm lacing her words.

Claire sat with one leg curled under her in the chair across from Mazie, her long cotton skirt tucked neatly against her knees. She looked like a Swedish doll with her long blonde hair plaited tightly in two French braids that brushed near her waist.

Even though she hustled and bustled about the busy

bookstore throughout the week—often working late into the night to shelve new stock and balance the books at her desk —today she was the picture of a carefree farm girl on a lazy afternoon. Not a care in the world. It helped that there hadn't been any patrons for the past hour. Sharing coffee and chatting with each other as they were, one could almost imagine they were just relaxing on the front porch next to a country road. It made Mazie feel happy…soothed.

She knew she should get up and start heading home. It would probably be a frozen hot pocket dinner night for her —nice and easy. She was plumb wore out after all the excitement and tension of the morning.

She hadn't minded helping out really. The little ones, with all their energy and innocence, were dear to her and she always made it a point to stop by the classes on Sunday mornings as she made her way to the sanctuary. She soaked in all the hugs as the boys and girls ran to greet her. But Mazie had never had to be in charge of teaching small children, keeping them from beating each other over the head with wooden blocks or having to tie multiple sets of shoelaces all within one single hour.

She had plenty of experience caring for children at the hospital, but that was more of a one-on-one intimate experience with the kids, who were mostly feeling unwell and confined to a bed—a world away from the healthy whirlwind of a dozen spinning tops racing in all directions in a classroom.

Claire must have sensed their time was coming to a close because she untucked her leg from under her and gave it a gentle massage to work the blood back into circulation. Then, she stood and reached a hand out for Mazie's empty cup.

Mazie stayed seated. She needed just a moment longer. She wanted to take advantage of the pleasant mood before the spell was broken.

"So…what did you think of my neighbor, Brian? Sweet young man, isn't he?"

Claire had her back to Mazie while she stacked their dirty cups in a basket that she kept for cups to be washed later. Mazie felt honored that the other customers got disposable paper cups for coffee while she was privileged to have a real ceramic coffee mug adorned with a photo of the majestic Grand Canyon. She watched Claire's back for any noticeable reaction to the question. There was none.

After what felt like an eternity, Claire glanced back over her shoulder.

"Oh, he was nice. Kinda quiet, though. Which, I'm sure, is ideal for you, since you have to live next door to him."

She reached down to a lower shelf and grabbed a canister of disinfectant wipes. Tugging one from the top, she wiped off the coffeepot and counter before tossing the cloth into the trash.

Mazie huffed. "Well, yes, Brian is quiet. I hardly notice

he's over there. He's probably used to discipline, having self-control, keeping to himself with, well…you know, his job and all."

Handing Mazie her cane, Claire walked with her toward the front of the store.

"Yeah…I'm sure his work is important. I remember you mentioned that he did some kind of undercover work or something, but, when I asked him about it, he acted like he didn't know what I was talking about."

The *tinkle* of the bells on the door alerted them of an incoming customer—and saved Mazie from trying to explain her misrepresentation of Brian's employment.

A tall young man with dark features, a muscular build, and a strand of black hair loose across his forehead greeted them with a charming smile. An expensive looking leather bag hung at his side. *Was that a purse?* Mazie scowled. She'd never get Brian and Claire together with guys like this dropping in. *He probably doesn't even read books.* She briefly considered hanging out a bit longer.

"Afternoon," the charmer nodded.

Claire nodded back and turned to squeeze Mazie's hand and lean in for a quick hug.

"See you next week?"

She stepped back and made her way to the door. Mr. Charming was browsing a fountain pen display by the front window. When he noticed Mazie was leaving, he rushed over to open the door for her. She gave him her ugliest scowl—making sure it wasn't in Claire's line of vision, of course—and mumbled, "Thanks."

She couldn't resist leaving one last parting remark.

"Maybe you and Brian can come for dinner again next week," she called back to Claire as she brushed past her doorman.

CHAPTER 10

MAZIE's first stop after getting her duty assignment from Rebecca was to swing by 144B to check on Lena Thomas. Rebecca told her the surgery had gone well but that Lena was still being closely monitored.

"Lena's gonna be on the floor at least another week or so," Rebecca told her. "Let's just hope she keeps up the great progress so she can go home and try to live a normal life."

Mazie was woefully clueless about most medical jargon, but what she'd gathered from Lena's nurses and from Rebecca was that Lena had undergone what they hoped would be her last surgery—for a while at least. The Fontan procedure, a final step in rearranging how the blood pumps through the heart, would help relieve the enormous stress Lena's heart was under.

She didn't understand how it all worked but was glad to

hear the procedure had gone well for Lena. Mazie hoped her prayers had made a positive contribution to the surgery.

After dropping off a stack of waterproof bed pads in room 132 and delivering IV tubing to the head nurse in another room, she was finally on her way to check on Lena. Mrs. Thomas, Lena's mother, was just exiting the elevator as she approached, a large coffee clutched in her hand. Her face lit up as she made her way over to Mazie.

"Mazie!" Mrs. Thomas leaned in for a quick hug, careful not to tip the coffee on them both. "I missed seeing you the other day, but Lena told me you dropped by. She was so excited about the candy that you left for her. I put it on the shelf right under the TV so that she has something to look forward to—she can't eat sweets just yet. I just wolfed down a hamburger in the cafeteria downstairs so I wouldn't have to eat in front of her."

She pointed to Lena's room just ahead and led the way. "Rick is on duty at the station tonight. It's just me and Lena for a few hours."

Mazie was grateful that Mrs. Thomas was walking slowly, since she didn't have her cane with her. She tried to limit her use of the cane at the hospital because it got more in her way than helped when she made her rounds. Her responsibilities as a volunteer were light and rarely involved any emergencies that would require her to hustle around the ward. The hospital floors were nice and level and fairly clutter-free. Besides, she had on her trusty loafers with the solid rubber bottoms.

Mazie was sure Rebecca only allowed her to keep volunteering at her age because she kept the little ones entertained when no one else could be with them.

When she'd started as a volunteer at this hospital, she was a spry sixty-two-year-old with a lot of zip and zing still left in her. The foreshadowing of arthritis in her knees and hips was easily dispelled with the swallow of two ibuprofen tablets and a few minutes with her feet up on a footstool. Somewhere around year sixty-nine, she started needing her "third leg" to descend stairs and to keep her steady on the uneven turf of her property so she could do her gardening.

Mrs. Thomas continued to lead the way until they arrived at Lena's room, Mazie trailing in her wake. She heard the rhythmic beeping of the monitors before they even came into view.

She had witnessed a lot of hard things over the past ten years—things that could make a person lose sleep at night —but it never failed to steal her breath when she saw her youngest patients with tubes and surgical tape draping over every part of their fragile bodies with hardly an inch of space to get closer to them due to all the machines and poles blocking the way.

Lena's faded green hospital gown was put on backward to allow easy access to the incision on her chest. An angry rust-colored wound, stretching from her collar to her diaphragm, peeked from the folds of the opening. Mazie shuddered as she stood in Mrs. Thomas' shadow.

"Hey, Lena girl! Guess who I brought with me to see

you?" Mrs. Thomas padded softly to the heavy linen drapes and tugged them aside, the flood of warm light dissipating the dungeon-like darkness that permeated the room.

Now that she had adjusted to the sounds in the room, Mazie heard the faint hum coming from the television above her head and shifted so that she could look up at it. A gaggle of rowdy kids ran around a playground on the screen, flittering from the swings to the slides to a hazardous-looking metal merry-go-round. And they were singing the whole time.

Must be one of those Disney shows...they're always singing.

She looked back at Lena.

Mrs. Thomas was bent over her daughter, stroking her hair and kissing her forehead. Although she could tell that Mrs. Thomas was being strong for Lena, Mazie saw the fatigue and worry etched on her face. She heard the shared whispers between them and kept her distance to respect their privacy. Then Mrs. Thomas stood and waved Mazie over. The surgical tape securing the tubing to Lena's nose wrinkled in tiny folds from her smile as Mazie made her way over.

Mazie couldn't imagine going through all the poor dear had been through and still be able to put on a brave smile like she was. Mazie felt a stab of guilt. Here she was, ready to bite the UPS driver's head off if she had a headache and he dared to ring the doorbell.

Children are God's little messengers to remind us not to take life so seriously, she thought.

Lena's gaze drifted to the far wall. She pointed to the small plastic baggie sitting on the shelf under the TV. A box of disposable gloves sat next to it.

"Look, I still have my gummy bears," she said. "I can't eat any yet—I'm not allowed. I didn't tell the other kids like you said." Her brows crinkled and her expression fell. "I have to stay in my room, so I can't go to The Treehouse yet. But...did you bring more candy?" She glanced down at Mazie's side to see if there was anything hidden there.

The Treehouse was a large playroom on the cardiac floor for children who were still hospitalized but were well enough to play and be around other children.

Patient artwork decorated the walls, along with colorful murals of mystical fairies and 3D butterflies made from transparent acetate. IV poles were secured to the backs of tricycles and dragged around the playroom as if they were just a minor obstacle to overcome in pursuit of fun. The kids endured their IV poles, bandages, oxygen tubes, and whatever else was strapped to them like soldiers hauling battle gear. There wasn't much that could stop their fun when they set their mind on it.

Mazie looked back at the bag on the shelf.

"Looks like you don't need more candy just yet, you saved that whole bag—*course if she'd had a choice, it would have been consumed that same night*—but if anybody deserves it, you do!" Mazie moved closer to the bed and, carefully wiggling her fingers under a pair of tubes fed to her chest, squeezed Lena's hand.

Wanting to distract the girl's mind from the candy she couldn't have yet, she changed the subject.

"Tell me the first thing you're gonna do when you get out of here and go home."

Lena didn't miss a heartbeat.

"Ride my scooter!" she blurted out. She attempted to sit up. "Daddy bought me a scooter for my birthday!"

Mrs. Thomas, who'd been sitting in a nearby chair listening to the exchange, stood and went to the bed, her hand gently restraining Lena. "No, Lena, you have to lie down."

Mazie tried to keep her distracted. "Your birthday! When was your birthday, Lena?"

Mrs. Thomas chimed in with a chuckle, "Not for a few weeks yet but we thought it would be fun to give her something to look forward to. She's turning *five,*" she said, giving Lena's cheek a pinch.

"Ah," Mazie grinned, "an *early* birthday present! You lucky girl! Tell you what, if you are still here next week when I come, I'll bring you a special present. I can't tell you what it is, though—it will be a surprise."

The little girl wiggled against her pillow and looked between her mom and Mazie, her lips forming a perfectly adorable "O" shape. Mazie could have just scooped her up into her arms right then with all her cuteness.

Lena squeezed her hand back. "Really? But"—the troubled look crept back into her eyes—"what if I go home and you don't see me?"

"Don't you worry." Mazie winked. "I'll make sure someone gets it to you."

As she finished her rounds and assisted with small housekeeping tasks on the floor, Mazie fussed over what she could get Lena for her birthday. She really had no clue what kids liked these days. Outside of a sprint as an elementary school secretary and her years of volunteering on the pediatric cardiac ward, Mazie had very little real-life, everyday knowledge of children. If her brief experience in teaching Sunday school was a peek at what parenthood would have been, she shouldn't complain about what she missed.

Except for Jacob... If I could do it all again.

No! She wouldn't think of that right now. Her heart wasn't ready—wouldn't *ever* be ready no matter how many years passed...even if she lived to be a hundred.

Whack! A stack of patient files landed on the counter in front of Mazie, breaking the spell that threatened to strangle her.

"Hey, Mazie." It was Olivia, one of the nurses that she didn't know very well because she normally worked the night shift.

"Can you let Rebecca know that I dropped these off?"

"Sure, I'll make sure to let her know." Olivia scooted away without another word and Mazie fixed her thoughts back onto safer ground: what to get Lena for her birthday.

～

MAZIE PUSHED the cart slowly past each room. She was in no hurry as she peeked in to see what was going on in each one—who was awake, who had visitors... But that was not the reason for her careful pace. On her cart was a mixture of puzzles, games, stuffed animals, and books. But, today, there were also two boxes containing hot, soft pretzels balanced on top of the upper level of the cart and she didn't want them to tumble to the floor.

She had first stocked the cart with the assortment of entertainment choices several years back so that the kids could choose something for the two of them to do while she sat with them. As she'd grown older, it also served as extra balance for Mazie as she made her rounds. More often than not these days, she noticed that the kids preferred the portable video game console for entertainment and she'd had to settle for trying to talk to kids while they stared at a screen or tapped away at the controller in their hands.

Maybe she wouldn't even be needed in a few years, she mourned.

But, this morning, she was still needed.

Mazie was on her way to visit Ashton Carter, the new patient who had been on and off the floor the past few weeks. She had already learned of his love for soft pretzels and puzzles, two things she happened to love herself, and was bringing him both this morning. Ashton's parents were out of town overnight and it would be his first day alone on the floor.

It was her job, and the whole reason she volunteered

here in the first place, to spend time with the children on the cardiac floor, helping to keep them entertained and distracted. Mazie doubted her ability to entertain them much anymore, especially since she was ages past their generations, but she was patient and never in a hurry to leave like most other adults. Plus, she was a great listener and an attentive audience to the younger patients' endless stories and incessant questions.

That, she felt, was one of her most valuable assets to the children on Magnolia Children's Hospital pediatric cardiac floor. Unless she was mistaken, she felt like many of the kids would agree.

Her cart preceded her into the room, but as the head of the bed came into view, the first thing she noticed was his scorching red hair, sticking up in every direction and reminding Mazie of a volcanic eruption. His hair was a stark contrast against the bright white mound of pillows under him. Feral green eyes, opened wide as saucers, stared up at her, in anticipation—or fear, more likely—of her purpose for being in his room. Mazie guessed that he hadn't even looked at the cart and noticed its cheerful contents.

He probably thinks I'm here to poke him with another needle or wheel him down for more chest x-rays.

They hadn't been properly introduced yet because he was either asleep or the nurses and doctors were with him whenever she had passed by previously.

"Well, hello there, Ashton! I'm Mazie. I just wanted to come by and sit with you for a little while. Is that okay?"

The saucer-eyes blinked once but never left her face. He was a petite boy, sunken into his bedsheets like a marshmallow cocoon, and he looked scared to death. Mazie knew she needed to step up to the challenge. She reached for one of the small, square boxes from the top of her cart.

Giving it a gentle shake, she smiled, "Someone told me that you like soft pretzels. I just happen to have one on my cart. Would you like to have it?"

Ashton's eyes snapped to the box, then down to the cart, then back to her. The tiniest perceptible nod was all the encouragement she needed. She nudged the cart aside as she reached over and set the pretzel box down on the rolling table next to the bed. Turning, she reached for the second box.

"Oh, look, I just happen to have a pretzel for me too." She looked back at him and grinned. "That means we can have a picnic right here in your room!"

Setting the second pretzel on top of the first box, Mazie crossed the room to pull over a chair for herself. Settling it close to the bed, which was still a bit higher than her, she pulled a wad of napkins from her sweater pocket. The young boy's eyes softened as he scanned the contents of the cart. The dread in his eyes from a moment ago had shifted to curious interest, all threat eliminated. Mazie followed his gaze.

"I brought some fun things for us to do too. Do you like puzzles?" she asked, already knowing the answer.

The beautiful green eyes turned on her. Up close, his freckles were like miniature sunbursts dancing across his cheeks. Mazie's heart warmed in her chest. She knew instinctively that she'd made a friend today. Then Ashton smiled, and the freckle sunbursts danced up into his eyes, giving her a peek into the endearing boy who lay under the mask of fear and uncertainty of being sick and trapped in an unfamiliar place away from home and family.

"Do you have mustard?"

With his rolling Irish accent, it took a moment for it to register that he was asking for "mustard." There was also the slightest trace of a lisp when he spoke, and Mazie noticed that his two front teeth were missing. She grinned, remembering that most kids are usually missing their front teeth around this age. She was missing hers as well—all of her teeth, in fact, now that she was endowed with dentures —but she doubted Ashton cared to hear about it.

With his unruly red hair and adventurous eyes, he reminded her of Calvin and Hobbes, the comic strip about a young mischievous, blond-haired, six-year-old and his stuffed tiger, Hobbes, and the adventures they shared. Harold had loved the antics of Calvin and had even picked up a book filled with a collection of the endearing comic strips at a yard sale one weekend.

The book was somewhere on a shelf at the house.

Maybe she would bring it to show Ashton if he was still here next week.

Mazie's hand slid down into her pocket, where she retrieved several plastic packets and held them up like a magician pulling a magic card.

"A man after my own heart."

BRIAN WAS PAINTING the living room wall when the doorbell rang, surprising him so much that he almost dropped the loaded brush.

He looked for a place to set the dripping brush down and ended up balancing it across the top rim of the paint can. With a quick wipe on his jeans and a brief check on the bottom of his sneakers for paint before stepping off the plastic lining, he made his way to the front door. Before he could reach it, the doorbell rang again.

"On my way!" he hollered. He really needed to get a "no soliciting" sign posted on the door.

He didn't take the time to look out the door peephole—didn't want to risk the person ringing the doorbell again in their impatience. He yanked the door open.

Mazie stood before him in her blue sweater, the hem of her long denim dress brushing the tops of her white tennis shoes. In her hands she also balanced two plates, one on top of the other. The one on top was covered with foil over a mound of something, and the red plate under it looked like one of his own.

"Oh, uh, hello Mazie. How are you today?" He stepped back from the door to allow her to enter. "Won't you come in?" She didn't move but peered around him.

"What's that awful smell?" *So much for a greeting…*

He followed her gaze. "I'm painting."

"Oh, that's wonderful! I'm glad you're getting around to giving this place a fresh face." She thrust the plates at him with a toothy smile. "I thought I would drop off some homemade glazed donuts."

Brian reached for the plates.

"Extra glaze on them too. Mind you, I had to walk over here extra careful. Didn't bring my cane. I couldn't hold two plates and a cane too." She pointed to the stack in his hands. "I brought back your plate from when you came for dinner. I hope that you don't mind that I tossed the rest of the peanut brittle. It was getting stale."

"Oh, wow…you shouldn't have." He stared down at the plates.

Really…she shouldn't have. She was one of the reasons he had needed to start jogging.

Lifting an edge of the foil, the sweet yeasty smell hit him and he felt the saliva already pooling in his mouth. "These smell great. You know," he said, tapping the red plate underneath, "you could have just put the rolls on my plate instead of dirtying up another one."

She brushed him off. "*Tsk.* Just bring it on over when you're all done."

Her face brightened as a thought occurred to her. "Actually, even better, why don't we have a barbecue at my place this weekend?

He had no idea how the conversation had drifted this far off course. He was quick to shut her down.

"Mazie, your grill was burned to a crisp, remember?"

The look on her face made him regret reminding her. Her expression fell, dragging her wrinkles down with her frown, until they piled along her jawline. She plucked at the buttons on her sweater with nervous motions. His heart skipped in panic, thinking that she might break down crying right there on his doorstep.

"Oh," she nodded. "I did forget about that."

The plucking fingers moved from the sweater buttons to her bottom lip. Brian was ready to jump in with a "Thank you, anyway, but I must be going…" when she looked up at him with a hopeful expression.

"Do you happen to have a grill?"

Brian blinked down at her.

"Uh, yeah, sure. I do…but…"

"Well, then, we could just have the barbecue here!"

She was almost glowing with joy and her wrinkles lifted with her cheeks. Brian reeled from the sudden turn of the tide. Frantically, he thought ahead to the weekend.

Am I doing anything to get out of this or do I flat-out lie?

Looking at the joy on Mazie's face, he would have to break it to her nicely.

"This weekend? Actually, Mazie, no. I'm sorry. I got things going on."

"Perfect!" she chirped, his refusal ignored. "I'll pat up some hamburger patties and—do you like potato salad with olives and pickles?" He nodded dumbly. "Wonderful! I'll make dessert too. Maybe you could toss up a green salad?"

"Wait, I'm not sure you understand. I have things to do this weekend, Mazie." While he was on a roll, he might as well bring up her other infraction. "Also, I've been meaning to ask you why you told your friend, Claire, that I was working undercover or whatever it was you told her. She asked me about it at your place."

Mazie's face deflated as she gazed up at him with sorrowful eyes. "Oh, goodness. I don't remember telling Claire anything quite like *that*. I do remember mentioning that you don't talk about your work much...but, oh dear...." She put a hand to her chest. "Are you angry with me, Brian?"

Angry seemed like too strong of a term. *Irritated* was a better description. However, the way Mazie was looking at him made Brian feel like a bully who had just pushed her down on the playground.

"No, of course not, Mazie. I'm sure it was just a misunderstanding." He chuckled thinking about the conversation now, wondering why he had let himself stew over such a trivial thing. "It's alright."

Mazie reached a timid hand toward him and patted his sleeve. "I really am sorry, dear. Is that the real reason you don't want to have a barbecue? Were you just afraid to tell me?"

Brian was stumped. "No, Mazie. Honest, I really am busy."

She nodded. "I understand. Maybe some other time." She gave his arm another pat and turned to go. He stepped forward to guide her down the steps, balancing the plates in one hand, while he cupped her elbow with the other.

"It's alright, dear. I've got this. I made it over here and up onto your porch with a plate of donuts without falling flat on my face," she said.

Brian knew he should be glad the subject was dropped and should just let her go, but with the mention of the homemade glazed donuts he held, he felt like a self-centered jerk.

"Hey, um, I might be available next weekend," he said. *I'll regret this later, guaranteed.*

Mazie paused and turned back to him, a flush of happiness on her face.

"Oh, that would be wonderful, Brian! I'll get back to you next week to make final plans," she said. "You don't mind if I invite a friend to join us, do you?"

Something nagged at the fringes of his reasoning but Brian struggled to recall it. He shrugged, distracted.

"Okay, sounds good, I guess. Salad, right?"

"Yes. I'll get everything else together."

Mazie stared at him like he had just rescued her from a fire-breathing dragon. Adoration shone in her eyes. He flinched when her hand came up, thinking she might actually attempt to hug him. She pointed at his face.

"You have paint on your cheek." She grinned and made her way off the porch. Mazie was halfway down the sidewalk before the nudge he felt transformed into a foghorn blaring in his head.

How much do you want to bet her "friend" will be that woman, Claire?

CHAPTER 11

Brian had been dreading the get-together the entire day, this whole week, come to think of it.

How he had been baited into hosting a barbecue at his place for a meddling old woman and her bookstore friend, Claire—who had acted just as surprised and miserable as he was the last time they'd met—he still couldn't figure out.

He heard a muffled knock on the door just as he hung up the phone with Mazie. He was starting to regret sharing his number with her, but she couldn't very well hobble over here every time she needed him and, after the grill fire, having a way to get a hold of him in case of an emergency seemed logical.

Mazie had phoned to inform him that Claire would be carrying over the potato salad while Mazie waited for the cobbler to come out of the oven. Then, Claire would head back to help her bring the cobbler as well as a few other things over to his place. Brian guessed the knock at his door was Claire now.

"On my way!"

He maneuvered around the large kitchen island and made his way to the door. He was still wearing socks and had already experienced on numerous occasions what happens when you try to rush around in socks on a slick tile floor.

Which Brian was reminded of when he tried to put the brakes on in the middle of the living room as the front door yawned open and Claire popped through his doorway with a large metal bowl cupped against her. He just stood there staring like a stunned donkey, unsure if he should be offended with her bold entry or laugh it off. The expression on her face told him she was second-guessing herself as well.

"Oh, uh…did you say to come in?" she stuttered, the color leaving her face as she realized her error.

Brian recovered and hustled toward her, reaching for the large bowl.

"Sure! Come in, come in. Let me take that."

Brian reached around Claire as she stood awkwardly in the entryway and pushed the door closed. She followed him to the kitchen and stood quietly while he made room for the bowl in the refrigerator.

"Would you like a drink?" he called over his shoulder, reaching for a can of Dr. Pepper from the refrigerator door. When she didn't answer, he glanced back and noticed her bending over to sniff an unlit candle on the table. His mom had sent it to him—not that he ever burned candles.

He tried again. "Do you want a drink? I have Dr. Pepper, iced tea, and lemonade." Claire straightened and walked toward him.

"No, thanks anyway. I better head back over to Mazie's and see if that dessert is ready."

Brian pulled out another can of Dr. Pepper and held it out. "You sure? You could carry it over with you." Claire shrugged and reached for the can.

"Okay. I guess I have a few minutes before I need to head back over. Mazie said she needed about fifteen more minutes on the dessert anyway."

As she popped the soda tab, Claire gave the room an appreciative glance. "Nice place for a bachelor."

Her smile was genuine and was obviously meant to disarm any assumption that she was being rude. Brian didn't think anything of the comment.

He attempted to look at the kitchen through her eyes: freshly painted bright white cabinets, a $22 black coffee maker with two plain black coffee mugs stored next to it (the only mugs he owned), a drop-leaf bamboo dining table from IKEA with one chair on each side, and a bowl of shrunken bananas that looked like they should have been tossed days ago in the middle of the kitchen island. Oh… and the single bare kitchen window. He'd been meaning to put blinds or some kind of curtain up but hadn't gotten around to it yet.

"Thanks. I've been doing some painting, mainly in the living room"—he nodded at the cabinets—"and a bit in here. The place still needs a lot of work, and that doesn't even include the outside. I do what I can when I have time."

The soda bubbles tickled going down his throat and he had to swallow hard to stop from coughing. He didn't know what to say next. He couldn't remember the last time he'd been alone with a woman, and certainly never in his own house. Thankfully, Claire picked up the conversation.

"I know you mentioned that you weren't in law enforcement…secret service…or whatever Mazie thought you did for a living, so what is it that you actually do? You work from home, right? I mean, that's also something Mazie mentioned, not that you even have to answer that question." Claire shook her head and chuckled. "Sorry. I'm not making a bit of sense. Let me try again. So, what do you do for a living, Brian? Again—you don't have to answer if you prefer not to."

Brian laughed too. The air felt a little lighter now that they'd broken through the thick fog of tension.

"I don't mind at all," he answered. "I'm a graphic designer and, yes, I do work from home. Mainly, I work nights. It's quieter and I'm a night owl anyway. To be honest, I'm not sure where Mazie got the idea that I did undercover work or had anything to do with law enforcement, although that sounds a lot more exciting than what I really do."

Claire grinned and shook her head. He noticed that she had the deepest dimples when she smiled.

"Ah, Mazie. No telling what she has up her sleeve, but you gotta love her," she said.

She took a sip of her Dr. Pepper. "So, a graphic designer, huh? My little brother dabbles in some graphic designing on the side. Nothing major, it's just a hobby for him. He helped me set up my website for my bookstore. I've been bugging him about maybe updating my business cards next to something a little more modern. Maybe even give the website some upgrades too. So...how did you get into graphic designing?" Claire moved to lean against the kitchen island across from him, looking much more relaxed than she had five minutes ago.

He enjoyed the work that he did but doubted Claire would be all that interested in hearing the whole background story of how he moved from doing the nine-to-five grind for an advertising agency that was leading him *nowhere* to making the leap to starting up his own gig, getting a small business loan, purchasing software and computer equipment—the whole nine yards.

Way too many details.

"I was already in that field and decided to go into business for myself," he said. "I should have taken the leap years ago but was scared I couldn't pull it off. I'm glad I did, though. I like being my own boss."

Claire raised her Dr. Pepper in a toast. "Same here!"

"That's right! You own that bookstore. Mazie mentioned that—"

He was interrupted by the tremolo of a mandolin and strings echoing throughout the kitchen. It was the theme song from *The Godfather*. The haunting melody originated from Brian's back pocket. Claire moved quickly to set her drink on the counter, remembering she was due back at Mazie's. Brian fished his cell phone out and hurried to silence it, feeling embarrassed by the sappy ringtone. Glancing down at the screen, he recognized Mazie's number.

"Hi, Mazie," he said as Claire swept out of the kitchen.

"Hello, Brian!" Her voice boomed in his ear and he jerked the phone back. "Can you let Claire know that I'm ready?"

Brian watched the front door close.

"She's already on her way."

MAZIE COULDN'T FIGURE it out. She'd felt like a game show host last night trying to keep things rolling at dinner.

She'd lost count of the times she had excused herself to the bathroom to give Brian and Claire time alone. She hoped they just chalked it up to the fact that she was in her seventies and that it must be true that older women can't hold their bladder very long.

The two of them never made it past lackluster table talk

—How long have you lived in Magnolia Springs? Do you have siblings? Can you pass the ketchup, please? —and not in the least sincerely trying to get to know each other better. Mazie was starting to feel like matchmaking just wasn't high on her list of talents. When the evening ended and she'd made her last attempt at getting them alone by offering to wrap up all the leftovers, Brian had insisted on helping. Like he couldn't wait to get the night over with so he could shove his company out the door.

Oh, he'd been polite and was the perfect host—setting up a folding table and chairs on the back porch, grilling the hamburger patties and corn cobs she'd provided, complimenting Claire and Mazie on their desserts, laughing and smiling at all the right times. He'd even made a decent attempt at putting together a hearty green salad, although he'd made enough to feed the entire neighborhood.

But Mazie was keen enough to notice that his smile never reached his eyes and that his thoughts were off somewhere else. Claire was also reserved but Mazie thought she could feel at least a spark of interest on the young woman's part.

Oh, well. I tried, Lord. If you want these two together, you're gonna have to take it from here. Playing matchmaker is exhausting.

"Ouch!" Mazie drew her hand back from the sharp thorn that had attempted to embed itself in her palm. She frowned down at the velvety dark-burgundy rose stem that had dared to use its weapon against her.

"You didn't have to bite me, you temperamental rascal."

The Black Pearl hybrid tea rose bush was her favorite in all the garden. Harold had surprised her by planting it for her on their fortieth wedding anniversary and waiting for her to notice it during her morning flower-tending. It hadn't taken her long to spot it, since she knew every living thing in her precious botanical paradise as well as she imagined Adam had known the Garden of Eden.

She often clipped a few Black Pearl stems to arrange in the vase on her porch table so that she could enjoy the deep beauty of its silken blooms.

Huh, she thought, *I might just have to teach this little lady a lesson and adorn the table with the yellow Floribundas for a week or two until she changes her attitude.*

Resting her cane against the honeysuckle vine shading the porch steps, Mazie pulled out the napkin left from breakfast that she'd tucked into her arm sleeve. She pressed it against the prick, where a small bubble of blood had risen.

It was time she went in anyway. There was that pile of *Woman's World* magazines she had been meaning to go through and she promised to make a batch of lemon sugar cookies for a baby shower they were having at the hospital for one of the nurses later this morning. Marie, a sweet young intern from the morning shift, had offered to pick her up for the occasion.

Lemon sugar cookies. She sighed, lifting the napkin's edge to see if the bleeding had ceased. A tiny bead of blood appeared. She pressed the napkin back down.

Harold's favorite.

She remembered the first time she had baked lemon sugar cookies for him. It was on their second wedding anniversary. Harold had gotten in late from a choir performance and had come in looking disheveled, tossing his book bag on the floor by the front door. She was sure he had forgotten their special day until he slipped up behind her while she was at the stove and presented her with a small white box.

Inside was a delicate gold locket on a thin gold chain. When she unloosed the latch, Harold's face smiled up at her from a heart-shaped cutout he'd taken from a photo from their wedding day. She smiled down at the bright red face in the picture, sunburned from Harold going swimming just hours before standing at the altar.

"That's not all," he told her as he sat on the kitchen chair to take off his work shoes. "You'll have to wait for it, though." A few days later, a lovely salmon-pink Camelot Rose bush appeared in the garden—her first rose bush. She was smitten.

Her anniversary gift to him was a special dinner she'd prepared and a large plate of tart lemon sugar cookies— her grandmother's recipe. They instantly became his favorite and stayed that way until he no longer recognized his bride, much less his favorite cookies.

Mazie was anxious to get started on her baking this

morning just so she could revisit memories of making them for Harold. Peeking and seeing that the bleeding had stopped, she folded the napkin and tucked it back into the sleeve of her sweater. She moved toward her cane.

As she started to reach for it, she noticed movement coming up the road from a few houses down. She had to squint her eyes to bring the object into focus. A head was bobbing up and down as it made its way toward her yard. She lost sight of the person for a moment as they weaved in and out of the spaces between the broad trees lining the sidewalk.

Mazie stood rooted, watching with growing curiosity. The figure was rather tall and, as it drew closer, she also noted it had a head full of black hair. As it passed her neighbor's goliath-size oak tree, she got a better view.

Brian?

Sweat poured down his temple as his head sagged. His light-colored T-shirt was sucked up against him with moisture. Mazie thought he looked perfectly miserable. Brian must have sensed someone was watching because his drooping head lifted and he looked straight at her. One hand lifted in a half-hearted attempt to salute. *Salute?*

Mazie grinned and twiddled her fingers at him, restraining herself from asking the obvious.

She watched as he looped around the white picket fence their properties shared, swept through his open gate, and slowed to a walk. She lost sight of him as he moved onto his porch.

Huh...I wonder what that's all about, she mused. She'd never even seen him up and about this early in the day before.

Well, she'd have to bring that up with Brian some other time. She would also have to save the chore of going through those magazines for later too. She had to get started on those cookies before Marie showed up.

CHAPTER 12

MAZIE's back was killing her. Twisting her body to the side and arching her back, she attempted to scoot half of her rear end into the slight curvature of the seat to relieve the pressure on her spine from the rigid wood under her.

Why in the world do people assume that old people must love rocking chairs? This wretched block of wood—probably pressboard at that—should have been made into a coffee table instead of a place to sit the soft parts of the body on. Mazie tried not to grunt as her hip started to lock up on her when she moved.

Least she could've done was throw a cushion on this thing.

Her neighbor, Janice, sat across from her in a lawn chair, which looked a whole lot more comfortable than what she was sitting in. Janice's mother was down for a nap in a recliner in the living room. She had propped the door open so she could listen for her through the front screen should her mother need her.

"Oh, Mazie," Janice sighed. "I'm at my wit's end. I love my mother and wouldn't have it any other way, but sometimes I feel so overwhelmed. She can't hardly eat anything most days and it takes us over an hour to get her showered properly. Thankfully, I have a caregiver that comes in twice a week to give me a break but..."

She reached for a cookie from the plate on the wicker table between them. "Thank you for bringing these, by the way. They're delicious."

Mazie had brought some of her favorite cookies to share: chocolate chip and raisin oatmeal. She hadn't really expected to stay for a visit, but Janice was on the porch and directing her to the rocking chair before she could squeak out a refusal.

She had planned to just drop the cookies off and arrange a time that she could come back for a proper visit. But since she had been coerced into an impromptu visit, she found that she didn't mind too much. It was obvious that her neighbor had been feeling pretty isolated and burdened lately and needed to talk.

Mazie felt bad that it had taken her so long to drop by. Janice had told her when they'd seen each other outside early one morning that she was moving her mother in with her. Mazie determined to be a better neighbor from now on and make an effort to reach out more often.

Giving a little nudge with her toe, Mazie rocked the chair a bit to loosen her stiff muscles and gave Janice a sympathetic nod.

"I couldn't imagine, Janice, how much you have on your plate right now with caring for your mother, but I'm glad she has you. There is just nothing like the blessing of a family. Still, I know it must be hard some days."

A slight tremble in her lips and the sudden sheen in her eyes warned Mazie that Janice was close to breaking down, but she rallied and shook it off.

"Yes...some days truly are hard, Mazie. But, I, well"— her chin jerked up and she stared right into Mazie's eyes— "I would never, I mean, wouldn't even *think* of putting Mother in a home." Her hands gripped the arms of her chair as she leaned toward Mazie. "Mom gave up everything to raise me. Putting her in a home would be like a slap in the face."

Mazie felt like *she* had been slapped in the face. Guilt coursed through her veins to the point that the ache in her heart far outweighed any physical pain she had from sitting in the stiff chair.

Oh, Harold.

The last few months of Harold's life were agonizing for her as they wrestled with the last stages of his disease. On more than one night Harold had disappeared from their bed and wandered around the house, trying doors to escape to the outside world. Thank God she had put padlocks on the front and back doors and hidden the keys and had locked the windows, or he might have succeeded. Then she would have been forced to call someone for help.

In the twilight of the final stages of the disease that stole him away from her, her six-foot-three, two hundred and fifty-pound husband became violent with her one evening when he thought she was a stranger in his house. On top of suffering from lack of sleep from twenty-four-hour care and endless worry, the fear of what he might end up doing to her was the last straw.

Alzheimer's is brutal and raw and had cruelly stripped Mazie, one painful layer at a time, of her soulmate and the love of her life as well as the dreams they had of making memories as they grew old together. She fought the bile of bitterness in her throat even now.

In the end, she had made the call. Had started the wheels turning for admitting him to a care home. Whenever she visited during those last days, Harold was not there. He had drifted away to an unknown land where she could not follow. Spread his wings in preparation for freedom from his deteriorated body. She had wept with relief mingled with crippling remorse when the call finally came that he had died in his sleep. A part of her died with him.

Yes, she understood what Janice was feeling right now, but she might not have a choice later.

Don't you shoulder more than you can bear, she wanted to tell her, but that's not what Janice needed to hear right now.

"Yes, dear, I understand how you feel."

～

MAZIE CLUNG to the smooth wood of the bedpost, her sweaty palms slipping downward as her body pressed hard against it.

Her chest burned as she struggled to draw in a deep breath, lungs quivering under the intense pressure. Images in front of her—the alarm clock, the empty water glass—shifted and swayed as dizziness and nausea engulfed her.

"God help me."

The episodes had been coming more frequently the past few months. She had been warned to expect them—these warning flags that danger was imminent—but she had dismissed them, brushing them off as universal signs of aging that she would just have to learn to live with. But they never failed to frighten her when they came, evoking mankind's age-old question as the familiar dread crept in: *Is this the end?*

It's not that she wasn't ready to meet her Creator and walk the streets of gold with Harold, but the process of getting there was disconcerting. Like everyone who faced death, she'd never been through that door before.

What is it like? Do you suffer mental and physical agony as you are dragged to the threshold, only to find that the door gently swings open and you step joyfully into the arms of welcoming angels?

A fierce *thud* punched deep inside her chest as her heart jolted itself back into rhythm. Gasping in a gulp of stale air from the musty bedroom, Mazie felt the pressure ease between her shoulder blades. She was suddenly aware of the moving air of the ceiling fan mounted above her bed as it flowed down on her, sending shudders through her body as the chilled air collided with the dampness of her exposed skin. Her nightgown was moist and clung tightly to her ribs and backbone.

She made no attempt to move—wasn't even sure she could—as she waited for her breathing to slow and her nerves to settle. After a moment, the dizziness passed and objects in the room came into focus again.

The cold tremors sweeping over her body forced her to push away from the bedpost. Her movement was slow, methodical, stiff from being in a cramped position for too long. She scooted closer to the edge of the mattress and explored the coarse rug fibers with her bare toes. Pressing down on one foot, she tested her ankle strength, keeping a firm grip on the headboard to steady herself in case she lost balance, before putting her full body weight on her feet.

Except for a few shaky breaths, she felt strength return to her body. When she felt ready, she stood, reaching back for the bedpost to stable her until she felt more confident. She waited for a moment more in the dark, getting her bearings, summoning her courage. The trembling in her limbs had a lingering effect. She attributed it to the after-shocks of the ordeal more than anything else.

She allowed herself to release the post and moved toward the bathroom, whispering her thanks to God—tinged with a slight disappointment—for sparing her one more time.

CHAPTER 13

THE CARDIAC FLOOR was quiet when Mazie arrived.

Rebecca greeted her with a smile and a typed list of the morning's tasks. Mazie glanced over the list, getting her bearings on how to plan her work. Her eyes were drawn to a handwritten notation at the top of the page that Rebecca had highlighted.

Lena Thomas had been sent home. Mazie rejoiced and mourned at the same time. Lena had been in and out of the hospital over the past several months before her surgery and she had developed a bond with the sweet girl. Mazie had always been very careful about not getting too close to her patients. She learned how necessary it was to keep her emotions in check when, during her first year volunteering at the hospital, she failed miserably and had come undone when two of her young patients had died.

Harold had been ready to demand that she pull the

plug on her volunteering at Magnolia, but she promised to work on it. She would *try* not to allow any of the children who she cared for on a daily basis into her heart. She would remain professional and keep her emotions at a safe distance. Naturally, she couldn't possibly keep that promise, but made it a point to break down only when she was alone so no one—especially Harold—would see her fall apart.

Mazie stared down at Lena Thomas' name. Lena was one of the many that Mazie had failed to guard her heart from.

I wish I could be there to see her face when she gets the birthday present I sent.

Mazie hadn't known what to get Lena at first. She had finally broken down and asked Claire for ideas. Her response was predictable, yet hit it right on the head. "Does she like to read?"

Together, they browsed the children's books, Claire suggesting several collections that were favorites for children Lena's age. Mazie settled on a few that looked interesting and handed them to Claire, who picked out two more books and added them to the stack.

"A little contribution from me," she said.

Mazie also noticed a small display of stuffed animals in the children's section. She settled on a brown bear holding a red plush heart. Claire carried their selections to the front.

Choosing a card from a greeting card rack by the register, Mazie signed it and added it to the gifts.

Claire had agreed to ship the package for her and dug

around in a back room until she found a box just the right size. There was no way to wrap the present, but she couldn't fret over that. Mazie handed Claire a twenty-dollar bill and the scrap of paper with the Thomas's address on it.

"Thank you, dear, for your help and for getting this sent off for me."

"It's no problem at all, Mazie." Claire smiled at her over the register.

But Mazie felt the need to explain anyway. "I don't make a habit of giving gifts to patients," she offered, fidgeting with a flower pen laying on the counter. "I know it's not the best practice but, well, this one was special. I've watched this sweet angel struggle since birth and we just connected…"

Claire came around the counter and gave her a hug. "You don't have to justify anything with me, Mazie. I understand."

MAZIE WAS ABOUT to put the phone down after the seventh ring—she had counted—when Brian answered with a raspy "hello" that sounded like he'd spent the night sitting next to a fire pit.

"Oh, good morning, Brian! I hope I didn't wake you…" She also hoped that he didn't sense the sarcasm in her voice because waking him up was *exactly* what she'd done.

"Um, who…?"

"It's Mazie, sorry, dear." She softened her voice, realizing she'd come on a little too chipper for someone who was a late sleeper. Besides, she needed to sound a bit remorseful before presenting her request. "I'm so sorry to bother you."

She could hear the shuffling of blankets as he cleared his throat. "No, it's fine. What's up?" A brief hesitation. "Are you okay?" A hint of concern in his voice.

He probably thinks I fell and need him to come get me off the floor.

"Oh, yes, dear, I'm fine. It's just that…well, I'm so sorry to ask, but I was wondering if you would mind taking me to church this morning? I usually walk, you see, but it looks like it might rain."

As she spoke, Mazie pulled back one side of the curtains and peeked out the window, her gaze avoiding the abandoned bird nest—it still made her sad to see it. She lifted her eyes to the sky. It *did* look a little dreary, but with only a few sparse clouds overhead, she doubted rain was in the forecast.

She didn't mean to be deceptive—not really—but she couldn't think of another way to get Brian to church. She doubted he would come if she invited him outright. He would probably feel odd showing up with her—like inviting the pizza delivery guy to church as a last-minute afterthought. But if Brian gave her a *ride* because she might get caught out in the rain, that would be a much more acceptable reason to be there.

The silence was long but Mazie was patient. She looked at the clock: *7:38*. They had plenty of time.

"Uh, sure, I guess so. What time do we need to leave?" He was definitely wide awake now. His voice echoed, like he was walking through a hallway or into the bathroom.

She was tickled. *Perfect!*

She mustn't let her excitement be too obvious in her voice.

"Thank you so much, Brian. I just hate to miss church. Service begins at ten, so we should leave around nine thirty. Does that work for you?" She knew she was talking too fast. Taking a deep breath, she slowed. "I appreciate this so much."

After hanging up, Mazie pranced her way through getting ready. As she pushed the bobby pins into the thin, inadequate bun she had tried to roll at the nape of her neck, she imagined Brian sitting next to her on the pew, captivated as he listened to Pastor Beckham deliver a heart-stirring sermon. She hummed as she patted cold cream on her wrinkles, attempting to soften their hard creases, and pictured Brian's eyes misty with tears as the Lord moved on his heart.

She beamed at herself in the mirror, not even minding the thin hair and wrinkles, admiring instead her best feature: her expressive green eyes. She did always think they made her look more youthful and drew people's attention away from the areas that were obviously aging.

In the kitchen, as she waited for her bagel to toast, she

puttered around the cupboards, sure she had another jar of instant hazelnut coffee around. Finding none, she peered into the almost empty jar on the counter.

Well, there's enough for another cup or two if I'm frugal. She would have to go to the store tomorrow. *Perhaps I can ask Brian to drive me after church today.*

No, that wouldn't do. She knew she was already pushing it asking for a ride to church. No sense in burning any bridges with him. Of course, bringing Brian along to church this morning meant she wouldn't be stopping by Emily's Book Barn today either.

Oh, well, Claire will understand when I explain why I missed coming by today.

She wished she could invite Claire to church as well but she was tied up with running the store on Sundays.

Twenty minutes later, coffee cup and plate washed, Mazie was proud to see Brian pull around to her driveway at 9:25 as she watched from her porch chair. *So punctual!*

When he parked, got out of the car, and helped her settle into the passenger seat, she was even more impressed.

And a gentleman.

She tucked her cane between herself and the car door and reached for the seat belt. She was a little surprised to see that he'd worn a pair of long shorts and a rumpled T-shirt for church but she supposed the Lord wouldn't mind.

The short ride to church was quiet. Except for when she pointed out where to turn, they spoke very little. She chanced a peek over at Brian and noticed that he looked like he wasn't fully awake yet. She felt a prick in her conscience. *Poor fellow probably worked half the night and here I am dragging him off to church. Hope he can stay awake through the preaching.*

She turned back to the window. Mazie didn't mind the silence really. She was getting used to the quiet in her life without the ebb and flow of Harold to fill the silence. Mazie studied the houses and landscape from her window. The world looked so different swirling by at this speed compared to her typical unhurried pace when she walked on Sunday mornings.

Somehow, she missed the old farm wagon with blossoming flowers spilling over its sides in front of the brick house. She had wanted to point it out to Brian because she thought it was so lovely. The darling poodle who always greeted her at the blue-and-white Victorian style house was a blur in her vision. Catching a glimpse of the chalk art that children often left on the sidewalk in front of the line of wooden mailboxes was an impossibility from her viewpoint.

Mazie was beginning to think she preferred walking over riding to church. She usually only asked for rides when the weather was contrary, not when it was as nice as this morning. She hadn't realized how much walking to church prepared her spirit for the word of God.

They had reached Grace Methodist. Mazie could see Karl greeting the Winston family at the doors with handshakes all around and his signature friendly smile.

"Turn right up there." She pointed toward the front

parking entrance. As Brian pulled into the parking lot, Mazie waved at Clayton and Logan, the Harrison twins, who were making their way to the Sunday school entrance. They waved back with puzzled expressions on their faces at seeing her in a car with a strange man. She imagined it would raise a few eyebrows when she walked into the sanctuary with him too. She was ashamed to admit it had been many years since she had brought a visitor to church and fulfilled the Bible's mandate to "go out into the highways and hedges" to bring the lost sheep to the Lord's house. She sat straighter in her seat.

Well, today that will be corrected.

Brian slowed at the sidewalk near the front entrance and guided the car to the curb.

"Here you are, madam," he announced with a mimicked British accent and swept his arm her way. Mazie was glad to see that he seemed more awake and chipper. "What time should I pick you up?" Putting the car in park, he reached for his door handle, preparing to come around and help her out of the car.

Mazie was stunned. *Pick me up? Did I misunderstand what he said?* She could feel the excitement from moments ago plummet like a bird struck down in midflight. She reached for his arm, stopping him from exiting the car.

"Wait! You mean you're not *coming in?*"

She knew she was probably squeezing his arm a little harder than necessary but didn't care—she was traumatized and close to a full-blown panic attack by the realization that

Brian was merely dropping her off on the curb instead of accompanying her into church.

The look on Brian's face reflected bewilderment and confusion.

"No…Mazie, uh, I just thought you needed a ride. I hadn't planned to stay," he mumbled. "Of course, I don't mind coming back to pick you up after service," he hurried to assure her.

The morning scenario flashed through her mind at a hundred frames per second.

Had I missed a cue somewhere? Did I really make it seem like I wanted to drag him out of bed for a lift to church because it looked like it might rain—and judging by the pleasant ride to church, it didn't look one bit like rain was heading their way and he had probably noticed—*and that I wasn't extending an invitation for him to join me?* In the flashing scenes in her mind, she realized what a pathetic mess she'd made of the whole thing.

No, you old crow, you never actually invited Brian to come to church. Only said that you needed a ride to get here.

And, speaking of *crow*, she was certainly eating it now, as she understood that she had acted deceptively and the Lord was surely displeased with how she'd gone about it. And it was her own fault for assuming Brian would be doing anything more than just dropping her off. Her cheeks grew warm as her hand slid from Brian's sleeve.

"Of course, dear. Maybe another time." She looked up through the front window at the clear sky, more for his benefit than hers.

"The weather looks very lovely now. I think I'll be just fine walking home after church— looking forward to it, in fact." She turned a brave, albeit wobbly, smile on him. "Thank you so much, Brian, for the ride. It was so kind of you."

Without waiting for his reply or his help, she pushed the car door open and swung her cane to the concrete.

"Mazie...hang on. Let me come help," Brian offered.

She waved him off. As if she wasn't humbled enough by her foolishness, and now appearing to be feeble so as to need a ride to church on a perfectly beautiful day, now Karl was making his way down the walkway to help her. What she wished more than anything right now was that she'd just stayed in bed and hadn't come at all.

No, Mazie-girl, if ever you needed to hear from God, you need to hear from him this morning.

CHAPTER 14

BRIAN FELT the tension creeping up the back of his neck from clenching his jaw.

Sam, Finn's younger sister, walked around his house with a large houseplant in her arms, one long green vine draping almost to the floor, trying to decide where the best lighting would be to place it. She flitted from one bright corner of the living room to a window in the office that faced the morning sun and back into the kitchen, where she stood nibbling the inside of her cheek while she judged the worthiness of the small kitchen window.

"Oh, dear, you poor thing, where should we put you?" she cooed down to the plant, its tapered leaves tickling the underside of her chin. Brian rolled his eyes at Finn.

Brian was less than thrilled to have something else to take care of in his life. There was a reason there were no other plants in his house. He could barely manage to keep the front lawn watered properly. Finn, who sat across from him on the couch sporting a wicked grin, winked at Brian as if to say, "Girls...aren't they the dandiest?" When Brian didn't crack a smile, Finn shrugged, then glanced to see if his sister was out of earshot.

"So, you wanna come out to my place next weekend? We could hit the racquetball courts, grab a tray of oysters and some fried pickles from Wintzell's, and go check out the girls at my cousin Greg's bike shop."

Brian couldn't resist cracking a smile now. He and Finn had always spent Fridays hitting seafood joints and staying up late playing video games at Finn's apartment, but Brian knew better than to believe Finn would be up to bounding around a racquetball court. He couldn't walk from a spot in the back of a Walmart parking lot to the front door without complaining.

"Seriously, Finn...picking up girls at Greg's bike shop?" Brian snorted. "Since when was Greg's a hot spot for finding dates?"

Finn stretched, his back arching over the arm of the couch, his denim shirt riding up, revealing a stark white round belly. "*Aaaa-haaa*," Finn yawned. "I don't know, Greg has a boatload of business this time of year and a lot of guys are buying bikes right now. So, girls flock around to see the guys. It's only natural that we show up to see the girls in turn..." He jerked his shirt back down over his ample stomach and nodded toward the kitchen and Sam.

"Unless you got a better idea for the weekend?"

Before Brian could spout off a response, Sam walked in —dragging a chair from the kitchen—and parked herself in front of them, stalling their conversation. Brian was glad she didn't try to sandwich herself between him and Finn on the couch, which wouldn't have surprised him. Instead, she situated herself primly on the chair and reached down to spread her flared skirt over her legs.

Her long golden hair was swept up into a high ponytail, a change from the single thick braid she normally wore. Pulling the end of her ponytail to the front, she twisted it in one hand and pinned Brian with a bright smile.

"What a darling house, Brian! So much potential!" The fingers of her free hand wiggled toward the window behind the couch he and Finn sat on. "Maybe a sheer curtain there and some bright throw pillows on the couch would make it more homey."

She nodded confidently as she mentally decorated the room, as if Brian should be running to grab paper and take notes. He hoped she wasn't getting any ideas about *living* in this house herself someday—it would only be a matter of Brian asking her on a few dates and popping the question and she'd already be choosing bridesmaids.

"Where'd you put that plant?" He steered the topic to safer waters.

Flicking the ponytail to the back, she pointed to the kitchen. "Oh, I decided to leave it at the kitchen window. I figured you would remember to water it if I left it close to the sink."

He ignored the sarcastic jab.

Sam leaned over to rub away a small water spot on the coffee table with one finger. "My students are learning about flowers and we planted petunia seeds in little plastic cups this week. We have a large window on one side of the class where we can watch them grow. The kids are so excited, but they think just because we planted the seeds on Friday that they will see sprouts on Monday."

Brian and Finn stared at Sam, the topic way out of their league. Finn did the honors.

"That's cool."

It's not as if Brian didn't like Sam. He'd known her since she was in the fifth grade, following him and Finn around when they hung out and even when they drove around town putting in job applications after graduation.

She was like a lost fawn and had an obvious crush on him, giggling at everything he said—funny or not—and finding every chance to sit by him. When she started calling "shotgun" for the front seat of his car when he came to pick up Finn, he was done with her admiration.

"Sam is starting to get on my nerves," he told Finn one night when Sam had asked to go miniature-golfing with them. "Can you drop a hint or something?"

Brian never asked him how he did it, but Sam started to back off and leave them alone, although he still caught her looking at him whenever they were in the same room.

When she reached high school, she had moved on to boys closer to her age and turned her attention to academics and social clubs. Brian rarely saw her after she went off to college, but after graduation and coming home to Mobile to teach elementary school, she made an attempt to reconnect with him. He wasn't any more interested than he'd been when she was in fifth grade. He had to admire her persistence, though.

Brian noticed that Sam was now staring at him, waiting for some kind of a response. Apparently, Finn's response was not the one she had been waiting for.

Uh, right, she was talking about seedlings and her students...

"Yeah," he coughed. "I remember growing beans in second grade, but I don't think we used dirt. We just grew them between two damp paper towels in sandwich baggies."

Turning to Finn before Sam could lure him into a further conversation about elementary school plant experiences, Brian nudged Finn's foot with his shoe.

"I think I *will* head to your place for the weekend. You've got me craving some of Wintzell's blackened redfish and fried pickles."

BRIAN WAS on his second mile and, surprisingly, wasn't gasping for air.

I'm getting better at this.

He had been trying to get a run in at least three or four times a week and was up to almost three miles now.

Although the neighborhoods were well-shaded with mature trees and the local landscape was pleasant to look at, it wasn't Brian's ideal running route. He would prefer to run somewhere out on an open dirt path or an empty back road. Somewhere quiet where he could think and avoid all the distractions.

And avoid an audience.

The gnome girl was sitting on the rock in her front yard again. Brian hadn't seen her since the last encounter when she had stared at him like he had a third eye. Instead of the pointy cap, she sported a wide red headband that stretched across her forehead and over her hairline, framing her face into a long oval. She wore a faded blue dress that looked to be a few sizes too big on her.

"How's it going?" He waved. Her expression softened but she offered no response. He should have taken the escape, but, for some reason, he tried again.

"Hello there! Good morning!"

Her eyes followed him as he walked along his fence toward his front gate. After a moment, she smiled shyly and gave a little wave before ducking her head into the collar of her dress and running back into the house.

What's the deal with this kid?

Brian shrugged it off and made his way up the walkway and into the house. He put the girl out of his mind. He had big plans with Finn this weekend and didn't want to think about the "creepy girl" across the street.

～

THE PARTY of ladies seated at the table next to them was rowdy, and the brunette sitting directly behind him laughed like a goose whose tail feathers were on fire.

But Brian didn't mind. He sat across from Finn at Wintzell's with a large plate of blackened red snapper laying on a generous bed of Cajun rice all smothered in a rich parmesan sauce in front of him. He'd only eaten half and had already given his coleslaw to Finn when he started getting full. Of course, he should have known better than to order the fried dill pickles appetizer. He just couldn't pack the food away like he used to.

He could see Finn was already eyeing his leftovers. *Nope, not today buddy.* Brian looked around for the waitress to ask for a take-home box.

Wintzell's Oyster House in Mobile, Alabama, had always been a favorite hangout for him and Finn. Whenever they got paid on Fridays, one would treat the other. Since Brian had moved to Magnolia Springs, his Friday nights had been filled with work, more often than not just to ward off boredom.

He studied the establishment walls filled with quotes and fun sayings that were a trademark of the Wintzell's restaurants, most notably here in the original Dauphin Street location in downtown Mobile. Originally a small oyster bar founded by J. Oliver Wintzell back in 1938, they offered their oysters with the slogan, *"Oysters—fried, stewed, or nude!"* and covered the walls with Oliver's own witty quotes as a personal touch.

When the waitress, a short robust lady with a booming voice and jolly smile, came over, Finn relented and asked for a box for his leftover chargrilled oysters-on-the-half-shell as well.

"Aren't those kinda gross heated up later?" Brian asked after the waitress walked away.

Finn gave him an incredulous look. "You serious, man?" He shook his head. "I probably won't reheat them anyway. I don't mind them cold."

It was Brian's turn to look incredulous. "That's just nasty, Finn."

Finn was his best friend in the whole world and hanging out with him this weekend had been great. He hadn't realized how much he missed *not working* and actually socializing again. It seemed like all he did these days was work on client projects or toil on tasks that needed to get done around the house. He had sat through dinner tonight listening to Finn lament about the fact that he couldn't find a serious date and that he would be single forever. Then he launched into stories of fishing with his dad at the lake and how he couldn't wait to have kids someday to do that kind of stuff with.

"I have no doubt you'll have a troop of rowdy offspring under your feet someday, Finn. Don't ask me to babysit either," he said.

Brian couldn't remember his own dad doing anything

as memorable as taking him fishing. He hadn't thought much of it until Finn had invited him to go along with him and his dad a few times and found that he really enjoyed it. He even made the mistake of asking his own dad why they never went fishing and was subject to a verbal diatribe about how he was busy providing for a family and didn't have time for "goofing off."

"If Finn's dad worked harder to take better care of his family instead of loafing around fishing, his family could have more to enjoy," his dad told him. Looking back, Brian knew his dad was wrong. In fact, if his father had spent more time with his own family, it might not have fallen apart.

Brian had no intention of putting himself in that situation. If—and it was a big *if*— he ever got married and had a family, he would work hard to be a good provider, but fishing and "goofing off" would be priorities too.

The move to Magnolia Springs had allowed him to put space between him and his uncomfortable memories and, most of the time, he actually enjoyed solitude and being unplugged from mainstream society. But there were a few times when he had gotten so desperate for human contact that he found himself looking out the office window, which faced the front of the house, to see if Mazie might be walking up with a plate of brownies or something interesting to eat.

That was another thing. Brian missed real home-cooked food. Back in Mobile, Brian and Finn were spoiled with home-cooked dinners at least once a week at Finn's parents' place. When his own mom wasn't working, they could drop by her place for more good food. He wasn't bad with a barbecue grill, but he couldn't prepare anything decent that required cooking inside the house on an actual stove.

It wasn't that he hadn't tried. His first few weeks in the house, he had purchased a book of easy crockpot meals from the bookstore and stopped at Walmart to buy a crockpot. It was his first one. He figured it couldn't be too hard to figure out three settings: *high, low,* and *off.* As he predicted, it was incredibly simple and he'd lived out of that cookbook for weeks, enjoying the smells emanating from the kitchen all day long.

But even the easy crockpot meals became redundant after a while. Half of the chapters in the cookbook were things he would never use a crockpot for, like desserts and appetizers.

And who cooks their breakfast in a crockpot? That was another chapter he'd skipped.

The waitress swung by their table and dropped off two boxes and their checks. After transferring his oysters to the box and securing the lid, Finn stood.

"Ready?" he said, reaching for his check from the table.

Brian had already packed up his food and was pulling his wallet out to throw a few bills on the table. He pulled out a few extra twenties.

"Guess you're gonna claim it's my turn to pay, right?"

He scooped up his check from the table and held out his hand. Finn didn't deny it. He handed over his check.

"Well, if you insist." He winked.

Snatching the slip from Finn, Brian shot back, "That's alright. You can pay for racquetball tomorrow." He already knew where this was going.

Finn turned to leave but not before Brian heard him mumble, "Yeah, right, do I look like I could run around a racquetball court?"

CHAPTER 15

IT TOOK Brian several minutes before he worked up the courage to get out of the car.

She was expecting him. In fact, he was surprised she hadn't already popped her head out of the door to see what was taking him so long—he knew she would be watching for him, waiting for him to pull up.

The car was off, the keys clutched in his fist, while he stared at the house. Brian studied the mud-colored paint curls that clung stubbornly to the aluminum siding of the old house and the crumbling edges of the concrete steps ascending to the broad porch.

His eyes drifted down the sides of the porch to the dark cavern underneath where he and his friends used to dare each other to crawl under to see who was the bravest. Brian always lost the dare. It was way too creepy for him under there. But instead of the ominous crawlspace, he saw that the bottom of the porch was now covered with a green lattice skirt.

Hmm, that's new.

It had been a few months since he'd been back home to visit yet it seemed like yesterday for the heaviness that hovered over him. He couldn't identify its source either. He had a lot of good memories living in this house.

He thought back to the sleepover in seventh grade during which he and his buddies had accidentally set the kitchen rug on fire trying to roast marshmallows over the open flame on the stove using wooden kabob skewers. When one of the marshmallows caught on fire, Robbie, the youngest and higher-strung of the group, threw the whole stick—burning marshmallow and all—onto the floor. The nearby rug tassels caught fire and Brian had thrown a pitcher of water on it to put it out. The fire fizzled out, but the kitchen floor was a mess and the fire alarm had brought his mom racing from her bedroom.

For his high school graduation, his mom had organized a party for him, with tables laden with nacho fixings and punch as well as a homemade cake in his school colors. She had even single-handedly decorated the whole yard with balloons and banners.

For all her hard work, Brian had still found himself a little embarrassed with its simplicity, which felt more like a birthday party than a graduation, compared to parties his other friends were attending and all the expensive gifts being lavished on them. But he never let her see his disappointment. It would have crushed her and he could never have hurt his mom like that.

Naturally, his father couldn't make it but sent along a card with some cash in it. Brian wasn't expecting him to show up to his graduation anyway, since he'd never made an appearance to any events in Brian's life after the divorce.

As predicted, his mother's shadow appeared behind the screen door and Brian waved to let her know he was coming. No telling how long she had been sitting there wondering why he hadn't come in yet. It was déjà vu of his teen years when his mom waited up for him to come home from a late night out with his friends.

Brian tightened his grip on the keys and stepped out of the car. A tantalizing aroma drifted to him from the house and he knew she would have cooked one of his favorite meals. He slammed the car door, a bit more eager to get inside and see what the tempting aroma was.

As he made his way up the walkway, Brian surveyed the tall patches of dead grass throughout the yard and chunks of a broken clay pot strewn along the side of the house. Not a speck of color in sight, if you didn't count the smattering of wild yellow dandelions along the neighbor's fence.

Mazie would be horrified at this yard.

He didn't know why his elderly neighbor popped into his thoughts right now. He guessed it was because of how much time and effort Mazie put into cultivating her garden and how he knew that his mom didn't have the time or energy for that kind of indulgence.

Brian found the unkempt yard and his gloomy feelings fading into the background the closer he came to the porch steps. By the time his mom pushed open the screen door and stepped out to greet him, his arms were already reaching to embrace her.

It wasn't perfect, but it was still home to him.

SARA LEANED in for a hug as she accepted the plastic bag Mazie offered. "Thank you, Mazie. The kids always enjoy your cookies."

Mazie winked. "I used a little less sugar…you're welcome. I know how wild the little ones get on Sunday mornings." They shared a laugh, remembering Mazie's experience in the preschool Sunday school class not long ago.

Thankfully, that was the only memory that came up in their conversation after last week's humbling experience with Brian dropping her off. Especially after the Harrison twins had plied her with questions after church about the man in the car. Mazie couldn't remember what muttered reply she offered before making her way out the side entrance, only to be horrified at seeing Brian's white car waiting by the curb in front of the church, right out where everyone leaving the church could see.

Brian stepped out to help Mazie into the car—again to

her mortification—and she scooted into the car so fast she banged her knee on the glovebox. The bruise was still there.

Brian said he had asked someone what time service let out so he could come back for her. He had apologized for misunderstanding her request for a ride as an invitation as well, to which she had replied, "No, Brian, I'm the one who should be apologizing for my attitude. I made a mess of the whole morning. I'm sorry."

But today was a new day, and the ordeal was behind her.

She walked this morning, taking an extra moment to linger over the wagon of flowers and offering the friendly white poodle a cookie. She would invite Brian to church the proper way soon, but needed to let her pride heal first.

Pastor Beckham's message struck a chord in her heart this morning as he spoke about how Jesus fed the five thousand with the meager offering of a boy's lunch of five loaves of bread and two fish.

"Before Jesus could perform the miracle," he said, "the disciples had to step out in faith to find a food source and then the boy had to be willing to give what he had."

It seemed to her that the Lord would have found a different way than to make his disciples run around begging for food scraps, but miracles don't come easy, she supposed. He planned to feed the people, but it would only happen if someone was willing to step out in faith. She knew what she had tried to do with Brian was not acting in faith by a simple invitation, it was trying to shove the miracle down his throat. And it had backfired on her.

When Mazie arrived at Emily's Book Barn, she was surprised to see a lanky young man lifting books out of a box on the floor as he stocked a shelf. A strand of brown hair draped low over one eye. When he stood, he swung it out of the way with a flick of his head.

"Good morning!"

Before Mazie could answer, Claire came around the end of a bookshelf hauling a cumbersome box in her arms. The young man rushed to help her with the load but Claire shook her head. "Nah, I got it." She set it down next to the box that he was working on.

"Hi, Mazie! I missed you last week!" Claire patted the young man's back and nudged him forward.

"This is Daniel, but we call him Danny. He's my nephew. I'm training him to help out around here."

Mazie gave the boy a polite nod. "Nice to meet you, Danny."

Danny smiled shyly, revealing a set of braces with blue wax pressed into them. "Nice to meet you too, ma'am."

Ma'am? She didn't think teenagers still had manners. There had been a few on her floor at the hospital who gave her such diabolic glares she wasn't sure if she should call the doctor or a priest.

Miss one week and see what happens?

She was hesitant to suggest coffee. Claire was obviously busy. But she was pleasantly surprised when Claire turned to Danny and asked him to keep an eye on the front of the store for a while.

"If you're busy, dear..." Mazie gave a pointed look in the boy's direction.

"No, Mazie, not at all. I've been moving boxes all morning in the storage room. I'm ready for a break."

Mazie made her way to the back. Claire had done some upgrades around the place: adding accent tables for book displays and a colorful bookshelf in the children's area that was the perfect height for little hands. There was even a rocking chair in the corner. Claire slipped up beside her and followed Mazie's gaze to the rocking chair.

"The rocking chair was my pawpaw's. I remember being rocked in it when I was young. Nana gave it to me when I stopped by her place on Saturday. I thought it would be perfect for children's story hour."

She turned to Mazie. "We need volunteers to read to the kids. Are you interested by any chance?"

Mazie imagined a dozen children seated on the large braided rug in front of the chair, all staring up at her as she read fairy tales, turning the book around to show the colorful illustrations as the children *oohed* and *ahhed*.

Yeah, right, she thought. *I can't get kids to sit still for a Sunday school craft, much less to sit patiently and be quiet. She'd have more luck roping the wind and locking it a jar.*

"Sure. I'd like that."

She didn't know where that answer had come from or why it had popped out of her mouth. Mazie refrained from pecking around to see if someone else had spoken for her. Then the bells on the front door jingled and Danny called out, "Aunt Claire! You have a delivery!"

"Be right back," Claire whispered, setting a cup of coffee down on the table as she swept past. She pointed back at it before rushing off. "That's yours."

Careful not to knock the table and spill her coffee, Mazie settled herself into the cozy armchair. She wondered if the chair could be exchanged for the rocking one in the corner—remembering the stiff chair on Janice's porch that had made her hips ache—if she read to the children. She leaned over and drew the warm coffee to her lips.

Mazie studied the books displayed nearby. Everything from murder and suspense, with obscure shadowed figures and dark sinister characters on the covers, to biographies. A vintage photo of Babe Ruth stared back at her from one cover. Another was titled, *A Woman of No Importance: The Untold Story of the American Spy Who Helped Win World War II.*

She couldn't imagine that a woman who reportedly helped win a war could be of no importance. She leaned forward to set the coffee back down on the table. A lone book on the endcap next to her chair caught her eye.

On the cover was a garishly dressed woman with a ghostly white complexion who appeared to have a peacock sitting on her head. Mazie tried to lean in for a closer look but the book was too low on the display. She settled back into the chair cushion. A moment later, Danny came by with a package of paper towels and set them on the antique sideboard next to the coffee machine. When he turned and noticed her sitting there, she stopped him.

"Excuse me, son, could you grab that book for me?" She pointed to the book with the peacock lady.

Danny bent, scooped the book from the endcap, and presented it to her in one graceful swoop. "Here ya go."

"Thank you, dear."

"Not a problem. You need anything else?"

"No, no. This is all."

After Danny disappeared, Mazie studied the book. It was a gently used copy with slight wear on the edges of the dust cover. Settling the book on her lap, she looked down at the woman on the cover again. Her face was pasty and colorless, except for the obnoxious bright red rouge that made her look like she'd been viciously slapped across both cheeks. Her tightly pursed lips also held a tint of blood-red coloring.

The Queen's Confession: The Story of Marie Antoinette. Mazie remembered learning about the Austrian princess turned French queen—who lived during the eighteenth century and helped spark the French Revolution—in history books growing up. She set the book on the table in front of her and retrieved her coffee mug.

When Claire made her way back, Mazie was almost done with her coffee. Claire stood, resting her elbows on the back of the chair across from Mazie.

"Sorry, Mazie, I'm pretty sure the delivery guy has a crush on me—he talks forever." Seeing Mazie's raised eyebrows, she was quick to set the record straight. "He's in his fifties, not happening," she said, pushing away from the chair and making her way to the coffeepot.

"Don't you worry about me," Mazie told her. "I've enjoyed just resting and admiring the changes you've been making around here."

Claire returned and sat across from Mazie, closing her eyes as she took a timid sip of hot coffee. "Ahhh, delicious." She glanced around. "Thank you. I'm just trying to do some upgrading."

Mazie patted the plush arm of her chair. "Just as long as you don't get rid of my cozy chair. It's my favorite parking spot between church and home."

The hint of a frown tugged at Claire's lips as she lowered her cup. "How have you been lately, Mazie?"

"Oh, busy as usual, dear. Things have been a whirlwind at the hospital with new patients this week and I baked two peach pies for the bake auction at church—Marg, the church secretary, picked them up yesterday."

She sighed, remembering that she had forgotten to add sugar to her list for Janice, who offered to pick up a few things for her at the grocery store. "What I really need to do is prune the rose bushes before—"

Claire held up a hand to stop her. "Whoa there, super-woman. I'm impressed, but what I meant was how have you been *feeling*?"

The knowing look on her face gave it away. Mazie knew where this was headed. She had shared with Claire a few weeks back about feeling extra tired lately and that she wasn't sleeping well. She thought she was just making conversation, like how older folks ramble on about the weather and all their aches and pains. Mazie was surprised that Claire even remembered her mentioning it.

"Well, I have my moments." She thought back to the terrifying episode a few weeks ago, including a few small ones since. "But I'm managing. Sure, I tire easier these days but I'm not a young woman anymore. Maybe I'm just pushing myself a bit hard and I definitely do not drink enough water—I hate drinking water. As they say, if you are even slightly dehydrated, it can cause all kinds of problems."

Claire was quiet. *Too quiet.* She stared at Mazie with a stern expression that made Mazie squirm like a guilty child sitting in the principal's office. She decided that she better not mention the shortness of breath. Claire would jump to conclusions and Mazie didn't want the unnecessary attention.

"Have you seen a doctor?"

"Oh, now don't you fuss, Claire. I'm right as rain. I'm just feeling my age, that's all. I do have a check-up coming up in a few months. I'm not good about remembering to take my vitamins every day either, so I'm probably a little low on iron."

Before Claire could see the guilt in her eyes, she looked down at the book with the pasty queen on it. Her skin was the color of death, her bright cheeks painted like a mortician's botched makeup job. Mazie shuddered and looked away.

The truth was, she *had* gone to see Dr. Patel a few months back and he hadn't liked what he heard under the stethoscope or the fact that she mentioned her heart feeling like it was flopping all over the place and that she had bouts of weakness and feeling tired. He had scooted his rolling chair close to the exam table and told her he was going to say it to her straight. She always had some trouble understanding Dr. Patel because of his prominent Indian accent. However, she understood him loud and clear that day.

"I'm referring you to a cardiologist, Mrs. Ellinger. At your age, and with your family history, this is something you would be foolish to ignore. If you have any trouble—pain or tightness in your chest, difficulty breathing, sudden weakness, dizziness—I want you to go to the emergency room or call an ambulance immediately. Do you understand?"

"Yes, Dr. Patel. I will."

"Do you want me to call and schedule an appointment or do you want to do it?"

She promised to make the call.

After instructing Mazie to see his receptionist for the referral, he gave her a scolding reserved for doctors alone. "And, Mrs. Ellinger, do not wait two years for your *annual* exam next time."

The referral was still sitting on her dresser. The message from Dr. Patel's office, reminding her to make a follow-up appointment, was saved on her answering machine.

Mazie could feel Claire's eyes still fixed on her. She knew the "low on iron" excuse was lame, but she didn't really want to talk about her health. It made her feel anxious and forced her to face unknowns she couldn't stomach right now. She heard Claire let out a huff of air, then clear her throat, giving Mazie a reprieve.

"Did I leave that book there?" She glanced up to see Claire pointing at the book about Marie Antoinette that lay in front of Mazie, a puzzled expression on her face.

Mazie reached for it. "No, I was looking at it while I was waiting for you earlier. I want to buy it."

She turned the cover to face Claire. "The Queen's Confession. With a title like that, I just have to find out what she plans to confess."

Claire laughed. "Yes, I've read it. Historical fiction is one of my favorite genres to read." She stood and reached for their cups. "I need a refill, how about you?"

Mazie held up a hand. "No, thank you. I don't want to have to stop off in the bushes on the way home."

Claire refilled her cup and rejoined Mazie.

The conversation shifted to Claire's plans for the children's section, including a mural she wanted on the south wall above the bookshelves near the rocking chair. When it was time to leave, Mazie made her way to the register and started to pull her coin purse from her sweater pocket. Claire refused the money and tucked the book into a bag, handing it to Mazie.

"I hope you enjoy the book. We can talk about it when

you come next Sunday. And I was serious about you reading to the kids after I get that section finished up."

Mazie reached for the bag and slid the handles onto her arm. "Thank you, dear. When I finish it, I'll return it to you to put back on the shelf. And, yes, next Sunday we can chat about me reading to the children."

Claire walked Mazie to the door and held it for her, the soft tinkle of the bells lingering between them.

Mazie looked around for Danny, but he was nowhere in sight. "Tell your nephew that it was nice meeting him. He's a sweet young man."

"Yes, he is and I'll let him know you said so. You be safe walking home," Claire told her. "And, Mazie, make that call to your doctor, okay?"

CHAPTER 16

THE HIGH WHINE of the trimmer as it ground through branches vibrated her old bones and hurt her ears. A few small black tarps lay scattered in her garden where the landscapers tossed the cuttings for easy cleanup later.

Mazie hated calling for someone else to prune her rose bushes. She had done it herself for as long as she could remember. Actually, that wasn't true. Up until a few years ago, she and Harold had worked together on the gardening chores and they had both loved every minute of it. It was really Harold's job to prune the rose bushes at the end of fall and in early spring. With Mazie standing back to eye his work, she would direct, "Cut a little more on that side" or "Leave some of the canes to grow back, Harold, you're butchering the thing!"

Harold would become so frustrated with her that he would throw the pruning shears to the ground and tell her to do it herself. She would snatch the shears up and start snipping here and there on the bushes until Harold wandered back over and held his hand out for the shears. "Give me that thing, woman. Now, get over there and be quiet."

It wasn't exactly an apology, but more of an unspoken truce.

They would snap and snarl at each other the whole season, but all would be well again when the job was done and Mazie whipped up a batch of brownies and carried out a pitcher of ice-cold milk while they sat on the porch and congratulated themselves on their hard work.

Harold had planted her first roses back in the yellow house—that's how she remembered it—the "yellow house with the board and batten siding."

While there, she went to work as a secretary at the same elementary school where Harold taught choir. They scrimped and saved every penny those two years to put toward a down payment on their first house. It was a time of fond memories for them as she and Harold made their lunches side by side every night and drove to work together every morning.

Mazie loved dropping by Harold's classroom when she had a few spare minutes away from the front office just to watch him interact with the children. He was so patient and always made the kids laugh with his silly jokes and funny imitations of cartoon character voices. He would wink at her when she came into his class and announce,

"Let's all say *good morning* to Mrs. Ellinger." Dutifully, the students would sing out, "Goooood morrrrning, *Mrs. Ellinger!*"

The children would always break out in irresistible giggles because they knew that she was married to their teacher, *Mr.* Ellinger, and got a kick out of connecting the two of them together, as if they had been privy to a secret schoolyard crush between classmates.

They had enough for a down payment on a house by the middle of May at the end of their second year in the board and batten house and moved into their first home over the summer.

Just before school started up again in September—and after four years of trying, and failing, to have children—Mazie found out she was pregnant. When she made her rounds to pick up lunch envelopes from the classes in the mornings, she could hear Harold singing louder than the kids when she passed the choir room.

When the school year was close to winding up again and Mazie was having a harder time walking around the campus with her protruding belly, Harold was hired as a band teacher at the high school, earning enough money to allow Mazie to quit her job at the elementary school.

She didn't know how he did it—all that clanging and clacking, tooting and ceaseless racket. She'd brought him his lunch one day at school and had walked into the band room to instant sensory overload. Her experience working as an elementary school secretary, with seven hundred boisterous children filling the halls, did not even amount to that much noise.

Jacob made his way into the world a month later at three o'clock in the morning after twelve hours of labor and forty-five minutes of pushing from his exhausted mother. Their long-awaited bundle of joy was the farthest thing from *joyful* from the moment the nurse swept him away to the nursery all the way into the first chaotic weeks at home.

By his third day home, Mazie was sitting on the couch bawling in cadence with her newborn son, whom she had propped up with a stack of pillows while she tried to nurse him. Jacob hadn't slept for more than two hours at a time and neither had she.

Harold had tried to help—changing diapers and walking the floors with Jacob tucked in his arm, whispering, "It's alright now. Shhh…Daddy's got you." It was all to no avail. Just as soon as they would lower the sleeping baby into his crib, inch-by-painstaking-inch so to not wake him, his face would scrunch up and he'd start howling again.

By the fourth night, Mazie told Harold to go to the store and buy formula, that she was sure her milk wasn't enough and the child must be starving to death. Knowing how much being able to nurse her baby meant to her, Harold tried once more to encourage her.

"Let's give it another night, honey. You nurse and I'll walk with him so you can get a little extra sleep in between feedings."

"And what will *you* do for sleep, Harold?" While he had taken a week off to be there to help after she and Jacob came home from the hospital, he would need to report back to work on Monday—two days away.

"I'll sleep when he sleeps."

Jacob squalled all that night too. The constant wailing reverberating off the walls and wood floors of the living room set her on edge until she almost started screaming along with him. Long after midnight, Harold scooped the still-crying infant from Mazie's arms as she sat in her chair, dazed by exhaustion and a face streaked with tears, and sent her to bed.

"Let me take him for a while."

She didn't resist. As she lay on her pillow, trying to remember if she had even showered that day, she heard the soft tones of Harold singing to Jacob as they made their paces back and forth in the living room. The fact that she was hearing Harold singing instead of her son screaming was balm to her frazzled nerves. It was only a matter of moments before sleep overcame her. Some time during the night, she felt Harold nudge her and tell her to feed Jacob. When she pulled back the blanket to get out of bed, he stopped her.

"Feed him here, you'll both rest better."

Harold rolled up a bath towel and pressed it between the two of them so Mazie wouldn't accidentally roll over on the baby. Taking another rolled towel, he tucked it against

Jacob's back so he was nested in a towel-cocoon as his mother nursed him. Within minutes, both were asleep.

"Ma'am. Excuse me…"

Mazie jumped at the sound of the voice coming from the edge of the porch. A short stocky man with an untucked flannel shirt and a straw hat looked up at her. She recognized him as the boss of the small crew working on her yard. Seeing that he had her attention, he motioned toward the front southeast corner of the property.

"You want us to trim up that tree for you?"

The cottonwood.

The pollen coming from it always made her sneeze in the spring and it left a mess of seeds everywhere, but she tolerated it. Harold had wanted it pulled, saying its roots would eventually wreak havoc on the front sidewalk. But she loved the shade it provided and had interceded on its behalf. The tree remained. Looking at it now, she saw that it did look unkempt and had several low branches that were wild and unsightly, but she was already paying more than her budget allowed to get the rose bushes tidied.

Besides, the man had caught her at a bad time. She felt like she'd just lived through an emotional hurricane as the old memories flooded over her. The cottonwood looked like she felt at the moment and she craved that validation— something that shared her untidy life.

"No, leave it. Maybe next time."

CHAPTER 17

THE POWER HAD GONE out an hour ago, right in the middle of an important book cover project for a curriculum designer company.

But that didn't bother Brian much. He had deftly switched to his laptop and continued working without so much as a hiccup. In today's modern world, everything was backed up to an internet cloud server and having his designing software programs downloaded on several devices made the shift a seamless process.

But now the laptop battery indicator was red and he would have to grab the power bank to plug into the laptop if he planned to keep working. A loud *bang* against the side of the house nearly made him jump out of his skin and he lurched back in his chair, sending it rolling back several inches. He saved his work and powered off the laptop.

"Okay, I'm done. I can take a hint," he spoke out to the dark room.

At that moment—as if to ensure that Brian kept his word—the office was illuminated with a blinding flash, almost immediately followed by a tremendous *boom!* that shook the entire house.

The storm is growing worse.

Brian stood and reached for the flashlight he'd parked next to the laptop earlier when the power had first gone out. He needed to go outside to find out what had hit the side of the house and see if anything had been damaged. He resisted leaving his warm, cozy house to expose himself to the elements and had almost talked himself out of it when another thought struck him.

Did I roll the windows up on the car? He groaned and headed toward the hall closet for a jacket, the narrow beam from the flashlight leading the way.

Another rumble rattled the windows in the living room as he slipped into his flannel jacket and grabbed his car keys from the kitchen counter. He wasn't looking forward to going out in the freezing torrent but dreaded having a flooded car even more if he had left the windows down.

Unlocking the deadbolt on the front door and turning the knob, a *whoosh* of icy air shoved the door open before Brian had barely pulled on it. His exposed face and neck were instantly covered in a fine mist that took his breath away and he shuddered before stepping out onto the porch and tugging the door closed behind him.

Taking the steps in two leaps, Brian ran to the side yard to see what had hit the house. A large branch from the backyard tree was laying next to the house. He didn't see any noticeable damage but would check more closely tomorrow. He turned and jogged across the lawn to the car and did a quick survey of the windows. The driver window was down an inch, enough to leave a sopping mess by morning if he left it.

By the time he yanked the door open and slid in to turn the key enough to activate the window switch to close it, the rain had drenched him and half the seat before he could jump back out and slam the door closed. A brilliant fork of lightning split the sky with a fearsome clap of thunder right behind it. *That's too close for me.* Brian sprinted back toward the house, not wanting to be caught standing out in the middle of an electrical storm.

He was halfway across the yard when he thought of Mazie. The fact that not one light shone from the nearby porches or from any of the streetlights within his view confirmed that the power was out throughout the neighborhood.

Brian slowed as he neared the porch and looked toward Mazie's house. It wasn't that he expected hers to be the only porch with a light on, but he just couldn't help thinking about her trying to make her way around a dark house.

It's the middle of the night. She has probably been in bed for hours. Riviera will more than likely have the power restored in a few hours anyhow.

However, judging from the intensity of the storm, Brian knew that Riviera Utilities—Magnolia Springs' local electric company—would have their hands full all over the city most of the morning.

When he felt the first sharp ice marbles pelt his wet skin, Brian bolted for the safety of the porch. The deluge of rain and, now, hail was deafening and the temperature felt like it had dropped ten degrees in the five minutes he'd been out here. He stood on the porch, pressing his now-drenched body against the door jamb, trying to decide what to do.

He wasn't sure why he felt the nudge to check on Mazie. He could almost guarantee that she was sleeping, or at least *trying* to sleep during the storm, and that he would only manage to scare the poor woman half to death by knocking on her door in the middle of the night. Not to mention that she might injure herself just trying to get to the door with no lights to guide her way.

He was starting to shiver under the saturated flannel jacket. He could also feel water puddles filling his tennis shoes. The lightning was still coming in rapid succession but the rumbles following seemed more delayed between flashes.

From where he was standing, Brian could no longer see Mazie's house next door but he could see the front of her yard. Already, there was a broken branch that had torn from the large tree near her front gate. Small pebbles littered the property on both their sides of the fence and he knew it would be a harrowing ordeal to run over there and cause a ruckus just to find out that she was fine.

Nah. I'll check on her in the morning.

He bent to remove the wet tennis shoes so he could leave them on the porch. He would deal with them tomorrow. All he wanted to do was to get out of these drenched clothes and crawl into a warm bed. He wouldn't even bother trying to shower in the dark tonight. He had practically gotten a shower just running to the car and back. The shoes made a sucking noise as he pulled them off. He peeled his socks off and stuffed them inside his shoes, setting them close to the door.

As he opened the door to go inside—a fine mist of cold rain in his wake—he tugged his jacket off and dumped it on top of the shoes.

He would deal with that in the morning too.

SHE WAS ALREADY AWAKE when the hail started.

She could hear the subtle change in sound from a thousand paper bags being crumpled in sequence to the louder pings in varying tones depending on what they struck: the wood railing on the front porch, the metal rain gutter below the roof, the plastic pot on the front steps that held her azaleas.

Mazie worried about how the hail would hurt her rose bushes and the delicate clematis vine trailing up the porch post. A severe storm a few years back had yielded nearly golf ball-sized hail that had shredded leaves, broken branches, crushed flowers, and all but destroyed the whole season's careful nurturing of her garden.

Mazie sat in the faded gray lounge chair staring out through the large bay window at the storm as it took its rage out on her back yard. The chair was stiff with a straight back that made her whole body ache the longer she sat. She had a perfectly comfortable recliner on the other side of the room that had been Harold's but she couldn't get out of the monstrous thing once she was in it.

She had considered getting rid of it since she rarely had company and really had no need for it, but found she just couldn't part with it yet. For the first few months after Harold died, she would sit on its edge to see if she could still smell him on the fabric.

She thought she detected the faint scent of English Leather cologne and coffee, both of them part of Harold's daily existence, but she couldn't tell for sure. He hadn't even worn the English Leather his last year before he took his exit from her life. Still, it was enough to imagine it smelled like him. The chair stayed.

She pulled the heavy throw blanket closer to her chin

CHAPTER 17 | 177

and leaned her head against the high back of the lounge chair. Storm or not, she wouldn't have slept much tonight. She had tried to lie down earlier but felt like there was a heavy boulder sitting on her chest. Rolling on her side had been worse. Sharp, stabbing pains between her shoulder blades had driven all hope of sleep away.

Mazie had sat on the edge of her bed for a few minutes and breathed through the lightheadedness, talking herself through the panic rising in her. After twelve minutes—she knew it was twelve minutes because she had stared at the digital clock on her nightstand and watched every minute pass—she stood and made her way slowly down the stairs to the kitchen.

She was reaching for the box of herbal tea bags when the power went out. Abandoning the task, she followed the illumination from the lightning coming through the front window to the lounge chair in the living room, grabbing the throw blanket from the back of the couch as she went.

Mazie knew she was playing a dangerous game of Russian roulette with her life by ignoring the signs. It wasn't like she needed the finger of God to write on the wall what was happening. In fact, it was *because* she knew what was happening that she kept putting it off. Her heart was failing her, just as Dr. Patel had warned her a few years ago that it might.

Harold had not even known, not that he would have remembered if she had told him anyway, with Alzheimer's stripping his memories from him. Even with the knowledge and the occasional attacks, she had managed to care for Harold until those last months before they moved him to a care center, as much for her safety as his.

It was wicked and appalling to think it, but somewhere deep down, she felt like she deserved it. She had shaken her fist at God when death had struck the first time, cruelly robbing her of her and Harold's only child, one they had waited so long for, prayed for, rejoiced over.

No warning. No last farewell. A flaming fire that had warmed everyone around him, reduced to a puff of smoke blown away in a moment of time. It was a cruel act of fate to pluck first one and then the other from her life, leaving her grasping the memories like a shipwreck survivor clinging to a piece of driftwood on a stormy sea. Maybe if she let go of it now, she too would sink beneath the surface and join them in their heavenly home where God had taken them...and had left her behind.

It's so cold in here.

She shivered under the delicate blanket, which was only effective as a couch decoration and for draping across one's legs more than a real source of warmth. The lightning had slowed and Mazie briefly wondered what she would do without the spurts of light now that she was stuck in the dark room. It was around two in the morning (it was 1:14 when she had finished watching the twelve minutes pass on her clock) and the sun wouldn't be up for several hours yet.

She glanced toward the dark shadow where the couch

CHAPTER 17 | 179

was and wondered if she could manage to prop herself up on it and try to sleep. She had never slept on a couch before, at least not on purpose, if you didn't count the time she'd fallen asleep reading a book while Harold watched the news or a football game on TV.

She didn't know how she would sleep with all that racket going on outside anyway. At least the pings of the hail pebbles against the house didn't seem as deafening as they had a few minutes ago and the wind was less fierce. She shivered and tried to tuck her slippered feet under the blanket wrapped around her but it was useless, the blanket was too short.

She knew she would never make it back upstairs without damaging herself, but Mazie thought she could at least reach the basket in the corner under the floor lamp.

There was an assortment of other blankets in the basket that, while she knew they were no larger or warmer than the one she had now, would make a nice pile of layers that would ward off the cold in the room. She would grab them and make her way to the couch to try to get a few more hours of sleep before it was time to get up. Today was Thursday and it would be a busy day at the hospital.

The children will be frightened in this storm, but at least the hospital has generators so they will still have electricity. I also hope that the weather will be clear by the time I need to leave.

The last time there was a heavy rain she'd had to traipse across flooded streets and endure spray from passing cars, arriving at the hospital a dripping mess. This storm would likely leave the streets and sidewalks in shambles with broken branches, trash, and other litter to get around, not to mention that the streets would be more flooded than before after this heavy downpour.

She would have to call Rebecca and see who was scheduled today. Maybe someone on shift this morning could give her a lift to the hospital. She also hoped the electricity was fixed in the next few hours or she would miss her morning coffee.

I guess I could see how hot the tap water gets. She pushed her icy hands under the blanket. *Nothin' I can do about it right now.*

Her last thoughts were of Janice's frail mother a few houses away, unable to care for herself, forced to depend on others for her every need. She hoped the woman wasn't too frightened by the storm.

THUMP... THUMP... THUMP!

Mazie jerked up in the chair and felt a sharp pain sear down her neck and left shoulder. She had to blink several times to clear her vision and she felt disoriented. She knew a loud pounding had woken her but she couldn't place where it was coming from.

Slowly, awareness came over her as she pieced together the long night with the storm, ending up on the chair—which she had obviously fallen asleep in, as her cramped neck was informing her—and, now, an unfamiliar knocking on her door. Fully awake and sitting up, she noticed the sky was light where the sun was trying to break through.

Dear lord, what time is it?

The pounding on the door was a little louder now and Mazie heard a voice coming through the heavy wood, though she couldn't make out what they were saying.

"Be right there! Give me a minute!"

Somehow, she had managed to wrap the blanket around her legs and under her right hip as she slept and it took several attempts to untangle herself. She stood slowly and nearly toppled over when her stiff ankles refused to bend so that she could walk. Holding to the edge of the chair, she lifted each foot, rotating it in a wide circle to loosen the muscles and give her joints some juice.

By the time she made it to the front door, the knocking had ceased and she saw a shadow cross her porch and hover near the window. She stood in frozen fear as she contemplated that the voice she heard at the door may not be someone she knew and now that *someone* was planning to break into her house.

Just as she started to back away—*where would she even go?*—she saw the silhouette of a man's head in the window from behind the sheer curtain and a deep voice call out, "Hello! Mazie?" Then, a soft tapping on the window and the full image of his tall figure pressing against the glass came into focus as he tried to peer through the opening in the curtain.

Mazie turned the deadbolt and fumbled with the doorknob lock. The figure shuffled back to the door and waited silently as she worked the door open. There stood her neighbor with his mop of black hair mashed flat on one side, dressed in a rumpled pair of jeans and open leather sandals.

"Brian?" Mazie squinted against a ray of sunshine that had snuck its way through the tight cluster of gray clouds that hung low in the sky. For a moment, she worried that she appeared to have just gotten out of bed and was mortified that Brian would think she had slept the morning away like a lazy bum.

Then again, she HAD been sleeping, come to think of it.

"Sorry to bother you, Mazie. I just thought I should check up on you, I mean, well, with the storm and all." He shrugged. "Not that you need checking up on. It's just that the power went out—well, I'm sure you already knew that…"

"Oh, dear, aren't you the sweetest?"

Realizing how cold it was outside, she opened the door wider. "Come on in. It's freezing out there." She beckoned, giving a pointed glance down at the open-toed leather sandals.

Brian shook his head. "No need to come in. I actually thought of you when the power first went off but I figured you wouldn't appreciate someone showing up at your door in the middle of the night."

He followed her gaze down to his sandals, then looked back at Mazie, probably realizing how odd he looked.

"I didn't want to wear any of my good shoes outside and my other shoes are wet from running out to my car to check my windows last night."

Mazie knew she probably looked a sight herself, but couldn't resist the dig. "I was thinking you were rehearsing for the role of Moses for a church play or something."

She got a belly laugh from him on that one.

"Nah, I don't wear long scratchy robes and beards make my skin break out. Besides, I don't even go to church."

Mazie cringed when she thought of the backfired scheme to get him to church not too long ago. She hadn't made any more attempts since. Now that Brian was acting so neighborly and she had his undivided attention, she figured now was as good a time as any.

"Well, since you mentioned church, I wonder if I could trouble you to be my guest this Sunday?"

She fluttered her green eyes just enough to appear as humble and sincere as she could fix her face to be. Brian rubbed his hands against the pullover sweatshirt he wore and gave her a thoughtful look. It took him a few heartbeats —she felt each one pound in her chest—to answer her and she was sure he was fishing for an excuse. She readied a way of escape for him, the suggestion of "maybe next time" on the very edge of her tongue, when he shrugged.

"Sure, why not? Be here at nine thirty to get you, right?"

If her teeth weren't chattering in her ear as she stood in

the cold doorway, Mazie was convinced she would be hearing the angels in heaven rousing up a holy chorus about right now. One thing she knew for certain, *her* heart was singing.

He's coming to church!

CHAPTER 18

MAZIE SAT across the table from Janice and her elderly mother and watched as Janice cut the chicken parmigiana on her mother's plate into smaller chunks, cooing to her as if she was speaking to a child, "Mother, you have to try to eat. You know you need to keep your strength up."

Spearing a bite-size piece on a fork, she held it close to the woman's lips, waiting patiently for her to take the bite. She refused, turning her head away, like a stubborn toddler. Sighing, Janice set the fork back down on the plate and turned to her own food.

"This is delicious, Mazie. I don't know when I've had a better meal," she said, as if she owed the praise to Mazie to make up for her mother's refusal to eat. "Is this mozzarella cheese?"

Mazie tore off a section of homemade sourdough bread and held it out to Janice. "Three cheeses actually:

mozzarella, parmesan, and provolone," she replied as Janice reached for the bread. Mazie pointed to a dish in the middle of the table. "There's butter if you want it. I don't use it."

She had planned the special dinner at her house so that she could get Janice and her mother, whose name was Amaya, out of the house for a while. It had taken some doing guiding Amaya down the front steps and setting her up in the wheelchair to push her to the house and then guide her up the steps into Mazie's, but it had been worth it.

Janice fussed that Mazie didn't have to go through all the trouble of dinner at her house when they could just as well have stayed at her house to eat. But Mazie had insisted that the two housebound women needed a change of scenery.

"Besides," she asserted, "I enjoy having company and I get a bit stir-crazy myself sometimes."

So, here they were, sharing a companionable dinner together. Mazie didn't regret the extra effort one bit. She rather enjoyed the whole experience: planning the menu —*it was nice to have someone other than herself to cook for*—shopping for the ingredients (Brian had been kind enough to offer her a ride), and spending the afternoon making a carrot cake that Janice had mentioned was her favorite.

Mazie had wanted to try her hand at a dark chocolate ganache tart but Janice said her mother was allergic to chocolate.

Maybe I could make a ganache tart to carry over to Brian…

Mazie found the visit very pleasant and chided herself for not doing it sooner. Even Amaya seemed to enjoy herself as she listened to her daughter and Mazie chatter on about goings-on in the local news and gossip about the neighbors.

Amaya's stroke had robbed her of many of her physical capabilities, including speech and certain muscle functions. In fact, doctors were still evaluating how much damage the stroke had caused against the onset of dementia that had been detected over the past few years.

But, tonight, there was clarity in her eyes and the slightest lift of one side of her mouth as she sat quietly— another skill that she struggled with—and watched the two women talk and laugh. If she retained a hold on most of her mental faculties—and Mazie sensed that she did—then she needed this "girl time" as much as she and Janice did. Mazie made herself a promise that she would make these get-togethers a regular occurrence.

It's not all about you, old girl, she thought, as she observed the joy reflected on Janice's face.

Janice was finishing telling how their mailman, who she guessed was somewhere close to her own age, seemed to find every excuse lately to hand-deliver her mail to her door rather than just put it in the mailbox at the end of her walkway.

"He claims that he didn't think a large envelope would fit in the box, so he thought he should carry it to the door."

She giggled like a sixteen-year-old who had just been asked to the prom. "Honestly, I think he likes me, Mazie." Janice glanced mischievously at her mother. "Don't tell my mom that the mailman has a crush on me."

Overall, Mazie thought the night was a success and she said so when she walked Janice and Amaya home and helped—*really just refereed and gave useless advice*—Janice situate her mother into a comfortable chair, then put the wheelchair in the hall closet.

"Gotta give mom a shower real quick before bed."

Janice pulled Mazie into a tight hug, lingering as she whispered into her ear, "You made my day, Mazie. How could you have known?"

Mazie pecked her on the cheek and blinked away the tears that lingered close.

"Trust me...I just knew."

MAZIE FELT like she was back in the preschool Sunday school class again.

Except there were more than just preschool-age children gathering on the large rug in front of her. Kids ranging from toddlers through early elementary grades positioned themselves to face her for story time.

She felt her palms beginning to sweat as nearly two dozen sets of eyes peered up at her, not including parents and other adults mingling around the fringes. Seeing that nothing exciting was happening yet, they giggled, wrestled, and complained while they waited for the reading to begin. Mazie held the books that Claire had given her against her chest and looked out over the crowd.

Am I supposed to just start reading or does someone get them quiet first?

She spotted Claire at the back of the group, chatting with a mother holding a squirming toddler on her hip. She mentally scolded herself for *willingly* volunteering—she hadn't even put up an ounce of resistance—to read to a group of rowdy kids on a Saturday morning. Reassessing the challenge in front of her, she decided she would explain to Claire after today that she wasn't ready to continue this after all.

She could tell by how engaged in conversation Claire was that there was no way she could get her attention any time soon, so Mazie took it upon herself to get things rolling.

"Ahem, excuse me!"

Two little girls—obviously twins—one dressed in a pink dress, the other in a yellow one, stopped poking at each other long enough to see who had spoken out. Looking up at Mazie and judging they could risk it, they resumed their silliness. A few of the other children glanced her way as well, but were soon distracted by a boy in the center of the group making fart noises by blowing on his bare forearm. The more they were entertained, the harder he blew.

"Hello! Good morning, children!"

The thought crossed her mind that she should have a foghorn or something ear-splitting to blow to get their attention. The twins jerked their heads up and stared at Mazie. Then the one in the pink dress stood to her feet and turned to face the group.

"Be quiet!" she barked. At least half of the children stopped and looked at her.

She had quite a booming voice for one so young. *Was she around seven?* Mazie tried to guess. Her pink-clad hero, small fists clenched against her sides, stood on her tiptoes and gave it another go.

"Be quiet, everyone! It's time for the story!"

With that, Mazie's self-proclaimed story announcer plopped back down and smiled up at her. "I think we're ready now."

Indeed, they were. At least ninety-five percent of the children pinned their stares on Mazie as if they were just noticing her for the first time. Several folded their hands in their laps—a polite gesture they probably had learned in school—with the only notable disturbance being a very small boy near the window who stood and loudly bellowed, "I gotta go potty, Daddy."

After the boy was ushered away by a red-faced man who Mazie judged was "daddy," she pulled the books away from her chest and rested them in her lap. Then she looked down at the first title: *Aliens Love Underpants*.

You gotta be kidding me…

Sliding the two books from underneath—she didn't

even want to look at their titles—she lowered them to the floor against the edge of the chair's rocker and gave her audience her most charming smile: perfect false teeth in all their bright-white glory.

"Good morning, children. Are you ready for a story?"

In a perfectly orchestrated chorus of voices, the group at her feet gave her a hearty, "Yes!"

And so she began… "Aliens love underpants, of every shape and size…"

At first, she was mortified to be reading a book out loud to kids about a bunch of aliens who decide to visit Earth. Not to have contact with humans as *normal* alien stories go, but to explore the underpants the humans had hung on their clotheslines.

As she read on, Mazie shook off the awkwardness and got into her reading, adding more dramatic flair to her voice as she went. The kids seemed to love it. Mazie couldn't help but chuckle herself as she turned the book around at every page to show the children the hilarious illustrations of aliens of various colors, shapes, and sizes trying on and traipsing about in equally colorful underpants.

They roared with laughter and broke out in fits of giggles until Mazie had to bring their attention back to the reading. When she read the line about "Granny's spotted bloomers," a boy two rows back called out, "What are bloomers?"

Mazie pointed at the picture in the book of a large blue

bug-eyed monster sporting a pair of long, frilly white underpants with red spots.

"These are bloomers right here. Basically, dear, they're just baggy underwear. Bloomers are just what people used to call them in the olden days."

"Do you wear bloomers, lady?"

The kids roared their approval and Mazie heard Claire's soft voice chide, "Quiet down, everyone. We aren't finished with the story." Mazie wasn't sure who had blurted out the question but she pretended not to hear and went on with the story.

My goodness, what would Pastor Beckham think if he walked in right now?

Predictably, by the time the book ended, the children had peeked curiously under their own dresses and down their pants to see what their underpants looked like and a few even announced that they had on "blue underwear" or "mine are white, what are yours?"

A mother on the sidelines finally took control, "Shhh, pay attention. We aren't looking at our underwear right now." That brought on more giggles, but the curiosities were eventually quelled.

The other two stories that Claire had provided were equally engaging for the kids but not near as fun as the underpants one. What kid wouldn't be excited to listen to a story that talked about a subject that was normally taboo to discuss in public?

Still, Mazie had won the crowd over and they begged

her to keep reading. By the end of the third story, both she and the children were getting antsy—they were too young and she was too old to sit still for very long.

She snapped the book closed and threw her hands in the air. "The end!"

Several kids were already up and starting to run around. The adults moved in to retrieve their young charges from the carpeted area. Claire made her way to Mazie and gave her a high five.

"You did great! The kids loved it!" she squealed. "I think the adults did too."

Mazie flushed from the compliment, feeling quite satisfied herself. "I think so too. But, really, Claire, the *underpants* story?"

Claire laughed and helped Mazie get up from the rigid chair when she saw her struggling to stand. "I knew they would love it. Besides, you have to admit, it *was* an adorable book."

Mazie's rear was aching something fierce and she had needed to use the restroom since the middle of the second book. Now that she was standing, the urge was even more intense. Two young boys approached them shyly and asked Mazie if they could see the books she had read. She pointed down at the floor where she'd set the three books. "Help yourself."

One boy told Claire that he was going to ask his mom to buy the alien book and wanted to know how much it cost.

That was Mazie's chance to escape. She pushed behind Claire—not so politely either—and made her way along the edges of the bookshelves.

She hoped that she would make it to the bathroom in time.

CHAPTER 19

EMILY'S BOOK BARN was down to a dozen customers left in the store.

Danny and Claire were hopping between the registers, helping customers find books, keeping the bathroom stocked and cleaned, and everything else that comes with managing a bookstore. But the happy flush on Claire's face and the way she laughed and chatted with the customers was proof that she was thoroughly enjoying it.

Mazie helped pick up books that were scattered around the children's section and put them back on the shelves. Claire had asked Mazie after she returned from the bathroom if she wanted to stay for another hour or so to keep her company.

"I thought I could order in a pizza. You know, to kinda celebrate our first successful story hour with the famous

Mazie Ellinger: Matriarch of Emily's Story Hour!" She bowed to Mazie, making her laugh.

"After lunch, I'll leave Danny in charge and give you a lift home."

Even though she was tired, Mazie was still humming with adrenaline from the morning. She hadn't realized how much she would actually enjoy reading to a large group of children. Sure, she had plenty of experience reading one-on-one with children all the time at the hospital, but the shared energy of the group today left her feeling inspired and youthful. She wasn't ready to go home to face a silent house after all that. She agreed to stay.

After the last chattering and squealing of children's voices had been ushered out and the tinkling song of the door bells had finally silenced, Claire called in their pizza order and went to pour coffee for the two of them. She offered to make a cup for Danny, who was wiping hand-prints off the door glass, but he declined.

"No, thanks," he said. "Unless it's an iced latte from Starbucks, I don't do coffee."

Mazie finished refilling the shelf under the register with white paper bags stamped with Emily's Book Barn logos and settled herself into the armchair at the end of the counter.

Claire returned with two steaming cups of coffee and handed one to Mazie.

"Thank you, Claire. I've been looking forward to this all morning."

"My pleasure!" Claire said. "You've certainly earned it today."

Danny tossed a wad of paper towels into a nearby trash can, making a perfect shot. "Score!" He grinned, pumping his fist. He placed the bottle of glass cleaner under the counter and walked over to open the cash register, scooping up a handful of coins to start rolling into wrappers.

All eyes turned at the sound of the familiar chiming of bells. Mazie was sure she spoke for everyone when she mumbled, "Oh, lord, no more kids." In a *whoosh* of crisp air, the mailman swept through the door.

"Hey, Carl!" Claire set her cup next to the register and wiped her hands on her pants. She reached for the stack of mail he offered.

"Afternoon, Claire." He nodded toward Danny, who had started dropping the coins in paper rolls. "Danny."

Danny nodded, pounding down one end of a roll of nickels. "What's up, Carl?"

"Just another day of work." Carl reached down for the mailbag at his feet and turned to Claire. "No packages today."

He glanced over to Mazie and waved. She waved back. Pointing to the cup on the counter, he said, "Coffee smells heavenly. Wish I had time for a cup." He turned and headed back to the door.

"We'll keep the coffee hot if you want to drop by after your route," Claire called to him. Carl gave her a thumbs-up and swept out as fast as he'd come in.

Claire pulled the rubber band off the stack of mail. She set the loose advertisements aside and quickly glanced through the other mail pieces before stopping at a large pink envelope.

"Got some mail for you here, Mazie."

Mazie set her cup down on a nearby shelf and scooted forward in the chair.

"For me? Why would I have any mail coming here?"

"Yeah, the sender's name is Thomas." Realization came over her face as she leaned against the counter, setting the rest of the stack down next to her. "Oh, I know who this is from! Remember how I mailed that little girl's birthday present for you, the one that was your patient? Wasn't her last name Thomas?"

"Yes. Lena Thomas." Mazie reached for the envelope Claire held out to her.

"I used the bookstore address as the return address in case you didn't want anyone to have your personal one," Claire told her, scooping up the remaining mail and carrying it into the office to go through later.

Mazie looked down at the envelope in her hand. It was addressed to:

Mazie Ellinger, c/o Emily's Book Barn

The handwriting was beautiful cursive, practically an antiquated form of writing for the younger generation and certainly not one a five-year-old could write so gracefully. Clearly, Mrs. Thomas had addressed it.

It was a homemade card made of heavy white construction paper. The front of the card was decorated with a hand-drawn creature that closely resembled an elephant with a thick tubular trunk extending out from a plump gray figure with four fat stubs that Mazie assumed were legs. A smaller lump at the top seemed to be the head because it looked like it had two beady eyes and there were two triangles poking out from the top of it.

Smaller than most elephant ears I've seen. She grinned.

There was a bright orange circle in the corner with alternating short and long black lines spreading outward from it—the universal representation of the sun for many children Lena's age and Mazie recognized it right away. Opening the card, the large letters formed with oversized curves and scratched lines caught her eye first.

It took her a minute to make out the *Thank you, Mazie, for the books! They are my faffrt!* that sprawled across both sides of the card and through the center fold. Her heart melted at the misspelling of "favorite," which her mother had obviously left as is. She would have helped her spell the rest of it but probably found the incorrect spelling just as endearing as Mazie did.

Underneath Lena's words, Mrs. Thomas added in her own graceful writing that Lena had loved the books and that you would hardly know she was recovering from heart surgery with all the energy she had. Below her name, she had added this postscript:

Thank you, Mazie, for making a scary time much less frightening for Lena. You'll never know the impact you made on her and—I'm sure—on all the kids on the cardiac floor!

Mazie swallowed a lump of happiness in her throat. She felt like she'd hit a home run of successes with children today.

Claire returned, dragging a rolling chair from her office, and scooted up close to Mazie. She sipped quietly on her coffee while Mazie returned the card to its envelope, laid it in her lap, and settled back into the chair cushion. She knew Claire was curious, so she offered, "It was a thank you card from Lena."

"That was sweet."

"Yes, Lena's a precious girl. Her mother wrote that she's doing well since her surgery. I hope things keep going well for her. I hate to see these kids go through things that we adults would barely survive ourselves." Mazie shook her head, fingering the edge of the envelope in her lap.

"Good for her," Claire said. "What a trouper she is—all those kids are, really."

Claire stood to reach for a candy wrapper someone had tossed on the carpet. She shoved it into her jeans pocket and sat back down. "Any word on that darling Irish boy you were telling me about?"

Mazie smiled at the mention of Ashton Carter, the bright six-year-old who, although quiet and shy, had exuded a presence that was deafening with cheerful joy. One couldn't help but feel delighted in seeing his radiant green eyes and vibrant hair and the adorable freckles that danced with every shift in his facial expression.

"The tests showed no issues with bacterial endocarditis, thankfully. His parents were so relieved, of course, and he looked much better than he had when he first came in. After the round of intravenous antibiotics, he was good to go."

"That's wonderful! I love happy endings," Claire said.

Although she was disappointed that she wouldn't be greeted by his sweet smile any longer, Mazie liked happy endings as well. More times than she wanted to admit, that was not the case.

They ranged in ages and personalities. Inconsolable toddlers who cried constantly and lacked the language skills to put their fears and hurts into words and didn't want, understandably, to be left alone. Or the brooding teenagers who refused to use their words, preferring instead to blockade themselves and their feelings behind thick stone walls of silence, resentful of being different, of feeling like an *invalid*.

Then there was the vast majority of kids who took it all in stride—as the young often do—and chattered away, making the nurses laugh, barely whimpering when they were poked with yet another needle or ushered off to lay still for another battery of x-rays and endless tests.

One young man, around fifteen, had spent over an hour explaining the tactics of the gruesome video game he was playing on his laptop with its realistic war zones, complete with violent explosions and blood splattering on the game screen. Mazie had to look away several times—she just couldn't stomach it—but she stayed because she sensed he simply enjoyed just having someone keep him company.

That's what she was there for. For *them*. For the kids who didn't have a choice about what happened to them, but faced with courage what was dealt to them nonetheless.

And, just maybe, Mazie needed the kids as much as they needed her.

THE PAIN STARTED in the middle of her turkey sandwich.

She wanted a light dinner and had thrown together the sandwich to hold her over. Claire had dropped her off only an hour ago and, after eating pizza with Claire and Danny at the bookstore, she wasn't hungry enough to rustle up a full meal. A sandwich and a glass of iced tea would curb any leftover appetite for the rest of the evening.

Before heading inside after Claire had pulled away, she had tugged the garden hose over to the front gate and left it on to give her roses a deep watering. She planned to let it run for fifteen minutes while she ate the sandwich.

A crossword puzzle from the newspaper she'd gotten from Claire sat half-completed in front of her. Mazie pushed it away and swallowed the last bit of sandwich in her mouth. She pulled her glass closer and tried taking a small sip of her tea. The pain was bad. It radiated from the middle of her upper back and laced its way under her left armpit, settling hard under her left breast. Setting the glass down, she pushed back from the table, unsure what to do, paralyzed by fear.

Maybe it's the pizza giving me heartburn. But pizza has never bothered me like this before.

She glanced to the telephone at the far end of the kitchen counter.

Do I call? What if it passes? How long do I wait?

A thin layer of sweat gathered on her upper lip and her hands grew clammy. She rubbed them slowly against the polyester fabric of her skirt. Her upper lip tasted salty from the sweat.

She was scared. Eyes now fixed on the telephone, which felt farther and farther away the longer she stalled, she reached one hand up to grip the edge of the table.

I better call someone for help. But…

She wasn't sure why she hesitated, what concern tugged at the fringes of her conscience, holding her back.

Brian is coming to church with me tomorrow.

There it was. It was foolish. She was reluctant to call because she might end up in the hospital and miss the opportunity she'd been waiting for—had blundered the first time—and wanted to make right so badly this time.

But hadn't this been what she longed for, to finally be free of this old body and the constant struggle with loneliness?

You stubborn, old goat. You can't have it both ways.

Mazie struggled to catch her breath through another crippling pain—tried to stand but her legs were limp noodles and wouldn't hold her. The movement made her feel dizzy and muddled, her thoughts misfiring. She blinked to clear her vision.

The phone was a mere nine feet away—by her calculation—but might as well have been on the other side of the street with how useless she felt.

The pain increased in intensity and her fingers plucked at the buttons at her chest as if she could somehow release the pressure building there. Her legs shook with a mixture of fear and with trying to hold herself in the chair as it began to slip from beneath her. She felt the warm wetness under her bottom where her bladder had failed her.

Decades of memories flashed through her mind like pages being flipped in a photo book: her mother tying bows on her pigtails before school, playing with her cousins at her grandparents' lake in northern Iowa, the first time she went to a drive-in movie theater, her father's funeral during the 1967 Chicago blizzard, her wedding day... *Harold, I miss you*...weeping over a small, lifeless body lying on a hospital bed... *No! He's just a baby...don't take him...Jacob!*

Her body hit the ground hard as the chair toppled over. Her frantic attempt to stop herself brought her tea glass down on her, soaking the front of her, icy cold mingling with the warmth puddled on the floor under her. She clawed at the boulder sitting on her chest and sucked for air through her open mouth.

I'm terrified, God. Harold…Jacob…they weren't aware…didn't know what was even happening to them when their time came.

She had longed for it. Dreamed about it. Cried endless tears over it. Even bartered with God that she would leave everything she owned to the church if he would take her home, as if she had any real thing of value to leave anyway. She didn't care what she left behind as long as she could be with her beloved husband and Jacob again. The only living things that really cared that she existed, that depended on her for *their* existence, were her prized roses…her budding crocus flowers…the fussy azaleas.

Oh, Harold, who will prune the rose bush you planted for me?

No, her reasoning felt scrambled and disorganized, her consciousness fading, *anyone could tend to them and meet their needs.* Yet Mazie had placed herself in this situation and no one would know that *she* was the one needing tending now as she struggled all alone on the kitchen floor.

Now, as she lay in a sticky puddle of tea and urine, sinking in a vortex of pain and fear, for the first time in all her years of longing, dreaming, crying…bartering, Mazie found herself fighting against it, her mind betraying her as it silently begged God for the one gift she never thought she wanted until this moment…*more time.*

CHAPTER 20

WHACK!

The ball came out of nowhere and smacked Brian in the back of his right shoulder. It landed at his feet and rolled out in front of him. Swinging around, he searched for its source.

She was standing at the fence again—the girl across the street—staring at him with her oval-shaped brown eyes, a mischievous expression etched on her face. Then she lifted one hand and *waved* at him.

What in the world…?

He looked down to the green tennis ball at his feet, then back at the girl. She was dressed in a drab brown corduroy dress with brown leather boots that laced up to the middle of her calves. Bright pink knee socks peeked out of the top of the boots. She was definitely grinning. She waved again.

"Hello," she called. The oval eyes were wide open with anticipation.

Brian reached down for the ball and held it up to her.

"Is this yours?"

She bobbed her head.

"Did you throw it at me?"

She chewed on her bottom lip like a guilty toddler but retained the sly expression.

"Yes," she grinned.

Brian was intrigued, almost humored at this point.

"Oh, okay…and, *why* did you throw it at me, may I ask?"

Her expression clouded and Brian thought she might bolt for the house again, but she didn't. Instead, she shrugged and went to sit on her rock, shoving her hands under her hips and locking them under her bottom. One leg bounced against the rock as she peeked up at him.

"Do you want to play ball?" She asked.

It was his turn to grin. He looked around for anyone else watching who might wonder why the lone girl was talking to a stranger. If there was anyone around, he hoped they had also noticed that it was *the girl* who had thrown the ball at him to get his attention. There was no one else around that Brian could see.

He glanced around again and took in the close proximity of the street to the sidewalk where he stood and considered how he and the girl could manage to toss a ball back and forth over the fence without it sending him running out to the street to fetch it every time. The prospect didn't look too good.

"Uh." Brian rolled the ball around in his hand and jerked his head toward the street. "Not too sure we can do that being so close to the street."

She pulled her hands from under her and stood quickly. "You can come in my front yard and play!" She was already making her way to the gate.

Alarms went off in Brian's head. There was no way he was going in that yard. He could just see her dad come flying out of the house with a shotgun, wondering what the neighbor guy was doing alone in the front yard with his daughter.

Not happening.

"Noooo, I don't think that's a good idea." He lifted the ball to throw it back to her. "Here, catch. Ready?"

The look of disappointment on her face was palpable. Brian felt like he'd just slammed the door on a Girl Scout selling her last box of cookies. The ball had already left his hand and landed with a soft *thud* on the grass near her feet. She hadn't even tried to catch it, or maybe she just hadn't been ready for it. Either way, it was obvious she felt let down.

Brian felt bad, he really did, but he also didn't want to stand around in sweaty running clothes any longer either. Plus, he had things he needed to get done before work tonight. He watched her slowly bend to retrieve the ball and hold it close to her chest as she looked back at him. Brian had never felt more like a jerk in his life than he did right now.

Time to go.

Tugging the zipper up on his jacket—more from nervous tension than necessity—he readied to leave. He made a mental note to start jogging either after dark in the evenings or getting up earlier. It seemed these late after-noon jogs coincided with the girl coming outside to observe the neighborhood. Not sure what else to do, he left her standing deflated in the middle of her yard.

"Well, sorry we couldn't play. Have a great rest of your day though."

He gave a short wave and started to make his way across the street, his pace quickening to haste his escape.

Behind him, he heard her call out. "What's your name?"

Brian acted as though he hadn't heard her as he jogged toward his house across the street. It was better that way.

HE WAS ALMOST to his gate when Brian noticed that Mazie's hose was flooding her side garden—something unheard of for her, as meticulous as she was about how she watered her flowers.

She probably forgot about it.

He veered off toward Mazie's driveway and slowed to a walk as he made his way to the porch. He wasn't going to just turn off her water without asking, even if it was spilling over and spreading dirt onto her driveway. It would be just his luck that her precious roses would suffer from getting less than their weekly quota of water and languish…and it would be all his fault.

He knocked on the door and stepped back. It often took her a minute or two to get to the door, so he didn't think much of it when two minutes had passed and she hadn't answered. He knocked again, a little more firmly, in case she hadn't heard the first time. After waiting another two or three minutes, he decided he would poke his head around the back and see if she was there, since it was obvious that she'd been outside and had turned the water on for her plants. It was possible she was working on something in the backyard and had forgotten about the water.

He stopped halfway down the stairs, an odd nudge tugging at his conscience. He stepped back onto the porch and looked around.

Was something out of place that had drawn his attention but hadn't registered in his brain yet?

The glass patio table with the wicker base and two matching floral chairs on either side were in their proper places, the neat pots of flowers across the railing of the porch were lined up impeccably, and even the floral doormat was squared perfectly with the door frame. Everything looked fine.

So, why do I have this erratic premonition that something is terribly wrong? I must be feeling weirded-out from that run-in with the neighbor girl, that's all.

He decided that he would check the backyard anyway. If Mazie wasn't back there, he'd come around front and knock again.

Brian strode off the porch and made his way around the side of the house toward the back. The yard was nicely landscaped and, except for an assortment of birdhouses hanging from tree limbs and the burnt-out grill she'd left against the back wall—he'd have to ask her if she wanted him to haul it away for her—everything was quiet.

"Mazie?"

He crept out to the middle of a grassy area close to the back porch.

"Mazie, you back here?"

The simmering dread in his gut escalated to a bubbling cauldron as Brian turned and sprinted back to the front porch. He didn't want to scare her half to death by peeking in the front window like he had when he checked on her after the lightning storm, but he had a sinking feeling that something was dreadfully wrong. He glanced over to the lake of water forming at the front of her yard for reassurance that he was on the right track.

Brian moved toward the wide front window. A heavier set of drapes were drawn over the sheer curtains this time with only a foot of an opening in the drapes to make an assessment through. He cupped his hands against the glass and tried to make out images in the semi-dark room. Just a sliver of the kitchen could be seen from his limited point of view, but he noticed that a light was on in the room. He knocked gently on the glass, sure she wouldn't be able to hear it, but he had to make the effort anyway.

An accent table was centered in front of the widow. He arched his neck to try for a better view over the tall lamp that sat on it. Brian could make out one end of a rectangular kitchen table against the far wall. On the table, there appeared to be a white plate at one end with a vase of flowers at the table's center where several leaves and flowers peeked out at him from behind the door frame of the kitchen. Stretching taller on his toes, he thought he could make out what looked like a chair laying on its side on the floor, a mound of blue floral fabric next to it.

Oh, no…

That's all Brian needed to push him into action. Leaping at the front door, he shook the handle and pounded on the heavy wood.

"Mazie! It's Brian! Can you hear me?"

His breaths came fast and his head was pounding.

Do I call the police? Would she forgive me if I broke the window?

The window could be fixed—he'd pay for the stupid thing himself if he had to. What he wouldn't do was waste any more time. Mazie very well could have forgotten about the water being left on. But it was unlikely that she wouldn't respond to someone pounding on her front door.

The burning in his stomach had crawled into his throat as he worked through his options. Knowing the window would be a whole lot easier to get through than the sturdy wood door, he went for that.

He could call the police afterwards.

CHAPTER 21

THE SOUND of ripping paper jolted Brian awake. Pulling his legs down from where they were propped on another chair, he sat up. Sharp pains raced through his feet and legs as the blood rushed back into them. Massaging his calves with his fingers, he looked toward the bed. It took him a moment to register where he was and where he had spent the night.

The hospital.

He looked up at the heavy blue curtain hanging from the ceiling in the middle of the room. There was a high-tone beeping coming from somewhere across the room that Brian recognized as a monitor of some sort.

The coronary care unit, second floor. He glanced back at the bed.

A young nurse stood on the other side of the bed tearing the paper off a package of gauze. She looked up from her task and smiled at him.

"Sorry to wake you," she said. "I tried to be quiet."

Still in its open package, she set the gauze on a nearby tray. Then, she reached for an empty syringe and tubing that were spread on the blanket. Making her way across the room, she walked to a disposal receptacle mounted on the wall and pushed the syringe down into it. On her way back, she dumped the tubing into a hazardous waste bin.

Brian watched her with disconnected interest, not feeling quite awake yet. Back at the bed, she picked up the roll of fresh gauze from the tray. Pulling back a corner of the sheet, she gently lifted the hand of the patient and proceeded to unwrap the old gauze from the wrist. Keeping her eyes on her work, she addressed Brian.

"Are you her son?"

Brian rolled his neck back and forth, trying to release the tension from sleeping in the hard plastic chair. He could feel a terrible headache creeping in. He looked up at her through puffy eyes.

"No, we aren't related. I live next door."

She nodded.

"Then you're the one who found her and called for help?"

Brian stood and walked to the bed to watch. "Yeah, I did."

She lay the arm back on the bed and opened an alcohol wipe, using it to clean part of the hand where some blood had leaked out where the IV entered under the skin, before she proceeded to apply a fresh layer of gauze.

"She's lucky to have you."

Brian had found Mazie in a crumpled heap on the ground next to the overturned kitchen chair. There was broken glass and a brown fluid all over the floor, which he assumed was from whatever was in the glass. He knelt in the wetness and slivers of glass and checked for a heartbeat.

For a second he couldn't find one and was ready to start CPR—*was it thirty chest compressions, then two breaths?* he found himself panicking—before sliding his fingers slightly upward and locating a faint heartbeat. Lowering his cheek to her lips, he detected the faintest of breaths. That's when he had pulled the cell phone from his pocket and made the call. It's also when he noticed the blood on his hand and upper arm from breaking the window.

The EMTs hadn't even questioned him about riding in the ambulance with her where she had temporarily gained consciousness but didn't seem to recognize him. She only fought the oxygen mask for a moment before losing consciousness again. One of the EMTs cleaned and dressed the cuts on Brian's hand and arm as they sped their way to the hospital.

He couldn't answer any of the admission nurse's questions nor was he any help to the numerous doctors and other staff that approached him to ask about medications she was allergic to or for phone numbers of immediate family. Brian didn't know a single thing about her family, just that her husband had passed away a few years back.

He had tried calling the office number to her church

after they arrived at the hospital last night, but an answering machine picked up. He left a brief message. The only other person he knew to contact was Claire, and he didn't have a private number for her. He would have to wait until Emily's Book Barn opened this morning to get a hold of her. At least Mazie would have another woman nearby when she woke up…*if she woke up.*

The doctor couldn't share much with him since he wasn't related to Mazie, but Brian gathered that she'd had a possible heart attack. At this point, it didn't appear that anyone really knew the extent of the damage she'd suffered and she was too weak and woozy from the drugs to talk much last night. After they had done numerous tests, poked her with needles, and taped tubing to her body, she had slipped away again around midnight.

Brian didn't know whether to stay or leave. Mazie was obviously in good hands and he had done the right thing by her, so why hang around?

The nurse finished changing out the bandaging on Mazie's hand and had carefully slipped it back under the sheet, pulling the sheet back up to her chin. Brian admired her compassion as he watched her reach for a thin blanket that lay at the end of the bed and tug it over the sheet for extra warmth.

She turned and checked the flow on the IV pole and looked over the adjustments on the monitor. Apparently satisfied, she smiled over at Brian once again and pointed to the window behind him.

"It's early yet. You should try to catch a little more sleep."

~

Mazie was still asleep and it was only a little after six in the morning: still too early to try calling the church or Claire.

Brian sat in the chair by the window for another twenty minutes deciding what to do. He felt obligated to at least stick around until he could get in contact with her pastor or Claire so that one of them could come and be with her.

Meanwhile, there's no way I'm going to get any more sleep in this lousy chair.

While he waited for someone from the church to call back or the bookstore to open, Brian decided to see if he could find the cafeteria or somewhere he could at least buy a cup of coffee and a pastry. He hadn't eaten since yesterday before his run and, if he didn't get some calories in him soon, they might find him passed out on the floor and haul *him* onto a gurney. That's the last thing he needed.

Passing the nurse's station, he saw the same nurse that had attended Mazie earlier staring at a screen behind a circular desk in the middle of the unit. He approached.

"Excuse me," he whispered, not really sure why he felt the need to keep his voice low thinking it might be an unspoken rule for a hospital the same as it was in a library. "Can you tell me where I can get a cup of coffee?"

Pointing toward the elevators at the end of the hall, she gave him directions. "Head down to the ground floor and turn left out of the elevators. You'll see a sign directing you to the cafeteria." She looked down at her watch. "They should be open for breakfast now. If not, they have vending machines in there that take debit cards."

Brian had no trouble finding the cafeteria and was pleased to see that the kitchen was open. He passed through the line, peering through the glass case at the various breakfast items displayed: a pan of scrambled eggs, layers of overcooked bacon, a tray of biscuits next to another pan of watery, brown gravy... As hungry as he was, Brian wasn't sure he could stomach anything on the breakfast menu. The smell of grease mixed with disinfectant permeated the air, making him nauseous.

"What can I get you?" A short woman with her hair tucked under a thin green cap and holding a spatula in one gloved hand stared up at him.

Spying a tray of pre-wrapped muffins at the end of the counter, he pointed toward them. "I think I'll just grab one of those muffins."

"Go ahead and move on down. The cashier can help you." She pivoted to the man behind him. "Can I help you?"

Now I know why I never liked to buy lunch in the school cafeteria, he thought.

He chose a banana nut muffin and ordered a large

black coffee from the young man at the register. The total was $4.79. Brian threw down a five-dollar bill.

"Keep the change." Scooping up his purchase, he made his way out before he lost his appetite altogether.

Brian planned to make the calls to Mazie's pastor and Claire after he returned to the room, but when he arrived, Mazie's eyes were open, fixed blankly up to the ceiling. Brian moved quickly to set down his coffee and muffin on the low table by the window and made his way to the bed.

"Mazie?" He studied her face for a reaction.

Her eyes found him, but her face was void of expression. Those green eyes, normally bright and always bordering on the edge of mischievous, now seemed hollow and dead, as if she were looking *through* him instead of *at* him.

She doesn't know me.

He was struck by the shock of the knowledge that she had possibly suffered some kind of brain damage as a result of whatever had happened to her, which he still didn't know for sure: *Heart attack? Stroke?*

He was no good at this. Crashing through her window like Superman and swooping in to rescue an old lady in distress came natural for him as a man. The protective instincts kicked in as he imagined what he would want another person to do if they found his mother lying unconscious on the floor.

But, staring down into her impassive face, her blank stare pinning him, making him feel like he was supposed to do something more, was unnerving. He felt compelled to comfort her in some way, to draw her out of her stupor and coax her back to the functioning world. It was an overwhelming feeling. He felt more comfortable with the physical responsibilities of life, not the emotional ones.

"Brian?"

The sound came out croaky and dry, but was like music to his ears for the joy it brought him. He surprised himself with the discovery that it mattered to him, but her response was like a small victory for them in the battle they had both endured together since last night. Brian could smell the staleness of her breath as he stood over her. But he was glad to hear his name come from her lips. It was like she'd risen to the light from a dark place. He smiled down at her.

"Yes, ma'am. It's me. How are you feeling?"

She didn't answer, but studied his face in quiet reflection. Her face seemed to soften as she took in his features. The fog lifted from her eyes and he could see one of her cheeks twitch.

Brian noticed movement from under the sheet. He looked down and saw that Mazie's hand was trembling, her fingers hobbling toward him. Gazing back into her eyes, he saw that she looked frightened. He looked around for a button to push that would beckon the nurse for her. He didn't see anything obvious.

Brian reached down through the metal bars of the bed and touched Mazie's trembling fingers. Their glacial chill penetrated his skin, sending a shiver up his arm.

"Everything's gonna be okay, Mazie," he whispered. "I'm going to call your pastor and Claire in a few minutes and let them know you're here. Is there someone else I could call? I don't think anyone knows who to call or where to look for any of your family's phone numbers."

She blinked slowly, trying to bring the world into focus. Her lips opened, closed, then opened again. It took a few attempts before the words came. "No…there is…no one."

Brian wasn't sure what she meant. He tried again.

"Do you have any family I could call?"

No one," she repeated, her voice barely above a whisper.

Brian thought about it. He doubted she had a parent still living. He tried to narrow it down so she would understand. "How about a brother or a sister?"

Her mouth lifted softly at the corners, her head rocking gently against the pillow. "I don't have a sister. No brothers."

Her smile wilted and Brian could tell she was growing weary. He didn't want to push her. He would just make the two calls that he'd planned and others could take it from there. This situation was out of his comfort zone.

Brian carefully pulled his hand back and was about to encourage Mazie to rest, but she reached for his hand again. Her brows puckered and she looked confused.

I pushed her too hard. Maybe I better go look for a nurse myself.

"No, I most assuredly do not have any siblings," she rasped.

The fact that she wouldn't let it go made Brian feel like she might be disoriented and confused and was becoming agitated by all the questions.

He patted her hand. "It's okay, Mazie. Don't worry about it."

"Why do you think I have a brother or sister?" Her gaze locked on him, and she had gone from looking confused to, well…almost offended.

He didn't know how to answer. It seemed like a natural question to ask in a time like this. Brian had instinctively assumed that her parents had already passed and that she might have brothers or sisters at least. He tried to explain.

"I just thought that"—*Sheesh, how was he even going to answer this?*—"people from your, you know, generation, had larger families. Well, not necessarily *large*, but I figured you had at least one sibling."

Mazie gave him an incredulous look just as a nurse walked in and noticed that she was awake.

"Hmph," Mazie grunted, closing her eyes. "I don't know about you sometimes, Brian."

She couldn't see it, but Brian had a big smile on his face. He had no doubt that this spunky matron was going to come through this just fine.

CHAPTER 22

Brian didn't want to make the call. To start with, he was tired and grumpy. He hadn't gotten much done with client work or gotten much sleep the past few days with everything going on with Mazie.

But today was his brother's birthday. He wasn't sure that he wanted to wade through the useless small talk that always dominated their brief conversations. Conversations that tended to center on Derek and everything going on in his life. Brian couldn't remember the last time he showed any real interest in what *Brian* was doing.

But it was his brother, and it just felt like the right thing to do.

Derek answered on the first ring. "Hey, bro!" Brian was thrown off by the greeting. He was almost surprised that his number still showed up on Derek's caller ID, since they hardly ever talked.

"Hey, Derek. Happy birthday!"

"Thanks! I appreciate it. Good to hear from you. What have you been up to lately?"

Brian shared about some of the client projects he was working on and a little about the new house, but glossed over any details because he didn't think Derek cared all that much. That fact was obvious when Derek offered the obligatory "That's nice" before launching into a play-by-play of all the exciting things happening in his own life, including asking his longtime girlfriend, Veronica, to marry him last week and a big birthday weekend in New York planned with their dad.

Brian found it interesting that his dad had found time to plan something fun with his insane schedule. *A whole weekend in New York just to celebrate Derek's birthday.* The bitterness crawled up into his throat and almost choked him.

"Wow, congratulations to you and Veronica! When's the date?"

"We haven't set one yet, but she's envisioning a fall wedding. Expect an invitation in a few weeks," Derek said.

In a normal family, Brian probably would have been one of the first his brother would have called with the news, maybe even asking him to be a groomsman, but that wasn't how things were with them. He should feel honored that he was even being invited. It would be a grand event too. He was sure of it. Dad had always poured time and money into Derek, neglecting him and Mom, having shaken the dust off his feet all those years ago and never looked back. Since moving to Florida with Dad, Derek had basically cut them off too, and Brian felt anger burn in his gut.

"Sure. Sure. Let me give you my address. Do you have a pen and…"

"No, man, it's okay. I'll give you a call later to get it." Derek chuckled. "If I write it down now, I'll probably lose it before I need it."

Brian rolled his eyes. Less than five minutes on the phone and he was already irritated. He might as well stir the waters so Derek could be irritated too.

"Sure, I guess that works. So, hey, have you checked in on Mom lately? She was telling me the other night that she was thinking of going back to college."

Derek made no attempt to mask the sigh. "Yeah, no, I haven't talked to her in a while. Been super busy. I'll give her a call next week and let her know about the wedding and all," he said. "College, huh? She's in her fifties, bro. Isn't that kinda old for college?"

Brian had never wanted to throat-punch someone so much in his whole life. *Yeah, super busy. Maybe Derek could call his mom on his way to New York for his exciting weekend.*

"No, Derek, I'm sure it's not. Lots of people go back to college at Mom's age. Anyhow, I'm sure it would mean a lot to her to hear from you."

Derek was quiet for so long that Brian had to pull the phone away and look to make sure the call hadn't gotten dropped. When he did answer, Brian could hear the coldness in his voice.

"She could call me too, bro. Don't act like I owe her anything."

"What's that supposed to mean?" Brian fumed. "Mom says she's called you tons of times and you never answer your phone. She'll probably be calling today to wish you a happy birthday too."

"Well, she never leaves a message or anything. I can't always pick up at the times she decides to call, which is usually when I'm at work…"

Brian cut him off. "Which means that you've *noticed* that she's making the effort, which is more than you bother to do." He was seething, unsure of what the true source of this depth of his really anger was. He wasn't the kind of guy who let things get under his skin and he made it a point to avoid confrontation. Well…except for right now.

Derek's last words before hanging up on him cut deep, deeper than he'd ever been hurt before. Maybe he deserved it since he had pushed Derek's buttons.

"Well, I got Dad, Brian and you got Mom. Who ended up with the better end of the deal?"

The phone rested against Brian's cheek for a full minute after the call was disconnected.

Was his brother right? Was it a thorn in his side that Derek had enjoyed a comfortable life with his dad while he and his mom had struggled for everything? Or was he wrestling with bitterness that Dad had fought to keep Derek but not him? He'd never really allowed himself to dwell on it or wallow in self-pity but that didn't mean it wasn't lingering in the shadows of his heart all these years. Derek's words had pierced that dark place, dragging the demons that taunted him out and dropping them at his feet, whether he was ready to deal with them or not.

More and more he was beginning to understand that biology alone doesn't make a family. He'd had more connection and less emotional baggage being around Mazie and Claire—shoot, even chatting with the mailman and the neighbor girl across the street—than he ever had with his family, including his mom. He loved her and they had a good relationship, but she had her own issues to deal with. Most of the time, he felt more like a big brother trying to protect his little sister from making bad choices. It was exhausting.

"…I got Dad, Brian, and you got Mom…"

Brian couldn't think of one thing that he admired about his dad, or the way Derek was turning out…just like him.

"You know what, Derek? I'm pretty sure I still got the better end of the deal," he said aloud. Derek would never hear the words, but Brian wasn't really saying it for Derek anyway. He was speaking to himself.

CLAIRE AND MAZIE were playing a game of chess that they'd set up on a TV tray on Mazie's lap. Claire had the worse end of the arrangement in that she had to lean over the cold metal bar on the bed to move her pieces. Mazie offered to let her put the bar down but Claire claimed it gave her something to lean on.

Neither one of them had ever played chess before today, so Brian was their coach. Mazie couldn't keep the moves for each piece straight in her head and kept trying to jump Claire's pieces on the black squares with her bishop on a white square.

"No, no, can't do that, Mazie," Brian patiently pointed out. "The bishop only moves diagonally on his own color. You can't jump colors like that."

Mazie sighed and moved her bishop back, trying not to jostle the game board too much and send the pieces scattering off the TV tray. She moved a rook instead and looked to Brian for his approval. He was concentrating on Claire's options as she planned her next move.

Well, I guess I went the right way this time.

Since they weren't paying attention to her at the moment, Mazie let her eyes roam over both of her friends' faces. Brian, dark and handsome, compassionate, but a loner who enjoyed the bachelor role a little too much. After coming close to the brink of death, she wanted to kick him in the head—with love, of course—and wake him up to all that he was missing about life by locking himself away and watching the world pass him by.

Claire, busy entrepreneur, friendly with everyone, giving to a fault, having dreams and big plans for her future with no one to share it with. Not that Claire had ever complained.

She probably just doesn't realize that she needs someone in her life, Mazie surmised.

Although Mazie wanted nothing more than to stitch the raw edges of these two young people's lives together and solve both their problems, she had done some growing up these past few days. In fact, now that she thought about it, a realization hit her.

Solving other people's "problems." That's where you are wrong, old girl. What you consider their problems may not be things that bother them at all.

The first moments after waking up in the hospital, she had felt an almost tangible disappointment that God had— yet again—cheated her out of death. But then she thought of the horror she'd felt laying on the kitchen floor, thinking that she actually *was* dying, and how she wasn't sure that's what she wanted after all. All that yearning for her life to be over, only to beg God to reconsider at the last minute.

Sorry, God. I guess I really don't know what to pray for anymore.

He must have understood her dilemma and sent Pastor Beckham this morning, who took her hands in his and prayed with her. In that prayer, she had felt God's voice speak to her heart as clear as if he had been standing by the side of the bed: "Your work isn't finished here, Mazie. When you've accomplished what I have for you to do, I will call you home."

The transformation in her heart had been immediate. After years of resisting, she was ready to submit her will to

God and had felt his peace. Since that prayer, Mazie felt like she had been resurrected from the dead—and she very nearly was. She had come close to facing eternity, but God had sent Brian to intervene because it wasn't her time to die. But what dawned on her—more like *slapped her upside the head* —as she became aware of the people and opportunities she would have missed, was the realization of how *alive* she felt.

For so long, she had felt dead inside—miserable, existing without purpose on most days—without a family to share her life with. She rationalized that God had mistakenly left her on Earth in this old, decaying body longer than was necessary instead of granting her release to leave this world. *What was the point?*

She often wondered why she was left here. She knew she made at least a modest impact on the children she cared for at the hospital, and her small circle of friends and church family made her feel like she meant something to them, but she never once believed that they wouldn't be just fine without her.

It struck her as humorous that most of her close companions were either too young to drive or, if they were old enough to have a license, were still too young to collect social security. In other words, she had no companions close to her age.

Maybe that was her fault. There were a few women her age at church and they often chatted and sat next to each other at potlucks, but that was the extent of it. She just naturally felt drawn to the younger crowd, drawing on their energy and their need for her.

Is that it? I want someone to need me? To feel like I have a purpose?

She noticed that Claire had taken her turn, deftly swooping her knight in to take out Mazie's bishop. Knowing they were waiting for her to move, Mazie scrunched her brows together as if she were concentrating on her strategy. Truth be told, she'd lost interest in the game.

Fate intervened when the sound of a pan flute came from the bench by the window. It was Claire's cell phone. She carefully stepped back from the bed and went to retrieve it. When they heard her say, "Hey, Danny, what's up?" Mazie turned to Brian and pointed down at the TV tray.

"Can you take this? I think my leg is getting a cramp."

"Oh, sure. I've got it."

Brian positioned himself to pick up the tray without toppling the chess pieces but Mazie told him she was done with the game for now, that she was declaring Claire the winner, which Mazie was sure was true anyway. By the time Claire had hung up, the game was cleared away and Mazie was yawning.

Looking from the tray on the rolling table—the chess game had already been returned to its box and sat on the tray—back to the end of Mazie yawning, she said, "Okay, I can take a hint. It's amazing how you got sleepy right when

I was winning." She winked at Brian. "Should we let this old lady get her beauty sleep?"

Mazie waved her off. "Who are you calling old lady?"

"Don't you try and deny it," Claire told her as she leaned over and kissed Mazie's forehead. "I'll call and check on you tomorrow after I close up shop."

Brian leaned over next and gave Mazie a hug. She could tell the first time he had done it a few days ago how awkward it had been for him to hug her, but it seemed to get easier for him each time he did and that fact made her heart content. When Brian hugged her, she imagined what it would have been like to be hugged by her son, Jacob, had he lived to be a grown man like Brian.

Brian stood and reached into his pants pocket for his keys. When he stared down at her, he looked amused.

"And I'll see you in the morning. Don't get yourself in trouble before then, so the doctor doesn't change his mind about releasing you."

Mazie grinned up at both of them. "Go on, get out. Let an *old lady* get some sleep."

"GOOD MORNING, MRS. ELLINGER," a voice called out from the kitchen.

Mazie sat on the couch trying to read *The Queen's Confession*, the book Claire had loaned her weeks ago. She'd forgotten about it. Now that she was home from the hospital and stuck doing nothing—at least until she built her stamina back up—she had all the time in the world for reading. She could hear Elizabeth, the caretaker she hired to check in on her a few times a week, puttering around and opening blinds in the kitchen, the bright sunlight making its way into the living room where Mazie was.

Elizabeth came around the corner with a small bag in her hand, which she held up for Mazie. "I picked up your prescriptions from the pharmacy."

"Thank you, dear. Just put them on the kitchen counter with the other hundred bottles of drugs sitting up there," she answered sarcastically.

She nearly gagged every time she took all those nasty pills. It didn't matter if she gulped them with orange juice or tried to down them with apple cider, she always shuddered for a full minute after they went down.

Elizabeth was a sweet young woman, albeit bossy at times. She was cheerful and full of energy, which tended to drain Mazie if she had to listen to her for too long. But, overall, she liked having Elizabeth around. Her presence brought instant energy into the house when she came, after all the silence and humdrum Mazie had to endure being home alone.

Not that she was alone for very long. Brian came by in the afternoons and dragged her on short walks with him to get her exercise. Of course, she only complained as if he was *dragging* her to do it but, in all honesty, she loved it and

Brian knew it. What old woman wouldn't want to be seen walking with a tall, handsome man?

They would talk about his family and how he and Finn —whom Mazie discovered was the same fellow that she had seen at his house on occasion—had always been in trouble as teenagers. On their walks, Brian often waved at the quiet little girl across the street when they passed her house. She would wave back and call out a hearty "Hello!" to them. When Mazie asked Brian what he knew about the girl, he shrugged and said, "She's different, but a sweet kid."

Even Claire came by most evenings with some kind of tantalizing dish that she'd made or picked up or Brian would come over and barbecue for them—lean chicken and lots of veggies for her, of course. He'd surprised her with a brand new barbecue grill when she came home from the rehab center and had promised to "properly train" her on how to grill when she was up to it. She planned to never be *up to it* so she would have the excuse to ask him over.

And Claire too. She made sure to always include Claire when she could make it so she and Brian could get better acquainted. She was careful not to make it too obvious to the both of them, though. While she had no intention of giving up on her plans to get them together, Mazie had learned to let God do things in his own time without too much interference on her part.

Elizabeth disappeared to put the pills on the counter and returned with a spiral notebook and a handful of brochures. She settled herself in the chair across from Mazie. *Harold's chair.* She sighed and set her book aside.

"Oh, what are you reading?" Elizabeth eyed the book.

"Do you know who Marie Antionette was?" she tested. *Why bother going into the story if she doesn't even know who I'm talking about?*

Elizabeth looked thoughtful for a second, then shook her head slowly. "I'm not sure. The name sounds familiar."

Mazie wasn't up to explaining. "Well, it's about her." She didn't offer any more explanation and the subject was dropped.

Elizabeth held out a colorful brochure to her. Mazie could see the picture on the front of a man and a woman standing on a golf course dressed in matching polo shirts, staring off at lord-knows-what in the distance. She made the effort to lean forward to peek at it, but made no move to reach for it or even act interested. She already knew where this was going.

Elizabeth thrust it closer. "I thought you might want to take a look at this."

Mazie shook her head. "No, thank you."

She heard the sigh but ignored it. "You should at least look at some of the brochures and pamphlets I brought you. Some of these places have a lot to offer as far as companionship and outdoor activities."

When Mazie didn't answer, Elizabeth tucked it inside the back of the notebook with a huff and opened the front cover. "Can we at least talk about how you are feeling?"

Mazie knew she was being obstinate. No matter how many times Elizabeth dropped hints or tried to slip brochures and pamphlets in front of her, she had no intention of packing herself off to a senior community.

But she knew she could be nicer about it. Elizabeth was just trying to be helpful and Mazie knew she was right in suggesting that this big house was too much for her. She had a housekeeping service come in twice a week but she really only inhabited her bedroom, one of the two bathrooms, and the kitchen and dining areas. The second bathroom and two other bedrooms were left untouched, except to be dusted and the vacuum lines refreshed.

Mazie wouldn't admit that the place was more than just a house—it had been her and Harold's *home*. Had been their home for the past thirty years since they'd moved from the yellow house, buying the larger home in hopes of their family growing. But no other children had come for them after Jacob.

No, she needed to remain here. To see Harold's chair sitting across from her, to have his dress shirts tucked close to her blouses in the closet, to *smell* and *feel* him in every fiber surrounding her here.

Still, she knew that it was time to make some tough decisions, so she would ask Elizabeth to help her bag up some of his clothes to take to the thrift store next week. But...she was staying in this house as long as her body would hold up.

Elizabeth was asking her if she'd been sleeping well and

how her appetite had been lately. Mazie coaxed her thoughts back to the present.

"I've never had much of an appetite anyway, but my friends and neighbors have been good about tempting me with some wonderful meals. As far as sleeping, well, not so good. I'm still adjusting to these medications they've loaded me up on."

Elizabeth jotted down a few notes in her book. "Yes, Mazie, it can take a while to adjust to medication and your doctor will probably need to do some tweaking to get the doses just right. See how it goes over the next week or so. When is your next appointment with"—Elizabeth glanced down at her notebook—"Dr. Patel?"

It was written on the wall calendar in her kitchen, so she wasn't positive. "Next week, I believe."

"Perfect. Let him know how you're feeling, which may be better by then, you never know."

They went over some healthy recipes for Mazie to try that were fairly easy. Elizabeth created a grocery list as they went and would do the shopping tomorrow. Mazie told her to add the ingredients for oatmeal raisin cookies—she had the recipe memorized—and had Elizabeth check and see how much instant hazelnut coffee was left in the canister.

"About a third of a canister left," she said, resuming her place across from Mazie. "Shall I add more to the list?"

"Of course," Mazie said.

Elizabeth didn't look up as she wrote. "Do you want me to see if they have it in decaf?

"Nope."

They shared a laugh.

"You got it. A girl's gotta have her caffeine." Elizabeth stood and went to check on toiletries and other things that Mazie might need for the rest of the week.

Mazie picked up her book but got bored with reading about Marie Antoinette's growing fondness for Hans Axel von Fersen, her Swedish love interest. She preferred reading mysteries. She had a whole shelf full of mystery novels in one of the extra bedrooms that she could read again if she got desperate.

Or maybe I'll sort through them and have Claire exchange them for new ones from the bookstore.

She set the book down on the coffee table. The ghostly pale queen stared back at her from the cover and Mazie shivered at how like death she looked.

Reaching for the book, she flipped it over.

CHAPTER 23

Brian walked to the end of his drive to grab the mail and noticed an older Asian man rolling up a garden hose in front of the house across the street.

The house where the odd, quiet girl lived.

The man's dark hair was balding in the front and his shoulders rounded close to his ears in a heavy stoop. On the front steps watching him sat the girl in a one-piece dress jumper over a sweatshirt and no shoes. Her hair was down and long tendrils curtained her face. The color was identical to the older man's. Brian assumed they were related.

Is this her father? Brian stood sifting through the few pieces of mail in his hand, peeking across the street without trying to be too obvious.

The man talked to the girl as he shoved the end of the hose into a plastic bin made to keep it out of view. Her head bobbed in response to whatever the man was saying.

Then she noticed Brian and jumped off the steps, running to the front gate. The man followed her with his eyes but didn't stop her. Brian knew he probably wondered what had caught the girl's attention so abruptly and sent her running to the fence.

"Hello there!" She turned and said something to the man, pointing over to Brian.

Brian thought about how much she had warmed up to him since he'd first seen her sitting alone on the rock, silent and broody. The girl standing at the fence greeted him as if he were a favorite uncle coming for a visit.

Brian lifted a hand. "Good morning!"

Her arms waved excitedly in the air as she yelled, "Good morning to you, too!"

The stooped man walked over and stood next to her. His expression was curious more than concerned.

Brian nodded respectfully. "Morning."

"Morning," the man answered, continuing to stare.

Brian closed the door on the mailbox and was about to turn back to the house when the girl called out.

"This is my dad!"

Well, that answers my question.

Brian paused, waiting to see if she would add more, but she didn't. The ball was in his court.

"Nice to meet you, sir. I'm Brian," he said. "You have a very sweet daughter."

The man looked down at the girl, who was barely below his shoulder height, a tender expression on his face. "Yes, she is. Thank you," he said, looking back to Brian. "I'm Kai."

With that, he patted the girl's shoulder and motioned her back into the house. Her face fell but she obeyed, giving him one last wave as she turned away. Her father followed, calling back to Brian, "Have a good day. It was nice meeting you."

Brian watched the two of them walk up the sidewalk, shoulders touching, the father speaking softly to his daughter, and wondered why the exchange had felt so peculiar, like an important pact between the father and daughter had come dangerously close to being broken by her speaking to Brian.

Well, he thought, *there's a strange family in every neighborhood.*

He had an important designing project to tackle tonight that he hoped would lead to a signed contract with a high-profile client if he did an exceptional job. First, he would shower and put a roast in the crockpot for dinner. After dinner, he planned to check on Mazie and then come home to work the rest of the night.

Another predictable, boring night.

MAZIE WAS SO EXCITED. Rebecca had agreed to let her come and spend the morning on the cardiac floor.

Of course, she had a list of restrictions for Mazie that

translated to "no working whatsoever." Her instructions were that she could visit the kids and nothing else. Mazie knew Rebecca was being generous in giving her even that much. She knew she would always be welcome to pay occasional visits on the floor, but her volunteering days were at an end. She suspected that would be made official at the annual volunteer appreciation dinner coming up in a few weeks.

Surprisingly, she was sad but not devastated. She still had the Sunday school kids and had even been recruited to help serve the kids during snack time, which gave her more time to spend with them. But she would miss her rounds at the hospital.

It had been years since she had picked up her knitting needles, but now she carried her craft bag out to the porch in the mornings and knit booties in various sizes for the children at Magnolia Children's Hospital to wear on their feet instead of what Mazie referred to as "those Martian socks," which looked just like the hair covers the hospital provided them, just cut in a different shape.

Once a week, Claire drove her to the hospital to drop off a stack of her knit booties and let her visit with the kids on the ward for an hour or so while she ran errands. Sometimes, Claire joined her and even brought along a few books to give the kids.

This morning, Claire had dropped her off, telling her that she would return after her dentist appointment. Mazie stopped by Rebecca's office for an update on the current patients. She was handed a clipboard listing several patient names and room numbers.

"You can just stop by a few rooms this morning and check on things," Rebecca said. She caught Mazie's eye and gave her a stern look. "A *few*. I don't want you pushing yourself too hard, Mazie."

Mazie scowled.

"There was a new arrival last night," Rebecca said, ignoring Mazie's unhappy look. "A ten-year-old boy named Jeffrey. He's scheduled for open-heart surgery tomorrow morning. The poor kid is feeling pretty anxious. I'm sure he could use a distraction."

Mazie looked on the list and located Jeffrey Salas in room 142A. "Poor darling. I'll go see him first."

There were two teenagers on the list, one fourteen, the other seventeen. She would check in on them too, but teenagers didn't take to her as quickly as the younger patients did.

The young ones don't notice the age difference as much as the older kids do.

She patted the bag at her side. She had brought cherry licorice to share with—or *bribe* rather—the children. Naturally, she wouldn't offer any to Jeffrey or any others who had restrictions, but there was always at least one child who was a lucky recipient.

She thought of the card that she had gotten from Lena Thomas and her mother. Just like all her previous patients, she prayed for her and always wondered how things went for them after they left the hospital. That's where Rebecca was helpful, often checking up on previous patients and their families to see if they needed additional support or resources.

"By the way," she said, "have you heard anything lately about Lena Thomas?" Mazie didn't need to clarify. Lena had been a return patient many times since her birth. Rebecca would know exactly who she was referring to.

Rebecca stood at the file cabinet, her back to Mazie, looking for a patient file while she chatted with her. When Rebecca failed to answer, Mazie assumed that she hadn't heard the question. But when she looked up from the clipboard on her lap, Rebecca had closed the drawer and turned to face her. She waited until she had Mazie's full attention before she spoke.

"There were complications, Mazie."

Mazie just stared. "Oh, I see." But, she didn't. Not really.

"What do you mean?"

Coming around the desk, Rebecca lowered herself into the chair next to Mazie and pulled herself closer. When she took Mazie's hand in hers, Mazie stiffened and a cold chill crept up the back of her legs.

"She didn't make it."

Mazie heard Rebecca whisper something about a massive pulmonary embolism and cardiac arrest but the words sounded foreign and the voice far away. She felt Rebecca wrap an arm around her shoulders and pull her into a hug. She didn't know if the tears were hers or Rebecca's when their faces touched and she felt the wetness against her cheek. Mazie took several deep breaths and pulled away. She tugged a tissue out of a box on the desk.

"You okay, Mazie?" Rebecca reached for a tissue as well.

Mazie breathed in deeply and hung her head. It never got easier. Every loss felt like losing Jacob all over again—like losing *every* child she had gathered under her wing on this cardiac floor—and it broke her heart anew.

No, she wasn't okay. But she would be after she worked through it.

The disappointment weighed heavy on her as she looked into Rebecca's eyes. Yes, Rebecca had been crying too.

"I've learned not to question God anymore, Rebecca," she said. "But I haven't learned not to disagree with him yet."

Rebecca hugged her again. "I know, hon. That's why I do what I do here. I can't change a blessed thing, but I can make it easier for some." She stood and patted Mazie's shoulder, then turned and opened the door.

"You stay in here as long as you need, Mazie. Then, you put on a smile for the kids that are still here, alright?"

Rebecca didn't expect an answer. The door closed softly behind her.

CHAPTER 24

BRIAN WASN'T sure exactly when he had stopped referring to the neighbor girl as "gnome girl."

The more he saw her as a real person—and a sweet girl —the more he found the term offensive, even if he was the only one who knew that's what he had labeled her in his mind.

He continued to make it a point to jog home on the opposite side of the street, but the girl was persistent in seeking him out the moment he came into view.

"I like your shoes," she called out to him one afternoon.

Brian had invested in an expensive pair of running shoes since he had gotten more serious about sticking with his running routine. He was up to five miles a day, three times a week now, and wasn't gasping for air at the end of his run anymore. He was pretty proud of himself. To celebrate, he decided to treat himself to the new shoes. They were red with a black stripe down the sides.

"Thank you!" he called back.

"Red is my favorite color!"

He looked down at the shoes and back to her. "Mine too!"

"What's your name again? I forgot."

He couldn't pretend he didn't hear her this time.

"My name is Brian." He didn't ask for hers. She offered it anyway.

"My name is Katy. I like your name...Brian." She pronounced his name slowly, stretching the vowel "i" out as if her vocal cords were trying the sound out for the first time.

Instead of the courteous "That's nice" that was on the tip of his tongue, Brian stood quietly, assessing the situation and his next move. It was dawning on him that what this young girl needed more than anything was a friend. I mean, why else would she position herself to watch for him during the times he usually went on a run? He didn't really think it was coincidence, although it could have been. It was as if she waited to see him just to have a few moments of being noticed, of being acknowledged.

"I like your name too, Katy." He searched for something else to add. "So, do you have any pets?"

He knew it was a lame question to start with, but it was the best he could come up with on the spur of the moment and it was a fairly safe question. It was safer than the questions that really picked at his brain like, "Why aren't you in school?" and "Do you have any friends?"

The sparkle in her expression seemed to fizzle out and he felt bad. Maybe he had chosen the wrong question to ask. She shrugged one shoulder and looked down at her fingers, cupped over the top of the chain link fence.

"I'm allergic to cats and my dad says dogs are too much work. I used to have a hamster that my grandma gave me, but my dad made me give it away because he said it made my room stink." She looked up with expectancy. "Do you have a dog?"

It was something that Brian had been considering. "No, I don't, but I'm thinking about getting one."

Katy's face lit up. "You should get one! A big dog that can go running with you."

Brian laughed. "Now that you put it that way, that's a great idea! If I take my dog on my runs with me, I could stop and let you pet him sometimes."

"Really!? I would like that!" She leaned into the fence as her excitement grew and Brian felt like he'd just handed the girl the winning ticket for a trip to the circus.

He almost hated to leave her standing at the fence when she had finally gained his full attention, but he really did need to shower and get dinner going.

"Well, Katy, I have to get inside now. I'm going to think about your idea about getting a dog." He waved goodbye.

Katy answered with two thumbs in the air. He couldn't help but laugh and give her a thumbs-up in return.

Brian chuckled to himself the whole way to his front porch.

A dog…why not?

BRIAN HAD NEVER LIKED KIDS—WASN'T sure he liked them even now—but Katy hadn't given him much of a choice. She had sat on her rock and watched him day by day, finally deciding "Yeah, he'll do," and started casting her spell on him.

When he went over to pull Mazie's trash out to the curb for her one evening, Mazie was sitting on her porch. She waved and called to him, "You are an angel, Brian! Thank you!"

He warmed under her praise. It struck him as he settled the bin close to the curb that a few months ago he would have never pictured himself helping out a neighbor—much less an old woman—and going out of his way to be kind to a lonely kid across the street.

Maybe I should have stuck it out in Mobile. The people in this neighborhood are making me soft.

Moving to close Mazie's gate, he noticed she still sat on the porch. He glanced back at the house across the street, then back to Mazie. *It will only take a minute.*

Brian stepped up on the porch and was immediately welcomed with a warm smile and an invitation to sit in the empty chair across from Mazie.

"Well, now, I suppose you came to spy if I had any cookies to share," she said.

He shook his head and laughed. "Busted." He pulled the chair out and made himself comfortable. He pointed to the house across the street.

"Actually, I had a question. Do you know anything about the family that lives in that house, where the girl you asked me about before always sits out in her yard?"

Mazie's eyes were tender and discerning, and Brian got the impression that her gaze was communicating more than she intended to say to him. Then her eyes turned to the house, one finger tapping her chin as she thought.

"They haven't lived there long. Maybe a year or two, if I recall. There was a woman that lived there for the first few months, and then she just disappeared. I haven't seen her since."

She shrugged and her face clouded. "I noticed the girl when I came home from church several times and tried to strike up a conversation with her but she wouldn't budge. She would draw back like a hermit crab scurrying to its shell. I kept trying, though, every Sunday afternoon that she was sittin' out there, but I wouldn't get much out of her."

Mazie stopped and turned her green eyes back on

Brian. Her face was tranquil, the pattern of deep wrinkles softening to the point that Brian caught a glimpse of the lovely young woman she had once been. She tilted her head and smiled as she studied him. "But she isn't like that with you, Brian. There is something about you that makes her feel safe, that draws her out of her shell." Mazie pulled her gaze back to the house across the street. "Oh, she did warm up to me a bit, telling me once that my flowers were pretty and saying 'hello' every so often when she sees me. I even brought over cookies one morning and met her father. He thanked me and said he would share them with Katy—that's her name by the way..."

"She told me," Brian interjected.

Mazie nodded and continued. "He said that she was in the middle of working on her schoolwork. Seeing him up close, I deducted that he is retired and is old enough to be her grandfather. I remember the woman who used to live there being much younger than him. For whatever reason, he is now raising her alone."

Mazie was quiet for a moment, then turned a sad smile on Brian. "I'm sure you can tell that Katy is, well...slow. I can't keep up with the terms they use anymore, but I guess you might say developmentally challenged."

Brian pulled a gulp of air into his lungs and sunk back into his chair. He knew something was off but couldn't put his finger on it. Mazie connected the dots for him. He chewed on his bottom lip and stared across the street.

"Yes, I could tell something…was off. I never see her with other kids, she's home all day… I don't know, she just seemed too friendly with me being a stranger and all. Besides," he said with a shrug, "I'm not really good with kids. I'm not even sure I like them half the time."

Mazie was smiling when he looked back at her. "Katy's mind isn't cluttered with all the stuff that bogs the rest of us down. She's innocent, free from many of the judgments and preconceived ideas that we harbor."

Mazie leaned forward and patted his hand. "For whatever reason, Brian, she chose you. Maybe she can see something in you that you cannot even see in yourself."

IT WAS at Mazie's birthday celebration that the idea was conceived.

Claire had put together a surprise party for Mazie at the bookstore, telling Mazie that she was picking her up after the store closed so she could help Claire choose books for the next few Saturday story hours. Claire had met a few of the nurses and Rebecca when they had dropped by to see Mazie in the hospital. Rebecca had given Brian and Claire her card and told them to contact her if Mazie needed anything.

"I know she's too stubborn to ask for help herself," she told them. He and Claire both agreed.

Claire reached out to Rebecca last week and asked her to invite any of the staff who Mazie had worked with and had even gone over and introduced herself to Mazie's neighbor, Janice, whom Mazie had mentioned often, and invited her to the celebration. Brian put in a call to Rev. Beckham, who showed up to the party with several members of the church, including a few families with children in Sunday school who were particularly fond of Mazie.

Someone at the church had even organized meals to be brought to the house after she'd arrived home from the hospital and coordinated trips to the grocery store or any other errands she needed done.

It was clear that a lot of folks cared about Mazie.

By the time Claire guided Mazie into Emily's Book Barn on that afternoon, her friends were waiting to shower her with love and gifts. Everyone yelled, "Surprise!" when she walked in, and the shock and bewilderment on her face was obvious. So much so that Brian was almost afraid they'd give her another heart attack.

The look on her face when she realized they were all there for her was worth every effort Claire had put into the party. With fingers pressed to her lips, happy tears slipped unabashedly down Mazie's cheeks, weaving gently through her wrinkles down to her chin.

Brian was standing close enough to hear her whisper to Claire, "I've never had a surprise birthday party before." Brian had to blink back a few tears of his own.

The store was closed to outsiders, so everyone who had not visited the bookstore before was treated to a quick tour. Everyone loved the children's corner, which Claire had finally finished decorating and now sported colorful mobiles of planets and aircraft hanging from the ceiling. The wall murals of forest animals were impressive as well and made the area feel even more cheerful and welcoming. The guests were especially impressed to hear that Mazie was a reader for story hour.

"Oh, Mazie is great with children," one of the ladies from the church remarked. "She's even helped out in Sunday school a time or two."

Mazie had piped up on that remark, adding, "Only to substitute, my dear, and that one event wore me plumb out too."

Brian looked around at the bright bookshelves individually painted in greens, red, yellows, and blues in the children's section. The shelves were set lower for the children to reach and there were stuffed animals and colorful books artfully arranged on the shelf tops. An enormous braided rug was centered in the middle of the floor in front of a sturdy, wood rocking chair tucked close to the corner beneath a mural of two frolicking deer. The area brought back fond memories of trips to the library with his mother when he was just a boy.

"The kids love listening to her read."

Brian spun around at the sound of the voice behind him. Claire stood next to a woman with vibrant red hair twisted into a thick braid that draped against her neck. Brian recognized her at once: Rebecca, the volunteer coordinator at Magnolia Children's Hospital. She faced Claire as Claire shared how Mazie wasn't sure she would like reading to children but seemed to take to it naturally.

"Oh, the patients at Magnolia adore her. Don't let her fool you," Rebecca told her. She turned to Brian and put out a hand. "Hello. It's Brian, right?"

She had a firm grip. "Yes, good to see you again, Rebecca."

He had meant to go over and say hello earlier, but she arrived just before Claire walked in with Mazie and everything got busy after that. He nodded toward the children's section. "This is a nice setup you've got, Claire. I'm sure the kids enjoy it."

A pink hue flushed her cheeks as she met his gaze. She quickly turned away and made her way toward one of the murals, leaving Brian feeling like he had missed an unspoken message somehow. He and Rebecca followed.

"They do. My nephew, Danny, painted the murals," she said. "He did a great job and saved me a fortune not having to hire a professional artist."

"Impressive. He's very talented," Brian said. He pointed toward the rocking chair in the corner. "Love the reading area."

Claire rubbed her hands together, her face aglow as she faced him. "You know, we are looking for more volunteers to read to the kids. I bet you would be perfect!"

Brian chuckled. "Yeah, right. My cousin's two boys never sat long enough for me to finish a story before they were running off somewhere else. I don't think I have that magic touch to keep kids' attention for very long."

Claire cocked her head and grinned over at Rebecca, who stood quietly listening to the exchange. "Fine, scaredy cat. But you're not off the hook yet."

"Uh, huh. Likely excuse," Rebecca added with a smirk.

Addressing them both, Claire said, "If you know of any children who might want to come to story hour, we have it every Saturday morning. I usually have a snack for the kids afterwards and we also have crafts sometimes."

Rebecca was all for it. "Absolutely! Do you have a flyer or anything that I can share with the families at the hospital?"

Claire's face lit up. "I do! That would be amazing! They're up front. I'll grab a stack for you." She turned to Brian. "I'll catch up with you in a bit."

He nodded. "Take your time. I'll stick around. I can also give Mazie a ride home so you don't have to."

She smiled. "Thanks, Brian. That would be great."

Brian looked back at the rocking chair in the corner, imagining himself sitting there frozen in front of a bunch of squirrelly, rambunctious kids. He shuddered. *Not in a million years.* He also didn't think he'd be much help in getting the word out either. He didn't know any kids who would be interested in story hour on Saturdays.

Wait. Yes, I do.

His little friend across the street. It would be the perfect opportunity for her to get out and meet other kids.

Do something besides sit outside in her front yard half the day. Surely her dad would bring her, right?

Brian made his way to the front to grab a few of those flyers for himself.

CHAPTER 25

IT FEELS SO good to be sitting in church again.

Mazie stared up at Pastor Beckham, noticing for the first time how kind his eyes were and how his voice carried so much compassion as he spoke. She heard the rustle of fabric behind her and smelled the faint scent of citrus before a hand came to rest on her shoulder and a voice whispered, "Morning, Mazie. It's good to see you."

She knew without looking that it was Margaret, one of the matriarchs of the church—older than Mazie by fifteen years—who always shuffled in fifteen minutes late to service and sat in the pew behind her. She reached up and patted Margaret's hand, whispering back, "Good morning, Margaret."

To her right, Anabel rose to take her fussy baby to the nursery. Mazie tried to peek over the blanket draped over the bundle in Anabel's arms as she scooted her way out of the pew into the aisle. All she could see was a tiny fist waving out from the blanket.

Little Grayson. He's what? Four months old now?

Mazie hadn't realized how much she had taken her little church family for granted. She had even chatted with Karl this morning as he walked with her into church.

Karl—who had lost his wife late last year—loved to talk and had installed himself as the official door greeter for Grace Methodist Church, sharing a smile with everyone who came through the doors of the sanctuary. Mazie suspected that no one minded since greeting gave him something to look forward to on Sundays.

It might be the most contact he has with people the whole week, she thought.

That first year without Harold had been tough for her too. Now that she thought about it, it hadn't gotten all that easier since then either, but the sharp pain of loss had at least dulled to a deep ache.

Mazie typically came in through the Sunday school hall so she could drop by to see the children as they gathered in their classes. It was one of her favorite parts of Sunday mornings. She always got lots of hugs and attention from the little ones and it warmed her heart. When she could, she would make cookies or bring candy to share with them. Even though she knew that the teachers planned for snack time, Mazie always brought treats anyway.

Going through that way also kept her from having to climb the stairs or walk up the ramp to reach the front entrance. But this morning, Claire had dropped her off on her way to the shop and Karl had insisted that he walk Mazie into church. He started to guide her toward the children's entrance, but she was feeling daring this morning. She pointed Karl toward the ramp leading to the main church entrance doors.

"Let's go in that way today."

Karl cheerfully obliged—it was a shorter path for him anyway—and led her up the ramp, guiding her as carefully as if she were the queen of England.

When they entered the foyer, Mazie untucked her arm from Karl's. "Thank you again, Karl." She nodded and started into the main sanctuary, then stopped. She turned back.

"And thank you for making everyone always feel so welcome at Grace Methodist. We don't tell you enough how appreciated you are."

Karl blushed and puffed up like a proud rooster, stammering out a "thank you" before turning to greet a family coming through the doors. Mazie hoped the compliment would carry him through his week. She knew that even the smallest gestures could make a world of difference.

Mazie listened with renewed interest to Pastor Beckham's summary of the story of Ruth and Naomi from the Bible, a story Mazie had memorized since childhood. Having felt like she had returned from the brink of death and was granted more time for some unknown purpose, everything felt new and fresh to her. Fragments of previously inconsequential details of life were being discovered anew for Mazie as her heart absorbed the hum of life's energy that she had given little notice to before.

The biblical Ruth had cared for her mother-in-law, Naomi, after Naomi's husband had died. Even when Ruth's own husband—Naomi's son—was taken too, the young woman had remained to care for the aging Naomi. She hadn't needed to. No one expected it from her.

Even so, when the day came that Naomi—now a broken woman after suffering such tremendous losses—humbled herself and made her way back to her native land, Ruth willingly left all she had known to follow her. The young Ruth, who was more than eligible to be remarried and start her life anew, had instead followed Naomi to an unknown country and unselfishly taken it upon herself to care and provide for her mother-in-law.

Mazie remembered reading the story for herself in the Bible and thinking that she would have never made that kind of reckless decision.

What if things had not worked out for her in the strange land? she wondered.

Hearing her pastor share the story once again from the pulpit, she felt her heart swell.

Yes, I understand it now, Ruth! Sometimes we make choices because we love someone and their needs are of greater value in our eyes than our own. "Where you go I will go…" you said. "Your people shall be my people…"

Mazie's fingers trembled as she reached to pull out the

small white handkerchief that she kept tucked in her sweater pocket. The tears flowed freely before she could put the cloth to her cheek but she found that she didn't mind. She had cried a lot of tears over the past two years, but instead of ripping away pieces of her that left her raw and wounded, these tears brought healing and restoration.

Like storm clouds parting to usher in the rays of warm sunlight, Mazie saw clearly how a person would be willing to give up their identity to embrace a new future, take a chance on investing in a path that you'd only heard about and had watched someone cling to with the smallest seed of faith, not knowing what awaited you when you took the leap.

Did it really take me all these years to get this? What have I missed in trying to cling to the past when I still had a future in front of me?

She thought of Claire and how she'd planned a surprise birthday party just for her—the first Mazie had ever had—and how she called to check on her every day, stopped by the house to bring food for her during the week, and had always taken time out of her work at the bookstore to just sit and have coffee with her.

Sure, it wasn't like Claire had dropped her whole life to care for her like Ruth had for Naomi, but she had still made sacrifices and had gone out of her way for an old woman when she had no earthly reason to.

Even Brian—who had tried to appear indifferent—had gone above and beyond to check on her and run errands for the many things she needed—goodness, the young man had even saved her life. What touched her the deepest was that he came over every day to water her plants and keep the flower beds tidied up between the times when the lawn service came by for the larger tasks.

Brian couldn't know how much that simple act of kindness meant to her. How it brought her joy to sit looking out over the porch railing and see that her little world was still intact—that someone cared enough to tend to the things that meant nothing to them... but everything to her.

Not that she didn't offer her input on everything. It just wasn't in her nature to sit back and hope for the best.

Mostly, she tottered around the garden with Brian, offering subtle suggestions on how to prune a wayward branch from the rhododendron bush or to show him how to pinch the tips off the basil to keep it full and thriving.

She tried hard not to sound bossy but the poor fellow had never tended a serious garden before. In fact, he'd never even heard of a Wandering Jew or Creeping Jenny before—both invasive plants that Mazie didn't tolerate and worked religiously to eliminate at first site. The neighbor over her back fence had the offenders growing in their yard and they had been a thorn in her side ever since they'd planted them.

Mazie looked around and realized that everyone around her was standing as Pastor Beckham offered the final prayer. Her cheeks felt warm as she reached for the pew in front of her and pulled herself up, hoping that no one noticed her awkwardness and thought she had fallen asleep during the sermon. To her relief, she noticed that most everyone's head was bowed and no one seemed the wiser. She hurried to bow her head as well.

As she made her way out of her pew, Pastor Beckham approached her.

"Mazie, dear." He wrapped an arm around her shoulders and gave her a gentle squeeze. "How have you been feeling, young lady?"

"Young lady?" Shaking her head, she chuckled. "Aren't you full of flattery this morning? I haven't been called *young* in years. But, I'm feeling real good, pastor." Her tone became serious. "And I appreciate what you had to say this morning. Sometimes we forget that we aren't the only ones hurting in the world."

Pastor Beckham returned her smile, but the way he looked at her made her feel like he was peering into her very soul.

"Thank you, Mazie. You know"—he paused, waiting to make sure he had Mazie's full attention—"the story of Naomi and Ruth can be seen from so many different perspectives. This story isn't just about Ruth's love for Naomi and her selflessness in sacrificing everything to care for her. It also gives us insight into how much God loved Naomi too by *giving* her a Ruth in her life."

Mazie could hear people greeting one another around them, but they were just blurs in her vision as she focused on what Pastor Beckham was trying to say. She didn't know where this was going yet, but felt the nudge in her heart from God that he wanted her to learn something in this moment.

Pastor Beckham reached over and patted Mazie's hand. "You and Naomi have some things in common, Mazie. She lost her only two sons and her husband. Even her daughters-in-law were a constant reminder of what she had lost. She probably felt she had nothing else to live for and planned to return home to at least grow old and die in her homeland. Naomi felt like she had nothing else to offer—no future sons for her daughters-in-laws and returning home empty-handed."

Mazie tried to speak, to at least squeak out some kind of reply, but she had choked up and the tears had come again. She didn't bother reaching for the handkerchief this time.

Pastor Beckham continued, "But that's not how God saw it. You see, he wasn't done with Naomi yet. He hadn't written her off. He still had work for her to do. That's why he gave her Ruth. He wanted to do a work in Ruth's life but needed Naomi's help in bringing it about. And, well, you know the rest of the story."

He winked. "One of the greatest love stories in the Bible."

It took her a moment to clear her throat. "Yes, sir. I think I see it now."

Pastor Beckham reached into his coat pocket. He pulled a tissue out and handed it to her.

"You can't always stay where you've always been, Mazie. If you do, you might miss out on doing God's work."

His words wedged themselves in her conscience as he patted her hand once again and turned to greet another parishioner.

Safe places. Missing out on doing God's work.

Was this what God had been trying to tell her?

God couldn't have been more clear if he'd knocked her upside the head with a sledgehammer. She nodded in response.

I have a lot of catching up to do, Lord.

CHAPTER 26

BRIAN NEVER THOUGHT he would ever end up hanging out in the children's section of a bookstore, much less during story time. But, here he was, driving Mazie to do exactly that.

Kai—Katy's dad—had promised to bring her this morning and Brian wanted to be there when she showed up. Pulling up to Emily's Book Barn, he helped Mazie in and made his way to Claire's office, where he had promised to do some updating on her website. He could work on it from home in his own office but, again, he was waiting for Katy this morning.

It was actually his idea to invite Katy. After jogging past the girl all these weeks and seeing her sitting in her yard, the sight started to bug him. He wondered if she had anything else to do with her time.

There has to be more to life for this girl, he thought.

Then, she'd thrown that ball at him, hoping to engage him, and he'd had to brush her off and try to avoid her for fear that someone would think he was a child stalker or some weirdo. He had even started crossing to the other side of the street before he reached her house in order to dodge her. But, then she had started standing at the fence to wave at him. He couldn't help but admire her persistence. He should have felt like a celebrity as hard as she was trying to get his attention.

Is that what it's like to be a dad coming home from work every day, watching your kids dance with excitement to see you?

He tried to think back to when he and Derek were young and if they acted like that with their dad. No memories came to mind.

Brian started waving back at her. Even that small token from him seemed to make Katy's day special and her face would beam even brighter.

After a few weeks or so, Brian found himself looking for her, anticipating her appearance, a heart-warming welcome home. It was as if this peculiar, unremarkable child waited for the moment that he would pass just so she could leap from her rock and greet him, the only bright spot in her whole day.

Brian sensed there was something unique about the girl, something that went beyond what she lacked in understanding. Her simplicity, the stillness about her as she took in the world from the view from her front yard. It made him sad that he never saw other children around, at least not with her. He'd seen kids playing in the street or running around neighbors' yards, but Katy was never included. Not that he had any real insight to what she did with the rest of her day. He only saw her when he went on his afternoon runs or was out and about on his property. Who knows if she waited for friends to come home from school and they went off to play or the neighbor kids invited her out for a game of ball in the evenings.

But, he doubted it. He just…*felt* that wasn't the way it panned out for her.

Brian believed now that was the reason why she'd thrown *him* the ball. Maybe that throw meant more than just a random act of boredom. Perhaps it was an intentional—even if she wasn't conscious of it herself—call for attention.

A cry for someone to notice her.

And there was no way that Brian *couldn't* notice her. He thought about what Mazie had shared with him, how she had felt that Katy had instinctively connected with him for some reason.

He also couldn't help but feel that a higher power had orchestrated him being there to save Mazie in her hour of need. Could it be that he was being called upon to do the same for this girl?

～

BRIAN SAT in Claire's office tapping away on the new MacBook that Claire had recently purchased. She had asked him to update her website so that she could start adding products to sell and to just give it a facelift. Along with a few renovations around the store, she was eager to take her business to a new level.

Story hour was due to start in twenty minutes and Brian was feeling anxious, hoping Kai didn't back down on his promise to bring his daughter this morning.

He had promised to bring Katy today when Brian handed him the flyer promoting the event after seeing him out watering his yard. He had watched for Kai—*maybe he had picked up the habit from Katy*—hoping to catch him outside. It just felt more casual than walking up and knocking on the door like a salesman.

Kai had perked up at the idea, saying he was always looking for things for Katy to do. Brian had never seen anyone else going in and out of their house, other than Katy and her father. It must be hard to have the full burden of schooling and caring for his daughter by himself. Brian knew there were special classes that Katy could attend at school, but didn't want to pry.

The door's bells jingled several times—and each time Brian popped his head out of the office door to see who the newcomer was—before he finally saw Katy's flurry of black hair jammed under a baseball cap coming through the door. She was trailed by her father, who gave a timid nod to

Danny, who stayed visible to customers in order to direct the traffic of children arriving.

Brian clicked the update button on the server website and logged out. He waited until the login screen reappeared and snapped the laptop lid closed. He rolled the chair back and made his way around the front counter.

"Hey, Kai!" Brian walked over and shook the man's hand. He smiled down at Katy.

"Hello, Katy! How ya doing today?"

Her face was beaming and she offered him a broad smile of perfect, white teeth. Brian had never seen her smile up this close. She had a beautiful smile.

"Brian! You are here too?" Katy glanced at her dad. "Daddy, Brian is here!" She looked back at Brian and reached over to pat his arm. "Do you work here?"

"No, Katy." He laughed and pointed at Claire, who was just walking back from the rear of the store. "See that lady right there?" Katy followed his finger and nodded. "Yes."

"That's Claire. She is the owner of this bookstore and my friend. I'm just here to help her today."

Claire walked up as he finished talking and was about to ask about Katy, but Brian beat her to it.

"Claire, this is Katy." Brian smiled reassuringly down at Katy, hoping to transfer courage to her. By the way she squared her shoulders and let go of her dad's hand, he knew he'd been successful.

"Hi…Claire," she stammered. "This is my dad."

Claire stooped down to Katy's level and shook her

hand. "I'm so happy to meet you, Katy—and your dad too." She smiled up at Kai and then looked back at Katy. "Are you here for story hour?"

Katy was already nodding. "Yes." She looked to her father and then at Brian before turning back to Claire.

"Are you going to read to us?"

"No, sweetheart, we have another special person who just loves reading to children. Would you like to go meet her? In fact, I think you two may already know each other."

Claire stood and reached out a hand for Katy, looking to her father for his approval. After a subtle nod down at his daughter, Kai rested his hand on her shoulder.

"Go on, Katy. Go have fun."

Katy put her hand in Claire's and the two went off to the children's section together. Brian could hear Claire and Katy chatting as they went. Kai met Brian's gaze, a slight lift at the corners of his mouth. He nodded toward the opposite side of the bookstore.

"I'll be browsing through the mystery section. How long will she be?"

Brian wasn't sure how long they went, but gave his best guess.

"I'd give her at least an hour. I think they offer the kids a snack and might have a craft planned."

Kai seemed pleased. "Good, good. I'll look around for a bit. You know where to find me if you need me."

Brian nodded. "Yes sir. You got it."

Brian leveled his gaze on Kai before he turned to go. "She'll be fine, you'll see."

~

MAZIE HELPED PICK out the books she would be reading for today and had already read them herself.

No surprises this time.

She had to snicker thinking about how petrified she had been that first time, taking in the children's expectant faces and feeling like she had to latch onto their curiosity or lose their interest entirely. It's not like she hadn't been around kids. She just had never experienced twenty or so of them all staring at her at the same time, expecting her to perform magic.

Mazie noticed a petite fair-skinned girl with jet-black hair standing with Claire.

Is that Katy? The little girl from across the street?

The young girl clutched tightly to Claire's hand, a shell-shocked expression on her pale face. The baseball cap pushed down on her hair was an odd choice to pair with the delicate pink jumper and white slip-ons she wore.

Brian hadn't spoken of the girl since they'd had their little chat on the front porch and she saw him almost every day. There were a few times, as she passed the front window, that she noticed him stop to talk to her when he returned from an afternoon run. But she never expected the girl would ever show up here for story hour.

Did Brian invite her?

The young girl looked like a frightened puppy as she stared up at Claire, her expression conveying she had no clue where to go or what to do and that she had no intention of letting Claire out of her sight. Claire leaned over and spoke close to her ear, nudging her forward and giving her a reassuring smile. When she didn't move, Claire stepped forward and gave her hand a gentle tug as she pointed down at a vacant spot on the carpet.

There were close to twenty-eight children here—Mazie had counted a few minutes ago—and they were a rowdy group this morning. She would need to corral their attention in less than two minutes so they could get started. She rolled her shoulders back and gave her neck a quick pull from side to side to release the tension.

The subtle scent of the perfume she had applied this morning drifted up to her. She hadn't worn perfume or even scented body spray for at least a year. Passing through her bedroom this morning, Mazie had spied the diamond-shaped bottle, still mostly full of rich amber liquid, sitting in its place on her dresser when she reached for her sweater from a nearby chair. The only time she touched the bottle was to dust the dresser, which she hardly did herself anymore since she had a housekeeper come in now.

It was Harold's favorite perfume: Lancôme's Trésor, a choice he'd made for her birthday at the suggestion of the salesclerk at Macy's department store when she found him staring aimlessly at the perfume display case and had swept in to the rescue.

When he told her that his wife preferred floral scents but didn't like it too musky, she immediately reached for the Trésor. "Look no further," she told him. "She'll love it." And she was right. Wispy notes of rose and lilac—two of her favorite flowers—under a tone of apricot sweetness had instantly won her over.

Mazie had worn perfume every day since her teen years, having been reminded often by her mother that a lady must always be well-perfumed and smelling her best. She hadn't felt much like wearing perfume or doing anything special with herself since Harold had slipped away from her—mentally and, then, eternally. She had no one to impress and, if she were honest, there were some days she was lucky if she even felt like taking a shower, much less wearing perfume.

"I'm going to wear the Trésor, my dear. I hope you don't mind," she spoke aloud this morning, clinging to raw faith that Harold could hear her. Her voice had echoed back in the empty bedroom and she held her next breath in case, by some miracle, she might hear his voice answer back.

She heard nothing. But she imagined she felt his approval.

Mazie rolled the delicate, glass bottle in her hand, tugged off the top, and misted the air in front of her. Stepping forward, she let the mist settle over her.

A sensation of electricity had buzzed through her, tears welling in her eyes as his memory flooded over her. Tall, husky, with bold dark eyes. The teardrop-shaped scar on his chin when he'd run into a fence at fifteen. The way his mustache twitched when he was angry with her—which was rare. She stood for a moment, lingering in the intoxicating mix of floral nostalgia filling her nostrils, cherishing the memories this time rather than cringing from them.

I'm wearing this for you today, my love.

Brushing away her tears, she had pulled on her sweater and gone to sit on the porch to wait for Claire to pick her up.

Mazie realized she had been lost in her thoughts when she heard the children growing restless in front of her, waiting for her to begin the story. Taking a deep breath to clear her head, she leaned forward in her chair.

"Good morning, children!"

Her smile took them all in as they gave her their attention. She found the baseball cap first, then noted the dark raven hair of the girl sitting primly on the carpet where Claire had placed her. She was smiling now, clearly recognizing Mazie as her neighbor, and giving Mazie a little wave, looking for all the world like Mazie was about to announce her name as the winner of a pageant rather than just getting ready to read a few stories.

Just as Mazie settled the book she was to read on her lap, she noticed Brian standing among the moms and dads, babysitters, and other adults gathered. As if a curtain had been pulled back and revelation poured into her, Brian stood out like a beacon in the sea of faces, unaware of the indistinct signal he sent out, a cry for guidance and understanding, as if he felt led to go somewhere but had no clue how to get there.

Her eyes flickered down to the pale girl seated on the floor—another twinkle of light in the crowd.

Katy.

Mazie felt something awaken in her spirit—felt the subtle tug on her conscience. The fluttering of the voice in her heart swelled until it was as loud and clear as if it had shouted from a mountaintop.

These two, Mazie. This is the work I have kept you here for.

She gazed down at her lap to compose herself so she could go on with the story. The burden threatened to overcome her and she had to say a quick prayer to get her through it. She gulped the tears back and felt them lodge in her throat.

Okay, Lord. You have to help me. I have no idea what you expect…where to even start.

She lifted her head and smiled at the children waiting anxiously for the story. She didn't search again for Brian, but sensed he was still nearby.

Katy's smile remained intact, her eyes shadowed by the cap on her head. Mazie wiggled her fingers back in a wave, opened her book, and began.

"It was back in a time when dragons ruled the land…"

CHAPTER 27

BRIAN WATCHED as Finn entered the church escorting a
petite young woman with bouncy red curls and flushed
cheeks.

In spite of the occasion, Brian smiled to himself, a
sincere joy for his best friend filling his heart. Finn had been
dating Mindy for several months now and they were talking
seriously about a future together. In fact, Finn had already
asked Brian to be his best man.

But, today, they were sitting on church pews for a
different occasion.

The first chords of the organ were drifting over the
wooden pews and flooding the church as people made their
way to their seats. The scent of lilacs followed by a nudge at
his elbow made him aware of her presence before he even
turned to acknowledge her.

"Good to see you, Claire," he whispered.

Hair pulled into a flattering low twist at the nape of her neck, her soft blue dress with the gathered blouson sleeves and delicate loop trim at the neckline complimented her eyes perfectly. Brian lifted the edge of his tie between his thumb and index finger and held it toward her.

"I remembered...baby blue."

"Robin blue," she grinned. "It's *robin blue*. She was very clear about that."

Their attention was drawn to the front of the church, where Pastor Beckham was approaching the platform, stopping briefly to shake someone's hand. Brian reached for the coarse paper on the bench next to him. Resting the pamphlet on his lap, he stared down into the face of the older woman wearing a floppy straw hat, holding an armful of cut roses. Her radiant green eyes shone from under the shadow of the hat brim, staring up at him and piercing right into his soul.

"You get one shot, Brian. Don't look for happiness only on sunny days, but find joy even during the stormy ones. That's when you'll need it most."

It was the last words she had spoken to him the day before she died.

He blinked back tears. She would be disappointed that he was going to cry on her special day. The day she wanted the world to celebrate her happy reunion with her husband and little boy. Everyone was rising for the first hymn. Brian recognized several faces seated nearby, a few he'd met at Mazie's birthday party, including Rebecca.

He set the pamphlet back down on the pew and stood along with Claire. His eyes swept over the congregation of people, most wearing various shades of blue. His lip twitched.

Glad I'm not the only one who has no idea what shade "robin blue" is...

It didn't matter. What mattered is that they had remembered—had showed up. That they were here for *her*, that she had made an impact on so many lives, as Brian noted by the packed seats and, glancing over his shoulder, the few even standing at the back of the church.

Children. They seemed to be everywhere in the crowded sanctuary. There was a row of about ten older children seated at the front on the right side of the church. Brian remembered seeing something about a special song to be performed by the youth choir in the program.

He looked over to where Finn and Mindy were seated. Finn hadn't been around Mazie more than the few times he'd trailed along with Brian to check in on her and she had pushed plates of homemade brownies and lemon bars in front of him. Food...that's all it took to win Finn over to Mazie.

Brian had planned to save a seat for them next to him, but Finn had informed him that he and Mindy would be arriving late and not to worry about it. Brian hadn't even saved the seat next to him for Claire. It just happened to be vacant when she arrived, which suited him just fine.

The "homegoing celebration," as Pastor Beckham

called it, was a beautiful tribute to Mazie's life. Brian had no idea of the impact this kind, sometimes stubborn, endearing old woman had made on the people around her. Those who stood to speak told stories of how she'd brought them groceries when they'd lost a job and loaned her car to a family while they waited for their own vehicle to be repaired. In the end, Mazie had actually just given them the car, since she claimed that she never drove it anyway.

Pastor Beckham shared with the congregation that Mazie had named Grace Methodist as the beneficiary of her estate, with portions allocated to other beneficiaries. Brian had already been informed that he was on that list.

Nurses and other hospital staff shared how she always made the kids on the cardiac ward smile and how she calmed their fears when they had to stay at the hospital alone or were preparing for surgery. One after another stood until Pastor Beckham gently suggested they needed to move on with the service.

There was no casket at the front of the church, nor was there any kind of urn in sight. Mazie hadn't wanted a casket or an urn to be the last impression people had of her.

"It's just the shell of my cocoon I'm shedding and leaving behind," Mazie had told him. "The real me will be dancing on the other side of Jordan."

When she saw he was confused by the reference, she explained. "In the Bible, the children of Israel had to cross the Jordan River to reach the land God had promised them. That's what I will do, Brian. Cross from this earthly home to a heavenly one. Do you understand?"

He did. It was hard to accept...but he did.

As Pastor Beckham bowed his head for the benediction prayer, Brian closed his eyes and imagined a clear-flowing river with Mazie on the other side, running—no cane, agile as a young doe—toward her loved ones. The image in his mind was breathtaking and stirred a deep yearning in his heart to experience that for himself when his time came.

When the prayer ended, everyone turned to greet each other. A young woman had stopped to talk with Claire, so Brian made his way to a large wooden table in front of the pulpit where several photos were arranged. He knew that Mazie had chosen the selection and arranged with Claire to have them displayed.

There was one picture of a young woman with shoulder-length dark brown hair that was neatly clipped back with barrettes on each side, wearing a pleated skirt, knee-high socks, loafers, and a V-neck sweater with a small emblem embroidered on it. Brian guessed it was some kind of a school uniform. He recognized the half-grin as Mazie's right away.

Several other frames held photos of her next to a tall gentleman with broad shoulders who wore wire-rimmed glasses and a wide, mustached smile that made his eyes all but disappear in its wake.

Brian bent to study a gold double picture frame near the front of the table. A young boy, somewhere around two or three, he guessed, was pictured next to the tall man at a campsite in a wooded area. The left photo showed him in a pair of swim trunks holding a small ball in his hands. He looked to be in the middle of laughing at a funny face the man was making. In the right frame, the boy wore denim overalls with no shirt underneath and was barefoot. He stood with the tall man in front of a cabin waving at the person taking the picture.

Brian moved away from the table and made his way out of the church to the parking lot. Finn and Mindy had already left to go to a dinner for her sister's birthday, promising to drop by next weekend for a visit.

Brian had planned to say his goodbyes to Claire, but when he looked her way, he saw that she was chatting with several people. He knew she would be tied up for a while.

Guess that goes with owning a popular bookstore in town.

There was a large reception planned in the church fellowship hall but he wasn't feeling up to it. He wasn't one to mingle with strangers anyway but, this morning, he was feeling reflective and nostalgic and knew he wouldn't be good company. He planned to grab fast food and head back to the house to catch up on some work. It had been a long week and a few of his clients' work had suffered for it. They had understood when he explained his neglect, but he was determined to get caught up tonight. Besides, it would be good to keep his mind busy.

"Hey, Brian! Wait up!"

He heard the *clacking* of heels on the asphalt behind him

and turned. How Claire managed to jog in heels was beyond him but he wasn't going to wait until she twisted her ankle. He made his way toward her.

"You aren't staying for the reception?" She caught her breath while she adjusted a purse strap that had slipped off of her shoulder.

He felt bad for leaving without saying anything but was surprised she had made the effort to find him.

"Nah, I really gotta catch up on some work." He jammed his hands into his pants pocket, like a guilty teenager who had been caught sneaking out of the house. "Sorry I didn't say goodbye. You looked busy and—"

Head cocked, she gave him a scolding look, "Really, Brian? Are you running from your grief or from me?"

Whoa. This girl doesn't pull punches, does she?

"Neither, I promise. I'm okay. Actually, I'm happy for Mazie. She's right where she wanted to be."

He fiddled with the edge of his tie as he considered her words. "And I have no reason to run from you, Claire. Unless you know something I don't know," he said with a laugh.

Claire laughed with him. She tucked a lone strand of hair that had come undone behind her ear and reached into her purse for a piece of gum. She held the pack out to him but he waved it off.

"No, thanks."

"You know she tried every trick in the book to get you and me together," she said.

"Yes." He shook his head. "She was relentless."

He smiled and looked down at his dress shoes, unsure where she was going with this. He suddenly felt shy and gawky, like a boy with his first crush. But this wasn't a crush.

Or was it?

"I like the fancy clothes." He heard the humor laced in her tone. "Mazie would have been impressed."

He shrugged. "Yeah, I don't get out much, I guess. I had nothing decent to wear."

Determined to at least wear a dress shirt and nice slacks for today, he found himself running to a department store the day before for a hurried shopping trip. While there, he remembered Mazie's request for everyone to wear blue —*robin blue*—for her funeral, or *homegoing* celebration as she preferred it to be called. The male clerk at the store had called over a female coworker to help him find a tie that came close to that shade of blue. *Baby blue* was the best they could do. The clerk also reminded him he would need nice shoes to go with the ensemble.

In the end, he handed over the $137.42 for the clothes —socks and a belt thrown in at the last minute—justifying that he planned to attend Sunday services at Grace Methodist when he wasn't working and would need some nicer clothes to wear.

It seemed fitting that the first time he would wear his new dress clothes would be for exactly that: a church service, one just for Mazie. He felt the pang of guilt that he'd not shared this first time in church sitting next to her. He knew it would have meant a lot to her.

Instinctively, he knew what she would say: *Better late than never, Brian.*

He realized Claire was still standing in front of him and his thoughts had been elsewhere—which is why he had planned to escape from the reception in the first place—and raised his eyes to look at Claire.

Brian wasn't sure if she was grinning because she assumed he was failing at small talk or for some other reason. Either way, it was unnerving.

"What?" He pulled his hands from his pockets and raised them in the air. "Why are you staring at me like that?"

She gave his shoulder a playful punch. "It's fine, Brian. You're safe. We won't go there right now. Deal?"

For some odd reason, Brian felt a twinge of disappointment. He gave Claire his full attention. He wanted to tell her that he was ready to *go there*, if she was thinking along the same lines that he was. He wasn't entirely positive on what that meant to him yet, but he was sure that it would put a big smile on Mazie's face if she could see his heart right now. But, instead of speaking up and taking the initiative, stepping boldly up to the challenge like the man he was, he slithered back into his safe cocoon.

"Deal."

"You know," she said. "I was thinking of taking a crate of books to donate to Magnolia Children's Hospital next

Saturday after story hour. I've been training Danny on the register this week. He wouldn't mind watching the store for me for a few hours. You want to join me?"

Maybe it was the lingering scent of lilacs that drifted his way or perhaps it was just him feeling sentimental, but Brian warmed to the idea.

"What kind of books?"

"Children's books, silly. It *is* a *children's* hospital. Anyhow, I've been beefing up the stock in the children's area at Emily's, adding a new section and a few extra touches. I pulled some old inventory off the shelves to make room for the new books." A shadow passed over her face, but lingered only a moment. "The kids really looked forward to Mazie reading to them. Guess I need to find a replacement. I'll ask Rev. Beckham when I head back inside if he knows of any candidates."

Brian stayed silent. The fresh grief piercing the air between them. But, he didn't let it tarry.

"You wouldn't happen to be taking the books to the children's cardiac floor, would you?" He had to ask.

The glow crept back into her cheeks. "Why, yes…good guess! However, Mr. Smarty, I am dropping half of the books off first with the volunteer coordinator to distribute to kids in other areas of the hospital."

He nodded. "Of course. Rebecca, right?"

"Rebecca?"

"The volunteer coordinator for the hospital."

Her eyes lit up. "Yes! That's her. So...does that mean you're in?"

Brian pretended to consider her offer but had already made up his mind the moment she asked.

"Sure. Not too early, though. I work late Friday nights."

Shifting her purse to her other shoulder, she said, "Oh, yeah! Your undercover secret service work, right?"

Brian shook his head, amused. "Oh, lord, I had forgotten about that! Where in the *world* did that crazy woman come up with that story?"

Their laughter was cut short by a honk behind him. Turning, Brian saw that a car was waiting to back out of its parking space. Brian waved. "Sorry!" He scooted out of the driver's way.

Turning back to Claire, "Listen, about Saturday..."

He couldn't believe he was about to take the dive. He felt the twitch in his gut trying to warn him away but he decided to ignore it. He and Mazie had a lot of heart-to-heart talks the last few days of her life. In fact, she had been the only one who had gotten the message through to him that, in life, it was okay to take chances, that you might only get one shot at love.

Don't try to abide in the "safe places" Brian, where nothing can hurt you, she told him—her lovely green eyes sunken deep into the weary lines on her face as she struggled to help him understand. *Don't waste time living in the past and miss out on your future.*

Curiosity was etched on her face, but Claire waited patiently.

"What do you think about going to dinner later on that night?"

A smile teased the edges of her mouth, but the joy was clear in her eyes.

"I'd really like that," she said.

There's that awkward silence again, he thought. *This is going to take some practice.* He started to look down to avoid her stare, but forced himself to meet her gaze instead.

"Me too." It was the best he could come up with.

As if sensing he needed the encouragement, Claire gave him a playful wink and turned to head back into the church.

"Maybe we could talk about you reading to the kids for story hour over dinner," she called back.

He scowled. "Don't push it."

Her faint chuckle drifted back to him as he watched her walk away, the rays of sun reflecting off her golden hair.

How'd I do, Mazie?

He didn't need to *hear* her approval—he *felt* it. She had worked too hard to make this happen for him not to know she'd be thrilled.

Brian glanced around, trying to remember where he'd parked his car. He would be mortified if Claire knew how flustered he was from their brief encounter.

Walking toward the back of the lot, he finally spotted his car sandwiched between two large pickup trucks. He was wishing now that he hadn't used the excuse of work to leave and that he had stayed for the meal. He found himself wanting more than anything to turn around and spend the next hour sitting with Claire.

Next Saturday couldn't come soon enough.

BRIAN DROVE HOME SLOWLY, not thrilled about facing an empty house and the rest of the evening working in his office.

Before he got started, he planned to change clothes and head over to water Mazie's garden. He had been doing the watering for several weeks now but was planning to have the landscaping service put in a drip system sometime before the house went up for sale.

Mazie had always preferred to water by hand because she loved to spend time in her garden—fussing over every weed that had been missed, plucking fat caterpillars off her parsley, pushing her face close to the honeysuckle bushes to inhale their fragrance, whispering words of encouragement to the snapdragons and begonias as they withered at the end of their seasons.

She loved them all.

During the last few months, Mazie had pointed out several of her favorite rose bushes and told Brian she was having the lawn care crew transplant them to his yard and design a nice bedding area for them.

"You need some color in that yard, dear," she insisted one day as he guided her wheelchair carefully through her garden, stopping often to allow her to pluck off faded flowers and inspect the undersides of leaves for aphids. When they stopped by the Black Pearl rose bush, she stopped him again. Her voice grew tender and soft and he had needed to lean closer in order to hear her.

"That one." Her trembling fingers reached to caress the petals of a dark rose. "You must keep that one for me."

He learned that it had been an anniversary gift from her husband…her prized possession.

"I will, Mazie. I promise."

He couldn't have denied her anyway. When Mazie got something in her head you just went with it. A few weeks later, Brian inherited the Black Pearl bush and over a dozen other rose bushes as well as a few other plants, including the potted ones from her porch, that she thought he needed. She even managed to have a few rose bushes brought to Claire's, along with detailed instructions on caring for them. Brian knew all about how to care for them too. Mazie had been tutoring him for months now.

He had to admit, they added a nice touch to his yard. He had even taken to eating dinner on the porch if the weather was nice enough just to enjoy the scenery.

Pulling up to his house, Brian noticed Katy waving at him from across the street. He stepped out of the car and made his way over.

Gnome girl. He couldn't believe he had been so callous to

think of her that way when he now thought of her as the sweetest, most charming young girl he'd ever met.

Mazie had thought so too.

Kai had been grateful when Brian suggested that Katy tag along with Mazie to the bookstore on Saturdays. She could be there for story hour and then stay to help Claire around the store afterwards. Mazie spent that time knitting in her cozy chair by the coffee bar. Claire picked them up and brought them home every Saturday while Danny watched the store.

The girl was beyond excited to dust shelves and vacuum for Claire, who offered to pay her for helping. Claire had even given her the special job of decorating the tops of the shelves in the children's section with books and stuffed animals she chose herself. Katy was very proud of her bookshelves.

Brian had also seen Katy walking around with Mazie in the garden on a number of occasions—Mazie with her slow gait and Katy's unhurried wonder of the world around her. They were like two old souls on an afternoon stroll.

In her last weeks, she had grown weaker, her heart failing her. She had commissioned Brian to watch over Katy when it was her time to go—to help her father keep the young girl busy so she didn't just watch the world go by from her front yard but have the opportunity to experience life fully. She also implored him to check in on Claire and make sure she didn't work too hard. He could read between the lines on what she really meant.

"Get her to take a Sunday off once in a while and take her to church," she told him. "You *do* remember how to get there, right?" That had gotten a chuckle out of him.

He knew she was near the end when she didn't want to go outside any longer, preferring to sleep or have long talks with those who stopped by to visit if she was feeling strong enough. The hospital had brought over a special bed for her and set it up in her living room to make access to her easier.

Claire came a few times a week to spend time with her, often reading books to her and chatting about whatever ladies liked to chat about. Brian came over before work most evenings and sat next to her bed, listening to her talk about whatever she felt on her heart to talk about: her life with Harold, happy and sad stories about children at the hospital where she volunteered, the young son she and Harold had loved and lost...

"He wouldn't have been much older than you are now, Brian," she told him one evening, her voice barely above a whisper in her weakened state. Her eyes were glassy and sunken but still lovely as she reached a wrinkled hand to his cheek.

"I'm thinking that God sent you along to fill that empty spot for me, if only for a short while."

The tears had come for him then.

"My heart has been aching for years to see my boys again, but God had some things I needed to help him with first. So I did my best, and...I'm ready to go now."

Brian knew…*Claire, Katy, those sick children…me.*

For all the effort he'd made to avoid forming friendships and allowing someone into his heart, he had failed miserably and ended up plunging deeper in than he ever meant to. Placing his hand over Mazie's on his cheek, he was thankful that she had nudged herself past his walls of resistance.

Her last words would be engraved on his heart for the remainder of his life—a mantra he would live by.

"You get one shot, Brian. Don't look for happiness only on sunny days, but find joy even during the stormy ones. That's when you'll need it most."

The hospice nurse called the next morning to tell him that Mazie had slipped away sometime in the night.

He only allowed himself to cry for a few minutes before he pulled himself together and set out to keep the promise he had made to himself after talking to Mazie. He called his mom. She had left a voicemail the week before telling him that she'd received a wedding invitation from Derek and was excited about it. Brian assumed he had received one too. An envelope addressed to him in black calligraphy sat unopened on his desk.

I guess if Mom can let it go and move on, I can too.

When he heard her voice on the other end, he knew there was no backing out. And he had felt pretty good about it too.

He told her about Mazie, whom she knew about from past conversations, and she expressed her condolences. She knew he and Mazie had grown closer over the past few weeks. They talked about Derek's upcoming wedding and how she wanted to shop for a new dress. That gave Brian the opening he needed. He invited her to come to his place to spend the weekend so they could drive over to the outlet stores in Foley. They made tentative plans for the beginning of next month. Brian felt like there were a lot of new beginnings in his life recently. *Claire…Katy…his mom.* Maybe someday he'd include his dad and Derek on that list, but he was nowhere near ready for that yet.

After crossing the street, Brian stopped in front of Katy's house and leaned on the fence. She had gone over to sit on her favorite rock and had pulled her knees up to her chest, swaying gently as she smiled brightly up at him.

"Hello there, Katy! What are you doing on this fine day?"

Her hair was pulled into a high ponytail and she wore a wrinkled pair of blue jeans and a frumpy brown turtleneck. But the glow on her face was all he noticed.

"Hi, Brian! You are all dressed up! I like your tie."

Mazie had tried to tell Katy—tried to warn her in the most simplistic manner she could—and Katy had held her hand and told her it was okay. But she didn't truly understand.

When she didn't see Mazie after a while, Katy would ask again and they would cross that bridge when it came. But, today, Brian had a better idea of what to talk about. He knew Claire wouldn't mind.

Brian bowed deeply. "Why, thank you, madam."

Katy giggled. "What's a *madam*?"

He feigned shock. "Why, it's a fancy way to greet a lady."

Katy didn't look convinced but shrugged anyway. "Oh, alright."

"Hey, I have an idea," he told her.

Her feet slid to the ground as she leaned forward, anticipation glowing in her eyes. "What idea?"

"I was wondering—if your dad doesn't mind, of course —if you would want to go with me and Claire to take some books to some kids at the hospital this next weekend after story hour? You could help pass the books out to kids."

Her eyes widened. "Oh, yes! I would like to do that. Want me to ask my dad?" She jumped up and started to turn to do just that but Brian stopped her.

"No, it's okay. I'll ask him later. I just wanted to ask you first."

"I'm so happy, Brian!" She had moved to the fence and stood rocking back and forth like she wanted to climb over and hug him.

Brian reached out a hand to give Katy a high-five. She jumped high and slapped his hand.

"Awesome!" he said. "I'll talk to your dad this week and make sure it's alright with him."

While he was at it, he thought he might even see if Claire and Katy wanted to tag along with him to the animal shelter to find a running partner and a roommate to share his big empty house with. He might even let Katy name the dog.

It wasn't much to start with, but he had to start somewhere.

Brian hummed softly to himself as he crossed back to his house, his head full of ideas for the future.

DID YOU ENJOY THIS BOOK?

I hope you enjoyed reading this book as much as I enjoyed writing it for you. I've learned a lot from Mazie's story, as I believe all authors do from the characters they spend so much time with. If you enjoyed this book, I would be honored if you would write a review on Amazon. Reviews are so important to an author. Even just a line or two can make a huge difference!

WWW.AMAZON.COM/DP/B0986K97TB

GOODREADS.COM/REGINA_FELTY

JOIN REGINA'S NEWSLETTER: HTTPS://RLFELTY.COM/NEWSLETTER/

ALSO BY REGINA FELTY

WHILE YOU WALKED BY

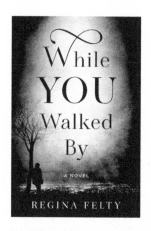

Terrified and naive to life on the streets, twelve-year-old Aden must forge his own survival in the face of dangerous predators and violence after his mother abandoned him. When an old man discovers him hiding one night in the alley, Aden is faced with a choice: flee or trust again?

www.amazon.com/dp/B086CWH6Y5